PRAISE FOR *A PLANET FOR RENT*

"Some of the best sci-fi written anywhere since the 1970s.... A Planet for Rent, like its author, a bandana-wearing, muscly roquero, is completely sui generis: riotously funny, scathing, perceptive, and yet also heart-wrenchingly compassionate.... Instantly appealing."
—The Nation

"A compelling meditation on modern imperialism.... A fascinating kaleidoscope of vignettes.... A brilliant exploration of our planet's current social and economic inequities.... Yoss doesn't disappoint.... Striking, detailed.... Yoss has written a work of science fiction that speaks to fundamental problems humans deal with every day. This is not just a story about alien oppression; it's the story of our own planet's history and a call for change."
—SF Signal, 4.5-star review

"Devastating and hilarious and somehow, amidst all those aliens, deeply, deeply human."
—Daniel José Older, author of the *Bone Street Rumba* series and *Salsa Nocturna*

"One of the most prestigious science fiction authors of the Island."
—*On Cuba* magazine

"A gifted and daring writer."
—David Iaconangelo

"José Miguel Sánchez is Cuba's most decorated science fiction author, who has cultivated the most prestige for this genre in the mainstream, and the only person of all the Island's residents who lives by his pen."
—Cuenta Regresiva

ALSO BY YOSS

FICTION

Timshel
I sette peccati nazionali (cubani)
Los pecios y los náufragos
El Encanto de Fin de Siglo
Al final de la senda
Polvo rojo
La causa che rinfresca e altre meraviglie cubane
Precio justo
Pluma de león
Interferences
Siedem Grzechów Kubanskich
Tropas auxiliares
Planète à louer
Mentiras cubanas
Super extra grande
Condonautas
La voz del abismo
Angélica

NONFICTION

La espada y sus historias
La quinta dimensión de la literatura

YOUNG READERS

Las quimeras no existen
Leyendas de los Cinco Reinos

A PLANET FOR RENT

YOSS

Translated from the Spanish by David Frye

RESTLESS BOOKS
Brooklyn, New York

First Restless Books paperback edition June 2015

ISBN: 978-1-63206-0-365

Cover design by Edel Rodriguez

Printed in the United States of America

3 5 7 9 8 6 4 2

Restless Books, Inc.
232 3rd Street, Suite A111
Brooklyn, NY 11215

www.restlessbooks.com
publisher@restlessbooks.com

Contents

A PLANET FOR RENT

For Rent, One Planet

Step on up, ladies and gents, right this way!

But only if you're xenoids, it goes without saying.

We don't want any humans...

A once-in-a-lifetime business opportunity!

An offer you won't be able to turn down!

For rent, one planet!

One whole planet, with its oceans and its mountains, with its glaciers and its deserts, with its plains and its forests.

For rent, one planet, with all its climates, its fauna, its flora, its minerals, and its moon.

And what's more, with all its intelligent populations.

A real bargain!

For rent, one planet, with all its history, with all its monuments and wonders. With its works of art and its pride, with its spirit and its faith in the future.

For rent, one planet, to the highest bidder, for an indefinite period of time, no conditions, no restrictions, no scruples.

For rent, one planet, whole or by shares. Whether you're an investor from Aldebaran or Regulus, or a tourist from Tau Ceti or Proxima Centauri, or a grodo or Auyar capitalist, you can't let this opportunity slip away.

For rent, one planet that's lost its way in the race for development, that showed up at the stadium after all the medals had been handed out, when all that was left was the consolation prize of survival.

For rent, one planet that learned to play the economics game according to one set of rules but discovered once it started playing that the rules had been changed.

For rent, one planet, for pleasure or spite, like an old social worker who's fallen on hard times and who'll let anyone be her master for a few hours in exchange for a couple of credits.

For rent, one planet whose inhabitants have stopped believing in the future. . . in any future, and all they have left is the pride of their solitary past to help them face up to their irksome, everyday, xenoid-filled present.

For rent, one planet, for you, innocent child of a culture and race that won the lottery, for you, privileged only because you're from some other solar system, because you grew up under the light of some other star.

For rent, one planet!

Cheap!

Don't miss your chance!

Sign your contract now!

Let's just warn you, in good faith. . . you might want to read all the fine print first.

Because maybe, thinking you've just rented the planet, you'll find out you've actually bought it. For all eternity. And, instead of paying with the credits you've rightly earned with your hard work and the sweat of your brow under the light of another sun, the purchase price was your soul.

But anyway. . . if none of that bothers you, come on: we're waiting for you.

Don't forget.

Tell all your friends, right away.

For rent, one planet.

Social Worker

The cybertaxi pulled up at the astroport entrance. Lifting the hatch, Buca extracted her long legs from the cab. First the right, then then the left. Then she straightened up with studied languor, hewing to her motto: Always be sensual.

On the other side, Selshaliman imitated her, and she envied his naturally dignified movements. With their shiny, grayish chitin exoskeletons, grodos had the rigid look of men wearing medieval armor. And majesty, plenty of it.

A Cetian would have looked nicer, in any case. Svelte, almost feline, so sensual; no wonder half the young people on earth imitated their way of walking.

But a grodo also had his advantages. She watched Selshaliman pay for the taxi with his credit appendage. His rapid, quasimechanical gestures were still extremely unsettling to Buca. Like he was a gigantic spider or praying mantis. But the image became more bearable when she recalled that she would soon have the human equivalent of a credit appendage: a subcutaneous implant reflecting the generous bank account that this exotic had just established in her name.

They went inside. Buca drank in the last terrestrial sights she would see for a long while. The microworld of the astroport.

The astroport and the neighborhood around it were swarming with traffic, as always. Xenoids just arriving, looking for excitement, and already being hailed by the network of tour operators from the Planetary Tourism Agency. Xenoids leaving the planet, exhausted and loaded down with cheap, picturesque souvenirs.

All sorts of them were there. Non-humanoids, like the enormous polyps of Aldebaran with their slow rolling motion on that one round, muscular foot; or the guzoids from Regulus, long, segmented, and scaly; or the Colossaurs, stout and armored. And also humanoids: Cetians and Centaurians. The former, svelte and gorgeous; the latter, blue and distant.

There were also humans, like that group getting off an astroport shuttle and practically racing to get inside. They looked like scientists, all of them very nervous. They were probably off to some conference, and they were all clustering around one fairly young guy who seemed to be the lead investigator. Though he looked pretty confused, too; this was obviously their first trip off the planet. But they were also privileged in their own way. Buca envied them a little. Earth allowed its citizens to leave only on very rare occasions, and only under very special circumstances. Probably some xenoid scientists wanted their human colleagues to attend their event and had paid all the travel costs and taken care of the paperwork.

You could even see a few mestizos here and there. Like that girl with the large eyes and the bluish skin. The Centaurian with her might be her father. Ramrod-straight, like all the rest.

The girl had to be famous, because her face looked pretty familiar to Buca. Maybe some simstim star, or a rich heiress... Or more likely a social worker like herself, but higher ranking. She couldn't quite remember. Bah, it'd come back to her later. It wasn't all that important, anyway.

Selshaliman moved his antennas nervously; he would rather have taken a teletransport booth to the central ring instead of crossing the whole thing on foot. He seemed uncomfortably aware of being the only grodo around.

These insectoids were crazy about security. They had their own network of teletransport booths and private communication circuits. A silly, overpriced whim, in Buca's opinion. But if they could afford it... After the mysterious Auyars, the grodos were the most powerful race in the galaxy.

They were telepaths. That was the foundation of their vast commercial empire. Maybe they couldn't read the thoughts of other species, but picking up on the moods and emotions of everyone they talked with put them at a distinct advantage in all their commercial deals.

She looked at him distrustfully. People said they were incapable of picking up and interpreting the thoughts of humans as sharply as they could those of their fellow grodos. But still. . . Selshaliman couldn't seriously believe that she might be in love with him. . .

But just in case, she closed her mind, humming the opening bars of a catchy current technohit. A trick she had picked up from her friend Yleka.

A freelance social worker had to be very careful. Never let her guard down. She couldn't rest till the hypership had taken off. So many stories were going around. . . Some social workers had put their trust in xenoids who later turned out to be humans, disguised with bioimplants. And they'd paid for their gullibility with months or years in Body Spares. . .

She looked around her. In the astroport, too, the unspeakable booths were everywhere. Inside them, bodies in suspended animation. Waiting for a client. . .

As if in reaction to her gaze, at that very instant the door to one opened and its occupant came wobbling out. Buca tried not to, but. . . she looked him in the eyes, as if hypnotized. She breathed a sigh of relief when she saw it wasn't him. Ever since Jowe had been arrested, every time she saw someone come out of a booth she was afraid of finding him with empty eyes.

Maybe it was stupid, but she couldn't shake her guilt complex. . .

Some races, such as the Auyars, were biologically incompatible with the terrestrial biosphere. To enjoy the tourist paradises that the planet had to offer, they had created the system of Body Spares.

All of the parameters of the "client" (memory, personality, intelligence quotient, motor skills) were computer-encoded and then introduced into the brain of a host-human. The xenoid gained both mobility and access to all the skills and memories of the "spare body."

There was just one "minor" detail: forty percent of the time, the person whose body and brain were occupied by the extraterrestrial remained conscious.

That must feel like being a marionette, moved by another's will. . .

When the process was in its experimental phase, being a "horse" (a term derived from Voodoo) was voluntary, and almost well-paid. But there weren't enough volunteers anymore, not once it became clear that there could be aftereffects. Nowadays, the sentence for any criminal offense was a certain number of days, months, or even years in Body Spares.

It was the modern equivalent of Russian roulette; not all "riders" took equally good care of their "horses." Some tourists pushed them to exhaustion, then simply paid the resulting fine. It was so cheap. . . Many humans lost their minds after being treated that way for five or six weeks. There were even rumors floating around that at Body Spares they tried to get all the spares to lose their minds. A suspiciously ambiguous law stipulated that you only had full civil rights if you enjoyed perfect mental health. Any obligation to return the use of a body to its legitimate owner would automatically vanish if he went schizophrenic.

Buca thought of Jowe, so sensitive and delicate. He wouldn't last two months. He was probably wishing he would die already. . .

But maybe—the idea was unlikely, she knew, but it was comforting—since he was young and graceful, some wealthy and powerful xenoid would have picked him. And now he'd be wrapped up in important negotiations with top officials from the Planetary Tourism Agency. That would be so ironic. . .

She only prayed that he wouldn't be "mounted" by an Auyar. They didn't mind paying the fines, no matter how steep, and they always destroyed the bodies they used as "horses." The grodos seemed trusting and naïve by comparison with the Auyars, for whom paranoia seemed to be second nature. They were ultraprotective of their privacy. Nobody knew what they truly looked like, or many facts about them. . .

Human and grodo, they walked through a giant hologram of Colorado's Grand Canyon. Ahead of them, two Aldebaran polyps were silently talking with their tentacle gestures, completely engrossed. Buca watched them in amusement: following the fluorocarbonate pollution of the twentieth century, and after being strip-mined for minerals by a mining corporation from Procyon, the place wasn't even a shadow of that image.

She noticed with pride that Selshaliman was also stopping to admire the panorama. One of the few things the terrestrials could feel proud of was the well-oiled machinery of their advertising and xenoid tourism industries.

Buca had been with an ad designer for a couple of months, and she knew some of the tricks of the trade. Colors imperceptible to the human eye. Infrasound and ultrasound. And recently, even telepathic waves for the grodos. . .

What's good for the goose. . . It was a bit of poetic justice if the Planetary Tourism Agency exploited the xenoids' special abilities to drain their bank accounts.

They were coming up to the first checkpoint, which was surrounded by the inevitable Court of Miracles: self-employed businessmen, illegal moneychangers, drug peddlers, and freelance social workers. And, standing discreetly apart, waiting for offers, very elegant in their tight black synleather clothes, the tall, handsome young men who did male social work. . . It was completely against the law, and Planetary Security cracked down hard on it. In theory.

All of them struggling against each other and with the tourists to earn some credits. Just a month earlier, in a different astroport, Buca had been part of the show, not a witness to it.

But the show was always the same, and with the same actors.

The Disabled Veteran who would show you his radioactive stumps for a few credits. The Victim of Body Spares, drooling piteously and holding out a trembling hand for alms. The Persecuted Believer, begging for help to finish his sacred pilgrimage. The Poor Mother And Her Dirt-Stained Daughter, lying in a corner, both watching everything with the eyes of abused animals. The Rich Man Down On His Luck, feigning dignity to sell his skilled forgeries, the alleged remnant of a family inheritance. The Endangered Species Vendor, with his hidden cages full of solenodons, talking parrots, or leopard cubs. The Orphan Girl, who for a hundred credits would show off her family photos. . . and everything else, and then she'd try to con or assault her extraterrestrial benefactor. The Fun-Seeking Young University Student, who wasn't poor (that had to be clear) but wouldn't sneeze at a few credits or a polite invitation to eat, if some generous humanoid who shared his same-sex tastes were to invite him. . .

The fauna that all the tourism guides warned about.

They only existed because they were tolerated: Buca recalled Jowe's words. A façade of false naturalness, a risky alternative for thrill-seeking tourists. The black market of self-employed tour operators. Their homemade products and services made the sophisticated efficiency of the Planetary Tourism Agency look good merely by contrast. . . and the agents of Planetary Security were keeping watch in the background, making sure the "self-employed" never became a real danger to the tourists.

Among them all, the freelance social workers stood out. Super-tall fluorescent platform shoes forcing them to walk with a gait that could look sinuous or simply unsteady, like balancing on stilts. Clothes tight as a second skin, too short, semi-transparent, or featuring a seductive play of light. Designs meant not to be suggestive but to put everything right out there on display. To leave just the smallest possible portion of the meat for sale to the client's imagination.

Buca looked at the women, half amused and half repulsed.

They were her past.

She compared them with her reflected image in the polished plastometal walls. She wasn't one of them anymore. She had ceased to dress in the lascivious uniform of desire.

She was wearing a pseudosilver ensemble that molded itself to her svelte form, suggesting it without clinging shamelessly to her body. The hues of the fabric shifted, interacting with her biofield. Only her face and hands were exposed; she had already displayed enough skin to last her a thousand years. This was the sort of dress the elegant humanoid ladies of Tau Ceti or Alpha Centauri wore.

Her skin was almost pallid enough for her to be taken for a Centaurian. . .

Maybe she should have bought that skin dye. Pastel blue. It would have heightened the illusion, and Selshaliman wouldn't have minded. Over and above the childish cult for xenoids and for imitating their looks and customs, xenoid women were simply more. . . distinguished.

Being with Selshaliman was all it took for her to breeze through the second checkpoint without being bothered. Only authorized social workers could enter this ring freely. Freelancers had to be accompanied, at least for the time being, by a xenoid to get inside.

The sudden pandemonium of colors and sounds bewildered Buca for a second, as it always did.

The middle ring of every terrestrial astroport was a zone of carefully controlled tolerance, restricted to travelers passing through or tourists eager to take advantage of the reduced customs duties. Social workers of every race and size, each dressed more provocatively than the last. And their male counterparts, in their black uniforms. Native crafts, souvenir shops, all the tourist paraphernalia you found everywhere, all over the planet. But more artificial, cheaper, and more concentrated.

Buca stopped in front of a hologram of New Paris. Before it was a half-melted piece of metal that, according to the sign, had come from the actual Eiffel Tower.

She had never been there. There were so many places on Earth that she might never get to now. . .

It didn't matter that New Paris was just a plastometal reconstruction of the old, authentic city, which had been leveled by a nuclear blast in the days following Contact. Like all terrestrials, Buca felt great pride in the Earth's past glory.

In Greece and Rome and the Aztecs and the Incas and Genghis Khan and the Mongols and the pyramids and the Great Wall of China and the Indian rajahs and the Japanese samurais and Timbuktu and New York.

The present was grodos and all the other xenoids.

Selshaliman also stopped in front of the hologram of New Paris. Hadn't he ever been there? It was ironic. Whatever the Earth was today, it was all due to them. . . and their money. And they didn't take advantage of it.

"Welcome to Earth, the most picturesque planet in the galaxy. Hospitality is our middle name! We're only here to make you feel better than you feel at home." Laughing, Buca recited one of the omnipresent slogans of the Planetary Tourism Agency.

Then her lips twisted into a bitter smile and she looked at Selshaliman with barely concealed hatred.

There was also the other past.

The one described in elementary school interactive texts. One of the few things the Planetary Tourism Agency handed out free to every inhabitant on the planet.

A relatively recent past. When people were already traveling to the cosmos in primitive ships, but many of them still refused to believe in xenoids. When Earth had different countries and lots of tongues instead of the one unified Planetary language. Cattle, crops, fish, and game in abundance, but also plenty of hungry people. When civilization was always on the verge of collapse. Because of nuclear war, pollution, the demographic explosion, or all of it together.

But Contact happened.

The minds of the galaxy had been keeping an eye on humans for thousands of years. Without interfering. Waiting until they were mature enough to be adopted by the great galactic family. But when the total destruction of Earth seemed inevitable, they broke their own rules and jumped in to stop it. Their huge ships landed in Paris, in Rome, in Tokyo, in New York. Their desire to help and their resources seemed endless. . .

Terrestrial leaders, jealously protective of their power in the presence of vastly superior minds and technologies, deemed this altruistic intervention an invasion. And their reaction was violent. Arguing that offense was the best defense, they sounded the trumpets and shouldered arms.

Nuclear arms.

The surprise attack caused a few atomic explosions, like the one that wiped out Old Paris. But there was no nuclear war. The xenoids prevented the rest of the missiles from going off, and then they revealed their full might. When they deployed the geophysical weapon, Africa disappeared beneath the waves. They gave one week's warning, but the obsession with secrecy among the governments and the disbelief of the masses were the real reasons for the deplorable disaster. More than eighty million humans perished in a matter of hours. When it would have been so easy to evacuate them. . .

After that horrendous incident, the extraterrestrials delivered their famous Ultimatum: since the terrestrials were incapable of intelligent self-government or of using their natural resources rationally, from that moment on they would cease to be an independent culture. And so they entered the status of a Galactic Protectorate.

To reestablish the damaged ecological balance, the planet's new masters instituted draconian measures: Zero use of fossil or nuclear fuel. Dismantling the great industrial and scientific centers. Zero demographic growth.

There were global protests, which were put down efficiently and bloodlessly. Total deaths: not even a quarter of a million.

Less than a century later, Earth was once again the natural paradise that had seen the birth of man. With practically all its non-green surface turned into a giant museum, tourism was the major (and almost the only) source of income for the planet and all its inhabitants. Tourism, controlled by the nearly omnipotent Planetary Tourism Agency, with huge investments of extraterrestrial capital and deep concern for the future of *Homo sapiens*. A brilliant future awaited human beings, under the benevolent tutelage of the galactic community, into which they would be accepted one not very distant day, with the rights of full membership. . .

At least, that was the official version.

Buca, like everybody else, knew that the truth was something else entirely.

If it were up to the xenoids, humans would never be a race with equal rights.

Xenoid altruism wasn't what had motivated Contact. And it wasn't the hope of saving humanity that had made them interfere, cutting off any possibility of the planet's independent development at the root.

Jowe had explained the real motives to her. He knew something about Galactic Economics—one of the subjects most strictly forbidden by Planetary Security. You could study it in the secret cells of the clandestine Xenophobe Union for Earthling Liberation. No wonder they were persecuted. Or that he had been condemned to Body Spares just for suspicion of having links to them. Though, most likely, the Yakuza had played some part in the affair. . .

Jowe used to say that the whole galaxy was engulfed in a cruel war. Like all wars, it had offensives and counter-attacks, diversionary movements and tactical retreats. But this was commercial warfare: for new technologies, for markets, for clients, for cheap labor.

Mankind had been a loser in that conflict from the get-go. And as such, it was condemned to be a client, never a rival, not even potentially. Earth barely produced enough food, clothing, and medicine to satisfy a quarter of its own population. And what it manufactured was of such low quality that it couldn't compete with the worst, cheapest products of xenoid technocracies. There was little use for earthly products except as folklore and tourist trinkets.

For commercial expediency, they turned the Earth into a souvenir-world—another of Jowe's phrases, Buca recalled.

Right. . . Because, no matter what the ads said, Earth was no paradise. Getting by was a day-to-day struggle. For every person like her who lucked out, thousands more were left by the wayside. Magnificent people, many of them. Like Yleka. Like Jowe.

Buca was almost sure that the real reason Jowe was arrested and sentenced had nothing to do with the Xenophobe Union, but something else much more petty. Until they caught him, Jowe was a freelance "protector." And one of the best; he raked it in. The protection racket was theoretically illegal, but it could be even more profitable than being a social worker. Riskier, too; if a freelancer got sloppy about paying off the Mafia, the Triads, or the Yakuza every month, tough luck. If Jowe gave her a half-price discount just two months after he started protecting her, only because he'd fallen in love with her beautiful eyes, maybe he'd been naïve enough to do the same for others. Too dangerous. Organized crime didn't like it when other people gave away their money. The arm of the Yakuza was as long as Planetary Security's. . . and they were tougher when punishing time came around.

Her conscience was clean. The truth of it was that she hadn't tricked Jowe. He had set his own trap. The overly idealistic kid believed that sex, cuddles, and sweet talk meant she loved him, too. . . She didn't force him to do it. He was just trying to do her a favor, relieve her debts. And since you weren't supposed to look a gift horse in the mouth. . .

She had liked him, too, but. . . Love your neighbor as yourself. But not more than yourself. That was another motto of hers. Even though Jowe was one of the few men who had known how to treat her like a human being, not like a beautiful piece of meat, an expensive toy with holes for satisfying his sexual desires. He spoke to her mind, which he thought was sharp, though uneducated. He was tender and patient. Really. . . Not like Daniel, the super-tall Voxl player. The hometown hero, the smooth talker who, years ago, had figured out the right lies and tall tales to take away the trophy of her virginity. . .

Now she was always hearing Daniel's name on the sports news. His rise had been meteoric; he must actually be a good player. They'd made him captain of Earth's Voxl team, and in a few days he'd be defending the planet's "honor," playing against a visiting team from the League. Biggest sports event of the year, though the humans had never won it. Yes, Daniel Menéndez had achieved his dream. He was in first place. Jowe, on the other hand, was just another loser in the pile. . .

But she'd never forget that last look he gave her when Planetary Security came to take him away. A mute plea not to forget him. The leathery face of the sergeant who arrested him. The face of a man who knows that somebody's got to do the dirty work, but that doesn't mean he enjoys it. Who's seen it all and doesn't believe in anything anymore.

Jowe. . . Saying goodbye: kissing him, crying with him, hugging him. . . and something like a knot formed in her stomach.

She gulped. Yes, it had been a sign of weakness. . . but it was the least she could do for him. She never could have made it without him.

Without what he'd saved her in protection money, she still wouldn't have saved up enough to buy the translucent leather dress that showed off her healthy animal body and her slender muscles to such advantage. And Selshaliman would never have noticed her at that party.

Getting picked by a grodo was one of the surest ways of leaving Earth... and one of the hardest. Other than luck, it required absolute health. Zero cosmetic or medical implants. Zero genetic or psychological disorders. Zero drug consumption, not even the soft stuff.

Even when Yleka made fun of her, she always kept faithfully to her daily exercise routine, and she detested the facile escape of artificial paradises. Chemical and electronic drugs went in and out of fashion. More and more expensive all the time, but always leaving a trail of incurable addicts in their wake. Telecrack yesterday, neurogames today, who knows what tomorrow. It was easier to replace one addiction with another than to recover.

Buca gave a pitying look to several boys hooked up to consoles. Neuroplayers. Isolated in the private worlds of their direct-access cortical implants. Rich kids, you could tell. By their tailor-made clothes and the fact that no burned-out street neuro would have access to the middle ring of an astroport. These guys had to have enough credits in their accounts to bribe the Planetary Security men. And to pay for hours, not just minutes, of time in play-cyberspace, where they could forget they were living on a planet with no future and a repulsive present.

Their philosophy was sound and darkly attractive: Reality is shit? Then run away from it. In the virtual world, time moved at a different pace. In it they could travel to planets they'd never see. In it they could be superheroes. Invulnerable Colossaurs, or beautiful, feline Cetians. Why risk real death by fighting with the morons of the Xenophobe Union for Earthling Liberation? In neurogames, they could enjoy a thousand synthetic deaths a day and liberate the Earth from the xenoid yoke a thousand times...

Convulsing with laughter every time they looked at each other, three authorized social workers passed by, swaying to the effects of what was no doubt one of the first times they had tried telecrack. Buca thought of Yleka. This is how it must start. . .

Telecrack was incurably addictive. Supposedly it heightened your telepathic potential, letting you establish temporary bonds of empathy, even exchange isolated thoughts with others. According to Jowe, that was all bunk. Human beings lacked telepathic receptors, and nothing could change that. The only effect of telecrack was to overcharge your neural circuits and cause hallucinations. Period.

Yleka used to take a dose before starting with each client. She said it "tuned her in," and she claimed she worked better that way. Maybe it was true. . . for the first two or three hours of the night. Later on she always ended up bawling and babbling incomprehensibly about an Alex guy "who was working on something hush-hush, very important." Her friend's secret bugged Buca a little at first (she had told Yleka her whole life story), but she soon came to the obvious conclusion that this Alex was just another dumb and meaningless lost love. And all that about his "important hush-hush work," just Yleka's romantic idealization.

Poor kid, she must have loved him a lot if she was turning to telecrack to try and forget him. Though perhaps the horse-pill doses she consumed were just an attempt to escape her own body while she was being subjected to all sorts of degrading manipulations. Being a social worker had a few points in common with being sentenced to Body Spares. In either case, a girl wasn't in total control of her body. . .

Yleka took the slow road to self-destruction. Her body deteriorating from addiction, she'd reached the inevitable moment when she could no longer attract clients the way she once had. At least she had managed to get that Cetian, Cauldar, to take her, and she left the planet with him. Where could she be now? And how was she doing?

Cetian humanoids were the galactic species most like *Homo sapiens*. But more beautiful, more seductive. . . and more dangerous. Males and females roamed all over Earth, always searching for candidates for their slave brothels. They paid very well. And nobody made love like they did. . . Buca had come this close to leaving with Yleka, going off with her and Cauldar. But she decided to take the rumors seriously.

There were horrible stories going around about the dives of Tau Ceti. About girls forced to couple unnaturally with the polyps of Aldebaran or the segmented guzoids of Regulus, leading to their death, mutilation, or exotic, repugnant, and incurable venereal diseases. And there were worse things than the slave brothels. Rumors told of lots of young people, seduced by the Cetians' angelic looks, who ended up on the organ traffickers' chopping blocks.

A lot of those stories must have been just made up. How could humans be of any interest, even zoophile interest, to beings that reproduced asexually, like polyps or guzoids?

But after prudently considering that there's a kernel of truth in every rumor, at the last minute Buca let Yleka leave by herself. Her friend, in a best-case scenario, would now be subject to Cauldar's every whim. All Cetians concealed an implacable iron will under their sweet external appearances.

A real pity: before she filled herself with drugs, Yleka had an enviable body. Maybe Selshaliman would have taken both of them. For a grodo, two would do better than one girl alone. . .

Almost without her realizing it, they had entered the inner ring of the cosmodrome, reserved strictly for arriving and departing passengers. The grodo's movements had grown calmer. He was much more familiar with this area, and he felt safer here than outside.

Though only a human who hated his fellow man would attack an insectoid. The only time a grodo had become the innocent victim of a group of armed robbers, the geophysical weapon spoke again and

New London disappeared, swallowed by a tsunami. Lesson learned. Grodos could travel safely anywhere on the planet.

Moreover, if anyone were crazy and suicidal enough to try harming one of these insectoids, he'd find it a hard job to pull off. Selshaliman's shining chitin carapace was practically invulnerable to every sort of projectile, and it was absolutely forbidden to own or manufacture energy weapons on earth. Planetary Security agents and their minimachine guns made sure the rule was scrupulously followed.

Armored, with four slender but incredibly strong arms and four matching legs, grodos were rapid fighters, with strength second only to that of the massive Colossaurs, and not by much. Besides, they had that stinger, good for injecting their lethal venom into their victims.

And for doing other things, as Buca knew all too well. . .

The inner ring of the astroport was empty of any sort of cyberaddict or social worker. Only travelers had access to this zone.

Through the large windows you could see the runway with the shuttles waiting in an orderly line, broken here and there by the occasional squat, aerodynamic suborbital patrol ship.

Buca smiled, amused: It appeared that, despite all of Planetary Security's boasts about "maintaining control," the problem of illegal departures from the planet kept getting more and more serious. They'd had to buy so many of these ships from the xenoids to control the fugitives that their own astroports weren't enough to serve them all.

Buca had never entered an astroport's last ring before. The simple fact that she was able to walk through these corridors was almost a guarantee that Selshaliman would make good on his promise. That before you knew it, she would be boarding the shuttle, and then the hypership, leaving Earth. Forever.

Nostalgia invaded her, with its troop of memories.

She remembered her birth on the small island whose name she would rather forget. Her mother, happy to finally have the daughter she had wanted, baptizing her with the name María Elena. Her father, a bearded astronaut in the satellite-hunting patrol, only an occasional presence at home, between one trip and the next. She remembered her childhood, free of poverty, free of dependence on Social Assistance, believing that Planetary Security agents existed only to protect her. Believing in terrestrial hospitality and the goodness of xenoids. . . And her mother, looking at her and sighing, as if to say, "Play and enjoy life now. . . There will be plenty of time for suffering later."

And was there ever.

But nobody could take those years of happiness away from her.

Later, everything came all at once. When she was ten, she discovered the lie of the Galactic Protectorate, the cruelty of the Ultimatum, what xenoids really were. Her birthday present was a one-week trip to Hawaii, all first-class. They even went to the astroport to take the suborbital shuttle. She loved it! Never suspecting that it would be the last time her whole family would be together. Her mother and father cried the whole time, whenever they thought she wasn't looking. They were hugging all the time, and Buca couldn't understand why.

Until, after they had been sitting for hours in the cosmodrome waiting area, it was officials from Social Assistance who came to pick her up. And she knew she would never see her parents again.

Driven to the brink by their mounting debts, they had sold themselves for life to Body Spares. In return for that farewell trip, and for a clause guaranteeing room and board for their daughter until she turned fifteen. And also for canceling the debt she otherwise would have had to pay in her parents' place, which would have made her a lifelong slave of the Planetary Tourism Agency.

She never forgave them.

Boarding-school hell, surrounded by kids rescued from the streets and marked for a life of crime almost from birth. A happy and sheltered childhood was a handicap there. Common girls, who had grown up keeping their distance from the turf wars between the Yakuza and the Mafia and making fun of the xenoids who prowled for healthy young native girls, had a mean streak that she lacked. They were as strong and aggressive as wild animals, and they hated and envied her for not being one of them. For being good-looking and having manners, for being tall and strong-boned. They hated her and they let her know it. Making fun of her. Humiliating her. Hitting her.

It was hard. But she adapted. Learned. Toughened up. So when the money that her parents (by then long dead, both driven insane) had gotten from Body Spares ran out, she ran away from boarding school rather than let other people decide what to do with her. She already knew what she wanted: to leave Earth, no matter the cost. She had no talent for art or sports, and nothing beyond basic education. And she sure wasn't going to risk her life on a wild kamikaze attempt at an unlawful space launch.

She knew what the surest way was to carry out her plan: become a freelance social worker and get a xenoid to take her. Galactic tourists really seemed to appreciate the sweetness and good cheer of human females, and especially their ability to pretend that their relationships were not mercenary. As for herself. . . She had ceased to be a virgin and innocent years ago. She was beautiful, cheeky, brave, and eager to get by. And utterly enraged at the world.

Without documents you could never become an authorized social worker. One of those who turn over part of their earnings to the Planetary Tourism Agency and in exchange get protection: a minimum salary, guaranteed retirement, and free medical care. Nor did she want any of that. Her way was to get by on her own or perish.

At first it seemed she wouldn't make it. Her first client, a deceptively friendly Centaurian, insisted on the full package. In his hotel room. And she, being treated like a lady for the first time in her life, naïvely agreed. . .

It was pretty nice at first. She had a few orgasms. But the xenoid kept going and going. . . and the act became a torture session that went on for hours and hours. She argued, kicked, and clawed, trying to get away, to no avail; the Centaurian was much stronger than she was. She screamed, crazy with pain, pleading for help. . . but the hotel rooms were soundproof, or else the human employees were too used to the screams of social workers. Nobody came.

The interminable and sadistic coupling finally made her faint. She ended up with her innards swollen, turned to jelly, aching for days. The worst of it was that the bastard took advantage of her unconsciousness not only to sneak off without paying but to steal what little she had saved, too. And he didn't even pay the hotel bill.

On another occasion she thought a particularly rank Colossaur had infected her with the incurable magenta illness, and she came close to killing herself. . .

But gradually she learned the tricks of the trade. After being robbed three times by amateur thieves, she contacted the pros to make sure her back was covered. Protection was expensive, but it worked. They never cornered her in a dark alley again. Or made her turn over her hard-earned wages at the point of a vibroblade. Or forced her to give herself up to enliven the night for her assailants.

Now she had triumphed. If she wished, she could come back anytime and walk haughtily through the seedy byways where she was once nearly a slave. If she wanted. But she never intended to return.

A teletransport booth opened right in front of her face, startling her. A grodo insectoid emerged in a gust of cold air. Apparently coming from some city in the far north.

She looked with curiosity at the empty booth. She'd never seen one so close, much less used one. They were colossally expensive. Completely beyond the reach of simple freelance social workers, such as she had been up until now.

It was time she started getting used to them. All the xenoids used them when they rushing. You got in, a flash of disintegration. . . and you showed up, with another flash, in a similar booth thousands of miles away.

They weren't perfect, however. You could only use them to get around on the same planet, and even so, they made small and regrettable mistakes on rare occasions. Very rare occasions, truth be told. For example, the grodos' private network had never had one of the accidents that periodically filled the news holovideos.

The Planetary Tourism Agency always paid compensation to the family members of the unlucky victims of dematerialization, giving the evergreen excuse that on Earth they didn't have enough experience managing such advanced equipment. . . because extraterrestrial technicians were reluctant to train human crews to run teleport booths. Maybe there was a bit of truth in that. Surely newly trained human teletransport specialists would pull every string and try every trick to get off the planet as fast as they could. Like any sensible person who had any skill that xenoids might value. Artists, scientists, athletes—they all ran from their birth world as soon as the dazzling glare of extraterrestrial credits made them understand where true happiness could be found.

Of course, they never stopped shooting their mouths off about Liberating the Earth, Fighting for the Rights of the Human Race, and other such hot-air slogans. Buca despised them. It was so easy to talk about ideals from the outside, on a full stomach. And so hypocritical. She'd never make fun of the people who stayed behind on Earth, and she'd never "show solidarity with their just struggle". . .

Blam. . . Blam. . . Blam. . .

Three isolated bangs.

Then the too-familiar rattle of small-caliber automatic arms.

Buca was stretched out on the ground before she understood what was happening. Her reflexes had betrayed her; you'd never survive in the suburbs if you insisted on standing up after you heard shots fired. A little annoyed over her broken dignity, she watched.

The Planetary Security men were cornering a lone terrorist. He was jumping from column to column with incredible agility, evading them

22

and firing a prehistoric repeating rifle. Doubtless he had taken an enormous dose of feline analogue, a non-addictive military drug that endowed any human with the tremendous agility and fast reflexes of cats.

The Xenophobe Union for Earthling Liberation guys often used it during their commando operations. The side effects were devastating exhaustion and depression, which left you totally defenseless. But a new dose would eliminate those effects. You could keep up the cycle indefinitely, or until you perished, all your physical and mental reserves drained, but active to the last second.

Beaten by numerical superiority and better arms, the man who thought he was a cat fell, hit point-blank by the Security agents' bursts of fire. They kept on firing until unrecognizable remains were all that was left of the body. The feline analogue also made you incredibly resistant to wounds. More than one agent had discovered in the flesh that a terrorist with a dozen shots to the chest could still open his belly with one blow.

When the astroport clean-up people picked up what was left of the body and traffic returned to normal, Buca got up and glanced around, looking for Selshaliman. She suspected a last-minute betrayal. That would have been the height of irony, to leave her stranded there in the middle of the astroport...

"Your identification, please," the Planetary Security agent's voice resounded behind her with a mix of courtesy and authority. The barrel of a gun, still hot, poked insistently at her shoulder.

Buca turned around, infuriated: if he had ruined her dress, that idiot would see...

"I thought freelancers weren't allowed in here." There was disdain in the voice that emerged from beneath the helmet covering the agent's features. Any courtesy had disappeared. "Pretty dress... Too bad a monkey's still a monkey, even in a silk dress. Come along with me, sweetheart. You and me are going to go clear up a few things in private... And you'd better be very nice to me if you don't want me to accuse you of being that poor moron's accomplice." He pointed with his minimachine gun at the pile of scraps that his buddies had turned the terrorist into.

"Wait, you're making a mistake, I came here with. . ." Buca tried to explain, trembling with fear and rage at once. That was the usual deal the Planetary Security guys offered women in her profession: sex for impunity. Didn't she know it. . . But how had he recognized her in spite of her super-expensive dress? She suddenly felt as naked and vulnerable as when she used to go around the other astroport dressed only in a translucent jacket and a scanty fluorescent loincloth.

"I don't care who you came with. You're going with me, princess," he impatiently interrupted her. And he stuck out his gloved hand to grab her brusquely by the arm.

Buca closed her eyes and cringed, like a child waiting for his father's belt to strike. Where had Selshaliman gone? Was it all just a dream? She should have suspected; it was too good to be real, for it to be happening to her. . .

Zasss. . .

The sound, right next to her, like a whip. Something fell.

The gloved hand had never touched her. She opened her eyes.

Selshaliman was at her side, antennas up and the light reflecting wonderfully off his faceted eyes. He had never looked so beautiful to her before. The Planetary Security agent, sitting on the floor several yards off, rubbed his aching chest.

"Are you all right, Buca? Did he hurt you?" the insectoid's vocal synthesizer chirped.

"Believe me, we are very sorry for this. . . incident. She is perfectly fine. My man didn't even touch her. We didn't know that she was with you. . ." The voice of another Planetary Security man, a sergeant to judge by his stripes, sounded conciliatory. "To make it to you, we'll give you top priority on the shuttle. . ."

"You had better do so. Come, Buca," Selshaliman pronounced

majestically, barely touching her. Buca leaned on him, trusting and deeply moved. At that moment she could even have loved him.

He'd hit a Planetary Security guy just to protect her! The sergeant and his man were nothing but trash to a tourist, especially a grodo. . . but it was the gesture that counted. She walked on Selshaliman's arm, feeling on top of the world.

But she didn't move away fast enough to avoid hearing what the sergeant said while he was helping his buddy back to his feet. Or maybe he said it so loud on purpose:

"Come on, to your feet, stupid. . . He hit you hard, but your armor absorbed it well enough. And you know what? You deserved it for being an idiot. For not paying better attention. That's not any old social worker. . . The grodo has picked her; she's going to be incubated, and that makes her a thousand times more valuable than you or me, or a hundred of us."

Buca didn't want to hear more. But Selshaliman's measured pace forced her to hear the rest, too. The expert sergeant explaining things to the rookie. What she had known from the beginning. What she'd rather not remember.

"No, it won't be like you're thinking." The sergeant had a decidedly disagreeable laugh. "Grodos are hermaphrodites. They only reproduce once, and then they die. But they have to deposit their eggs in another living being. The 'incubator' has to be warm-blooded, and as intelligent as possible. I guess that's so she won't kill herself, like a sensible wild animal would if it saw it was as good as dead. So she'll last long enough. . . So the eggs can hatch and the larvae can eat her guts without a care in the world. And apparently we human beings, especially if we're free of drugs or implants, are perfect fits. When?

Well. . . from the color of its carapace, it's got to have a few more years to go. Our girlfriend will have everything she wants until he-she feels it's time to worry about the continuity of the species. But I wouldn't want to be in her place then. . ."

Buca couldn't take it anymore. Removing her arm from Selshali-man's with a violent gesture, she gave a half-turn to face the sergeant.

The man had already taken off his helmet.

Those leathery features. . .

Buca gulped, recognizing him.

Those eyes, sick of seeing all the world's misery, gave her such a look that she was only capable of muttering, indistinctly, but with a calm that she never would have thought herself capable of:

"True. But I'm leaving, and you two are stuck here."

And she went back to her grodo lord and master. Rage and impotence burned in her eyes. Fortunately the makeup she had on was waterproof. Tearproof, too. And it formed a veritable mask over her face.

The day they took Jowe away she hadn't been wearing makeup.

It wasn't likely the sergeant had recognized her. . . Even so, the prudent thing was to get away.

As soon as she found an opportunity, she would beg Selshaliman to use his influence to have him. . . punished, somehow. She was sure he'd do it, to please her.

Just by thinking about this, she could feel the calm returning to her soul. Though maybe she would be coming down too hard on the man. . . He seemed to know a lot about grodos, and he had confirmed what Selshaliman had told her: until his grayish carapace turned completely dark, the time hadn't come yet.

Several years. And then. . .

What would it be like? Selshaliman had told her something. . .

The ovipositor stinger, smoothly and painlessly penetrating her vagina to deposit its precious cargo in the best protected of human organs, the uterus. It could even be pleasant.

And the eggs, so delicate they could take years to hatch. . . and for some girls, they never did. Maybe she'd be lucky, like she'd been so far. Or maybe even she could , with some metabolic poison. . .

She looked at Selshaliman out of the corner of her eye and went back to repeating the catchy lyrics of the technohit in her head. Better not to try anything. Better not even think about it. If the grodo suspected she'd even considered such a possibility, he'd drown her in acid. Or worse.

Several years...

It'd be better to resign herself to the idea right now. After all, she had enjoyed the best part of her youth. And as the saying goes, die young, leave a beautiful corpse. It wouldn't hurt; from what the grodo told her, the larvae secreted a very powerful analgesic. She'd enjoy it all right up to the very end, with the same dying vitality as a guy doped up on feline analogue...

And how she'd enjoy it! All her whims would be fulfilled. It was hard to imagine how big Selshaliman's fortune was. In any case, more than enough to buy the best dresses in the universe, to eat the most exotic delicacies, to travel to the most exquisite and most fashionable resorts. She'd have all the lovers she wanted... She'd already talked it over with the grodo: the very concept of faithfulness made no sense to a hermaphrodite being. She could even afford to take one of those pale, perverse, and beautiful Cetians.

She'd only be forbidden to have children. For the good of her expensive and precious uterus... But who would think of wasting time giving birth?

She'd learn to present herself well in galactic high society, to which Selshaliman, who no doubt had a prominent position in the caste hierarchy of his race, would be delighted to introduce her.

Of course, it was about time she convinced him to dump that horrible Arab name of his. He needed something trendier, more impressive, more modern, something to wow her girlfriends. Because he was going to pay to have some of them travel from Earth, you bet. And maybe, if he was still alive, Jowe... She owed him that.

Smiling, Buca walked through the last doorway in the astroport and boarded the shuttle that would take her to the orbiting hyper-ship.

A Japanese name would sound nicer. . . Those are all the rage now. Four syllables, the way they like. Horusaki, something like that. It was important to pick one, as soon as possible.

August 24, 1993

Mestizos

The genes of *Homo sapiens* are moderately compatible by nature with those of humanoid species with very similar biotypes and evolutionary histories, such as the Cetians and Centaurians. Species that, to be sure, cannot produce fertile cross-breeds with each other, a fact that has given biologists and anthropologists from across the galaxy a lot of room to debate about interstellar migrations of humanoid or prehumanoid races, and other more or less harebrained theories.

The possibility that two different germ cells could fuse and produce a viable zygote is vanishingly small. Of ten million potentially fertile couplings, only one will give rise to a hybrid.

Mestizos are always sterile, they usually lack developed sexual organs, and sometimes they do not even have a definite sex. But by the laws of genetics, they also possess what is called "hybrid vigor": they are more robust, more disease-resistant, and often more handsome than the members of either of the races that gave birth to them.

The Centaurians' blue skin and large eyes, combined with a human bone structure, produce spectacular results. Same with the feline elegance and vertical pupils of the lovely Cetians.

Likewise, hybrids seem especially gifted in the arts. Music, dance, visual arts are almost second nature to these exotic beings, whose ranks include some of the greatest talents in the galaxy today.

Cases of mestizo children can be found in every human social group. But, as is statistically logical, most mestizos are born to social workers, who are in most frequent contact with extraterrestrial humanoids.

It is a curious fact that, despite the risk of pregnancy, professional sex workers use no birth control methods in their relations with

Cetians and Centaurians. As they normally do whenever they couple with a native of Colossa...

There are two main reasons for this "carelessness."

The first is purely medical: while Colossaurs can transmit the incurable magenta disease, which is endemic among them and whose origins and structure are unknown, extraterrestrial humanoids suffer from almost no such illnesses. And any diseases they do have can easily be treated with conventional medicines, much like terrestrial syphilis, gonorrhea, or AIDS.

The second and more important reason is, well, economic. The Planetary Tourism Agency provides free medical care and pays large bonuses to any worker who gets pregnant by a humanoid—bonuses that grow even larger if the hybrid is born successfully.

In exchange for that generous pile of credits, the mother merely has to sign over all her legal rights to the newborn, who is handed over to the Agency's specialized teachers and experts for raising and education.

Young mestizos are given a costly and painstaking education aimed at developing their inborn artistic talents. An education that might go on for a few years, or for many, and that only comes to an end when a buyer appears.

Well-to-do xenoids are more than willing to spend large sums to acquire, more or less permanently, the talents of a humanoid mestizo. Mestizos, for their part, due to the exceptional peculiarity of their births, not only automatically enjoy all the advantages of double citizenship, terrestrial and xenoid, such as freedom to travel and so on, but in view of their valuable talents they generally also have much higher incomes and life status than any ordinary human.

The large number of credits that all mestizos must regularly pay to the Planetary Tourism Agency, regardless of where they live, is considered a tax on extraterritorial citizenship, perfectly legal according to galactic norms. Or fitting compensation for the huge investment made in their artistic education.

The rental-purchase of mestizo artists is currently one of the most significant sources of revenue for Earth, which is thus amply paid back for its investments in their education. In fact, the ineffable Auyars are investigating a project to achieve hybridization (artificially, at least at first) between non-humanoid races and terrestrial genes. Though the project is still in its experimental phase, they have already received thousands of requests for human-Colossaur mestizos, grodo-human mestizos, and other, yet more exotic combinations.

The Planetary Tourism Agency's only concern is the high risk of the "human" factor in their investment. The psychological stability of hybrids is abnormally low. Despite all efforts to the contrary, it appears that the predisposition of mestizos toward depression, neurosis, and other psychic complaints remains very high, though the relevant statistics are kept secret.

Some social psychologists hypothesize that the very sense of non-integration, of uprootedness, of having one foot in each camp, of not belonging, the very identity crisis that makes hybrids seek a solitary refuge in art, is also responsible for the fact that they have the highest suicide rate and the lowest life expectancy of any known "human" group.

Nevertheless, the Planetary Tourism Agency is conducting encouraging studies on the subcortical implantation of suicide blockers, similar to the blockers that xenoids implant in all humans who travel beyond Earth to prevent them from revealing what they've seen when they return.

Some behavioral specialists doubt the effectiveness of this method and suggest that depriving mestizos of the "relative escape" of suicide could result not only in the total collapse of their own psyches, but might also place their masters or purchasers in great danger. Unable to take their own lives, they might become highly aggressive toward others, seeking death by any means.

Despite these objections, which really come from a few isolated voices, the Agency is confident that this new technology will eliminate that deplorable problem forever and that it will no longer have to face claims for damages from xenoids who have seen the mestizos they paid so much for destroy themselves, without their being able to do anything about it. . .

Performing Death

"Being on top of game today. There being much audience," Ettubrute said on entering the tent, speaking in the hoarse rattle that was his voice. Then he added, standing next to Moy, who was adjusting the equipment for the umpteenth time, "Not needing more checking. . . Me having done it two times already."

"I'll be on the top of my game, don't you worry. And let me make one thing clear: I'll check it a thousand times if I feel like it; it's my life on the line—not yours, Bruiser," Moy grumbled without looking up.

The Colossaur growled, more out of habit than because he was actually offended. And it was a matter of habit: from the first, it had bothered him a lot every time the human called him Bruiser.

By the standards of his race, Ettubrute was small and weak. That's why he'd become an art agent. Like all professions that don't call for physical strength, dexterity, or aggression, the art business was held in low esteem by the natives of Colossa. The only honorable, ideal jobs for a "normal" Colossaur were bodyguard, law enforcement officer, or soldier. Ettubrute was a poor oddball, to his fellows.

The funny part was that Moy didn't call him Bruiser to mock him. The "weak" Colossaur who was his agent had a natural armor of bony reddish plates that few weapons could penetrate, and he stood nearly ten feet tall by five wide. Maybe he was a yard short and a hundred pounds too light to be normal-sized for his race. . . but he was way more than strong enough to beat any human into a pulp with a single blow from his arm, as thick as Moy's thigh.

"Being better if all turning out better today than ever. If you failing, contract ending." The Colossaur made a threatening gesture with his enormous tridactyl hand. "Not even earning returning ticket." He turned and stalked out so violently that the tent's thin, tough walls of synplast vibrated and nearly shattered.

"Idiot," Moy muttered, but only after the xenoid's heavy footsteps had faded away outside. Colossaurs had a keen sense of hearing, and they could be very spiteful.

What he was afraid of wasn't Ettubrute's armored fists and huge muscles—the Colossaur would never dare smash him. He was the goose that laid the golden egg, the Colossaur's best investment.

What truly terrified him was what his agent could do with his earnings, according to that one-sided contract he'd been forced to sign as a sine qua non for that ticket off Earth. Some of its clauses would literally make him Ettubrute's slave if the xenoid ever decided to put them into effect. And the worst of it was that, since Moy had voluntarily signed it with his fingerprints, voice print, and retinal ID, he had no legal standing to lodge a complaint.

Luckily, you might say that something like a. . . friendship had developed between him and his agent. Though that was too grand a word to describe any relationship between a xenoid and a human.

Even so, if Ettubrute ever wanted to hurt him. . .

Better not even go there.

"I'm trapped, trapped, trap-trap-trapped," he hummed, a habit he'd picked up through months of relative isolation. How long had it been since he'd laid eyes on another human face? Months. Since Kandria, on Colossa. And not even all human; she'd been half Centaurian. . .

His own face had even started looking weird to him in the mirror. Well, naturally, after seeing so many mugs covered with hair, or scales, or feathers, or stuff that was just indescribable, all up and down the galaxy.

"Didn't you want to see other worlds, kid? Be careful what you wish for. Tell 'em you don't want soup, they'll give you three bowls; tell 'em you do, they'll give you three hundred. To make you to stop wanting it," he thought sarcastically. "Only pity is, I'll never be able to tell anybody about it. I've seen so many things. . ."

His tour with Ettubrute had put him in contact with beings and places you never heard anybody mention on Earth. Some amazing, some terrifying. Beings any biologist or sociologist on Earth would have given ten years of their lives just to meet.

The morlacks of Betelgeuse, with their phosphorescent hides. The two-headed birds of Arcturus. The marsupials of Algol, with that natural teleportation. A hundred other races. The cosmos was a lot bigger than they ever supposed on Earth, and it held more beings that they'd ever imagined.

Beings he could never talk about: the laws of the galaxy kept strict control of the flow of scientific and technological information that was permitted to the "backward" races. For instance, *Homo sapiens*. And when he signed his contract, Moy knew that his memory would be blocked before he could return to Earth. To preserve the anonymity of races that didn't want *Homo sapiens* to know about them. To keep him from telling anyone about his experiences. A basic precaution to keep Earthlings from getting their hands on information and technologies that they weren't capable of using "rationally" yet.

"The important thing is what I've experienced and what I can remember, even if I can't talk about it," he muttered. "Lucky thing I never went to Auya. . ."

He stopped recalibrating the nanomanipulators for a moment and glanced outside the tent, over his shoulder. The blue, red, and black triple-diamond hologram rotated slowly, floating over the tallest buildings on the plaza. The Auyar symbol.

The wealthiest race in the galaxy. And the most protective of its privacy. Nobody knew what they really looked like. Nobody knew the location of their worlds. Those who visited them always got their memories completely erased. . .

Or they got death.

He stared at the triple diamond for several seconds, like a defenseless bird peering into the hypnotic eyes of a cobra. The Auyars paid really well. Better than anyone. A contract from them could make him rich forever. But at a price: being left with a mind as blank as a newborn child's. Stripped of the only true wealth he had managed to amass in his not-very-long life: his memory.

Moy trembled and tore his gaze from the triple diamond with an almost physical effort. "I should think about something else or I won't be able to do anything today," he mumbled, feeling beads of sweat slide down his forehead. "It'd be so nice right now to take a hit. . ."

A hit, a hit. . . *No.*

Shouldn't even think of it.

Telecrack had nearly scrambled his brain. Ettubrute had sworn he'd tear him to pieces if he caught him using it again, after all it had cost to rehab him. And the worst thing about Colossaurs was that they always made good on their promises.

"It was all his fault. . . He shouldn't have let me feel so lonely," Moy grumbled bitterly. "I had to find company in the tele—"

He gulped. Just mentioning the drug and remembering the incomparable feeling as it entered his veins had set him to trembling. He had to lean against a corner of the tent to keep from tottering over.

Of course it had been the Colossaur's fault.

Why hadn't he ever told him that telecrack's supposed ability to grant you telepathic powers was all a fake? If he was his manager, why hadn't he helped him manage his earnings better those first few months? Invest them, like he did himself?

Well, the truth was, the only thing Ettubrute could have done to keep him away from telecrack and the other easy pleasures would have been to forbid them outright. But Moy had been so eager to have credits and spend them however he wanted, maybe that wouldn't have worked either. . .

"It's hard to learn from somebody else's veins," he muttered, smiling.

With a sad smile, he recalled the consumerist frenzy of his early months. Amazed by the utter novelty of his performance, the xenoids were perfectly happy to lavish their credits on him. And he was perfectly delighted to squander them.

Everything he'd ever yearned for on Earth but had never had. Everything he thought of as a symbol of status, of power, of wealth. Expensive clothes. Exotic food. Sensuous Cetian hetaerae. He bought gifts for his whole family and sent them by teletransport. A condominium in the most expensive neighborhood. Credits, credits… And, finally, telecrack.

The excuse he gave himself for trying it was pitifully trite. It went something like this: after a certain point every creative artist has to develop his parapsychological faculties if he wants to keep going further. What great performances he could have created if he could read the audience's mind! The perfect, divine feedback loop…

"Ha," Moy laughed drily. "The divine zilch."

Deep down inside, he'd always guessed that telecrack was a fraud. Turning a human being into a temporary telepath was ridiculous, impossible. What he found attractive about the drug wasn't so much its dubious effects as its ability to create permanent addiction. And the brain damage it could cause as a side effect. Playing with death…

Hits and more hits. Russian roulette by drug.

Telecrack, even off Earth, was an expensive drug.

He spent thousands and thousands to fill his veins with venom.

Until one day Ettubrute, tired of bearing witness to his self-destruction, forcibly locked him up in a detox center. Moy was barely a shadow of a man, down to ninety wretched pounds and lucky he could even breathe.

They took care of him at the center. Real good care.

They freed him from his addiction forever.

Well, they were supposed to. That's what they were there for.

The incredible thing was, they did it in just eight days.

Eight days during which he came to know all the colors and flavors of hell. It had been bad. Real bad.

Knowing that was more than enough.

He didn't want to remember the details. . . Or, he couldn't. The Auyars weren't the only ones who could erase memories.

He got out, restored to health, having put on sixty pounds and gotten back almost all of his old self-control. Having gained total respect for xenoid medicine, which had done the miraculous and freed him from a drug that nobody on Earth ever escaped.

And a feeling of gratitude mixed with resentment toward Ettubrute. He'd saved his life, true. . . But he charged the full cost of the treatment to Moy's account.

It was only once he'd combed through his finances that he understood how much money he had wasted. Between the detox center's bill (effective treatment was expensive anywhere in the galaxy) and what he had spent on telecrack, he owed the Colossaur nearly half a million. And the worst of it was, his agent was close to washing his hands of the whole business and suing him for breach of contract. Leaving him stranded in a foreign world, without a credit. . . It would have been almost like murdering him.

It had taken begging, pleading, and invoking the "old friendship" between them — and a promise to pay off his debt in full, plus fifty percent — to get Ettubrute to loan him enough to be able to eat and fix up the equipment for his performance piece. The bare minimum he needed to start over. From zero. . .

The Colossaur had bled him with the skill of a parasite. And the ironic thing was, he was still supposed to be grateful to him for agreeing to keep on bleeding him for a while.

Naturally, he'd had to sell his tailor-made clothes and his luxury condo and give up the expensive whores and the exotic food. But, lesson learned. Once and for all.

"And here I am, in the thick of it," he sighed. At least he'd been strong enough not to give up. He'd already lived it up enough. Maybe too much. He knew everything you could do with money. And he knew he would be able to earn more. Next time would be different.

At least there'd be a next time.

He'd had to tighten his belt, the last few months. . . but he'd already practically covered his debt to the Colossaur. Before long, what he earned would be his again. . . minus the agent's usual twenty-five percent.

"Leech," he muttered, but without real anger. Yes, it was an exorbitant percentage. No xenoid artist turned over more than ten percent to his agent. But he was human, a terrestrial. . . Trash, that is. And he could never give enough thanks to his good luck and to Ettubrute for allowing him a chance to leave the cultural and financial hole-in-the-wall that was Earth.

There were thousands of human artists who would envy his situation, that he was sure of. Many artists, better and more original than him, would have sold their souls to the devil just to get out.

He thought with satisfaction about his upcoming triumphal return visit, with enough credits to buy a whole city on Earth. And enough firsthand experience of xenoid art to put his own work light-years ahead of any competitor's, in concept, theory, and development.

They could stop him from talking about what he'd seen, but they couldn't stop those experiences from seeping into his art. . .

He had nothing to complain about. It could have been a lot worse. Ettubrute, after all, was almost his friend.

He thought again about Kandria, that holoprojection artist he had met on Colossa. A beautiful mestizo woman, half-human, half-Centaurian, truly talented. Some of her "Multisymphonies" were genuinely good. And the girl was just fantastic at making love.

Too bad they'd barely had two weeks together. Moy wouldn't have complained about getting involved in a longer and more serious relationship with her. Though Kandria's Centaurian agent might have.

Her agent was her own father. And even though she swore to Moy a thousand times that the blue-skinned humanoid truly loved her, even a blind man could tell that her father's supposed "filial love" was nothing more than a well-planned maneuver to make tons of money off his bastard daughter's talent. Enough money to get his world's rigid society to pardon him for the sin of mixing his blood with a species as inferior as *Homo sapiens.*

The affection and considerateness Kandria's father showed her in public were too exaggerated to be real. Especially coming from a member of a race as cold and distant as the Centaurians. People said they had icicles for hearts and computers for brains. And in Moy's opinion, that was an understatement.

But he never commented on it. If it made the poor girl happy to believe her daddy loved her, he wasn't going to break the illusion. At least not while he was enjoying her splendid body every night.

He recalled those meetings with another sigh. Kandria. . . Her skin, that gorgeous turquoise hue, so flexible, her huge eyes. Her passion. . . Kandria was a magnificent example of what Ettubrute would cynically call "optimal utilization of installed capacities." Which were few: like almost all hybrids, she was congenitally sterile. The funny part was how, without a vagina or functioning ovaries, she could show such sexual enthusiasm. . .

"When it comes to sex, nothing is written in stone." Moy shrugged and checked the skinners. Everything was perfect. Ettubrute was not only a skillful agent (maybe too skillful) but also a very competent assistant when it came to technology. You could almost say he fully earned his twenty-five percent.

If not true friendship, the two of them had developed a very special relationship. Love-hate was too crude a term to define it.

It all started with the nickname Moy had given the Colossaur around the time he had signed the contract, when he admitted he was couldn't pronounce his real name, which sounded like Warrtorgrowrrtrehrfroarturr. "Et tu, Brute" was just a sophisticated way of saying "that old thing" or "you there." The Colossaur didn't really appreciate it. Since then, they had spent half their time making fun of each other, acidly. Maybe to forget how much they needed each other.

"Maybe if I stopped calling him Bruiser, the alien might stop mangling his Planetary syntax," Moy reflected out loud, checking the pendulums and bleeders.

Even though his race wasn't known for its language talents, Ettubrute had always refused to use a cybernetic translator. He preferred to mangle the Earthling language in his own barbarous fashion. Moy had finally gotten used to it, and he almost enjoyed it. At least it was more. . . personal, or Colossaurian?. . . than a translator's mechanically perfect pronunciation.

Though neither of them complained to the other, Ettubrute was as alone as he was. Or more so.

In Ningando, the Cetian capital, there weren't even five humans apart from Moy. Meanwhile, pairs of Colossaur police patrolled everywhere. But those perfect specimens of their race despised Ettubrute for his "weakness" and his "dishonorable" line of work. They even ignored him when their paths crossed, as if he didn't exist. To them, he was a virtual leper. Though Ettubrute pretended not to notice, he obviously found it much more painful when his fellows ostracized him than it would have been if they simply hadn't been there.

That's probably why the two of them ended up becoming so close.

"The solidarity of pariahs," Moy thought ironically, checking the explosive charges one by one and finding no mistakes.

He'd never found out whether Ettubrute was male or female. He'd always called him "he". . . He unconsciously identified his strength and brusque manners with maleness.

Not that it made much difference. From the little he knew, Colossaurs came in something like seven sexes. . . In any case, they kept their genitals hidden under the plates of their armored carapaces 99.99 percent of the time. In the rare moments of sexual intimacy they had shared, pretty much compelled by their mutual loneliness, the human had always found it safer and more soothing to let himself be caressed by those big tridactyl hands and that sensitive forked tongue than to pay much attention to the flaps of skin, tinged violet like faded flowers, that he guessed were his agent's genitals.

He'd never found out whether Ettubrute expected him to penetrate them or to let himself be penetrated by them. . . Nor did he have any intention of finding out.

Caressing Ettubrute's armor-plated bulk was a strange sensation. Like feeling a machine, or a stone statue. Moy always thought that Colossaurs had almost no sense of touch in their carapaces. But Ettubrute seemed to like that most of all. It wasn't much trouble to satisfy him. It was like petting a dog. Just slightly bigger. . .

From his earliest years, Moy, like all terrestrials, had discovered that sex was the common coin humans used to repay their obligations to the xenoids. Though it had never even crossed his mind to take up freelance social work, he figured the time he had spent satisfying the Colossaur's strange appetites was a valuable investment. . . emotionally. It probably had made the difference in Ettubrute's decision to give him a second chance with his debts.

In this life, everything has its price.

Everything was okay. Whistling, Moy left the tent and stepped out into the teeming plaza. The bustle, the noise, the smells, the colors hit his senses like a smack across the face. He took a deep breath and kept walking.

A short walk before each performance had become a habit. The lovely spectacle of the Cetian capital and its people calmed him—and motivated him, too.

It functioned more or less like: "Look at all the stuff you can have, if you work hard and don't spend too much."

Normally there weren't many pedestrians on the wide esplanade, but today was special. With the outrageous sense of aesthetics that only the Cetians could pull off (when they felt like it), a planetary-scale carnival was ringing in Union Day. The most important anniversary for every race. Commemorating the day they joined the community of the minds of the galaxy. Something like a coming of age.

Cutting through or circling around groups of Cetians and other xenoids decked out in exotic polychrome costumes, Moy wondered whether someday humans would be able to celebrate something like this, instead of Contact Day. Or better to say, Conquest Day?

"Karhuz friz!" He was so lost in thought, it took him nearly a second to become aware of the words a Cetian had enthusiastically directed point-blank at him.

He stared at him. The xenoid had used an ingenious system of holoprojections to make the right half of his body look completely transparent. The half-person had apparently mistaken Moy's human physique for a particularly hilarious costume and had made some witty comment on it. Or maybe he had only asked where he'd gotten it because he wanted one, too.

Moy only knew a few words in Cetian, and he didn't have a translator on him. Like the Colossaur, he wasn't crazy about them.

He hugged the Cetian warmly, almost yelling into his ear.

"Your half-mother sells herself to polyps!" And he laughed.

The humanoid looked at him for an instant. Then he shook his head sideways, the Cetian gesture for nodding in agreement. He let out a crystal-clear laugh and gamboled off, happy.

Seemed male. Pity.

Though ninety-nine percent of the time they were refined aesthetes who treated all beings other than their own race with distant, solemn, and courteously disdainful manners, on Union Day they let their hair down completely. For these twenty-six hours, every sort of joke was allowed, and the Cetians turned to amusements they would consider obscene to even think about the rest of the year.

The patchouli-scented aphrodisiac that he'd picked up by hugging the Cetian stimulated Moy's pituitary and nearly gave him an erection.

He stared after the Cetian, with half a mind to follow him.

He must be a male (and Cetians hated and punished homosexuality), and he had never much liked his own sex. But if everything was permitted today. . . why not?

The half-person had already disappeared among the crowd.

Moy sighed. Maybe after the performance he'd find a female who was more. . . communicative. And who wouldn't charge. Because Cetian hetaerae were magnificent but ridiculously expensive.

Cetian humanoids had a rare beauty that hinted at their feline ancestry. Terrestrials were especially drawn to them. When the first males of their species visited Earth they provoked true waves of enthusiasm and passion, next to which the cults of any of the music or film stars of the past paled in comparison.

And the females. . . Moy would never forget the tug on the groin he felt at the age of fourteen when he first set eyes on one of them, a female Cetian who had, probably by accident, attended an exhibition of his drawing teacher's works. Her tall, gracefully proportioned figure, the slash of the vertical pupils in her eyes, her lithe and nimble gestures, the caressing tone of her voice. That air of exotic sensuality, which seemed to emanate from her body. . . And her scent.

It wasn't much consolation to know that there were pheromones any Cetian male or female could produce at will. The effect was the same: a burning desire to rub against their skin, to pet them, to dominate them and be dominated by them. . . and at the same time, an almost divine respect for them, which kept anyone who wasn't a total idiot, or a sex maniac, or lobotomized, from ever attempting to have sex with a being born under the rays of Tau Ceti—unless you had a clear invitation from them first.

The most interesting thing was that this effect of respectful fascination wasn't exclusive to humans. Centaurians, Colossaurs. . . even the hermaphroditic, telepathic grodos seemed to lose some of their commercial aplomb in the presence of the exquisitely beautiful Cetians. One of the many riddles of the cosmos.

After living among them for several months, Moy had reached his own conclusion: the refined Cetians, those avid supporters of the arts, had perfected what they considered the highest art of all: the art of sexual attraction. Beauty-crazed, they had turned themselves into beauty itself. It was their weapon, their secret trump card in the great poker game of power being played out among all the races in the galaxy. Just as telepathy was for the grodos, total secrecy for the Auyars, and massive bodies for the Colossaurs.

But don't let their looks fool you. They were angels from hell. Underneath their distant, serene charm you would almost always find cruel, calculating minds that yearned to win it all, that shrewdly cashed in on the slightest advantage. Behind the mantle of beauty they were implacable beings, capable of seducing humans just to get them to work as slaves in their brothels or sell their organs for transplants. Or worse.

So, they might be the Judases of the galaxy. . . but nobody beat them in artistic sensibility.

It had been very clever of Ettubrute to pick Ningando as the grand finale of his tour. The capital of Tau Ceti was like the New York of Earth's golden age, the art mecca of the galaxy. If you made it among the Cetians, you had made it among all the xenoids (save, perhaps, for the enigmatic Auyars). And the reports he had seen seemed to speak very highly of him. Maybe his Colossaur agent didn't know much about art, but at least he knew where to find the people who understood. . . and who, moreover, paid well for it.

Paying for art. Money. Credits. Everything boiled down to that.

Moy strolled lost in thought, wandering down one of the streets that spun out like curving spokes from the wheel's central hub: the plaza. The shadows of the tall buildings lining the pedestrian avenue fell across him.

They were irregular structures, seemingly built in a thousand different styles, each one distinct. Yet the general effect was strangely harmonious. The Cetians had realized the impossible dream of Michelangelo, Le Corbusier, Niemeyer, and other great human city planners: the city as sculpture. The city conceived as a single whole, as a living organism that grows while maintaining a perceptible, natural order. After Ningando and the other Cetian cities, the cities of other xenoid races, no matter how magnificent, seemed identical to those of the humans: giant cancers, chaotic, sickly, putrid growths. Merely failed attempts at urban design.

Moy recalled Colossa, Ettubrute's home world, the first he had visited after leaving Earth. Massive city walls. Stout towers. Buttresses and bastions. Fortress-cities, conceived and built as temples to force and solidity by a powerful warrior race. Cities of excess, powerful but lacking any beauty, any grace, any rhythm. Any life.

Here, curved or straight, volumes and surfaces combined harmoniously yet dizzyingly.

Ningando. What wouldn't human artists and architects give to see its structures! How avidly all his friends would have drunk in all its glorious forms. How much Jowe, for example, would have enjoyed every inch of those buildings. . .

Moy stopped and looked back. Jowe. . .

Brilliant, delicate, sincere, pure, uncompromising. . . moron, misfit, destined for failure: Jowe.

The one with the most talent. The one with the original ideas. The one most loyal to his theories of art. The one who cared least about the market. The one with the greatest disdain for agents and dealers.

The one who sold the fewest works, because he never lowered himself to flattering the tastes of the xenoid tourists who came in search of exoticism and local color among human artists, and who kept his distance from testing or experimenting with form. The one who never wasted his talents on painting voluptuous social workers in provocative microdresses, or landscapes brimming with fake touristic radiance. The one who most hated the accommodating choirs of mediocre critics. Because his works delved deeper than empty provocations or the sterile masturbation of theory and countertheory. Because he made art.

Jowe was a born loser. One who had never come to terms with selling his work for a ticket from Earth to success. A failure proud of his losses. And happy.

Happy. . . The last Moy had heard of him, he was still creating, as tireless and unappreciated as ever. And to keep from prostituting his art, he had gotten into the semilegal protection racket. So he wouldn't die of hunger.

Hope it went well for him. Few deserved success more than Jowe.

But life had taught Moy that success never goes to those who deserve it, but to those who seduce and cheat and fight for it, whatever it takes. For those who wink at Mammon with one eye and at the Muses with the other.

Idealists like Jowe always fall by the wayside. The protection racket is tough. He probably owed megacredits to the Yakuza or the Mafia because his heart had gone out to some freelance social worker and her teary eyes. Or, much more likely, he was stuck in Body Spares for a few years, paying for his stupid collaboration with the dreamers in the Xenophobe Union for Earthling Liberation. . . a bunch of fanatics that Planetary Security only allowed to keep going because they'd have to give up most of their inflated antiterrorism budget if they broke up the gang once and for all.

Jowe. What a pity that at the crossroads of life he'd picked the wrong path, the one of defeated martyrs, not the one of triumphant heroes. Moy, himself, on the other hand, had only had a little talent and a certain business savvy. But together, the two of them could really have gone far...

And he would have loved just to be able to share Jowe's astonishment at the exquisite architecture of Ningando, at the delicate embroidery of the clothes its people wore, at the throbbing pulse of its cosmopolitan heart...

Absorbed in his memories, Moy nearly bumped into a group of Cetians whose somber gray clothing contrasted sharply with the explosion of forms and colors in the clothes of all their fellows.

Body Spares.

Earth wasn't the only place where races with physiologies incompatible with local biosphere turned to using native bodies to be able to walk around without cumbersome life support systems. But among Cetians and other cultures, candidates for Body Spares were well-paid volunteers who considered it an honor to serve as "horses" for representatives of other races. Not criminals atoning for their crimes, as on Earth.

And in Ningando, like almost anywhere else in the galaxy, the procedure was prohibitively expensive. It included incredibly stiff insurance fees, given the possibility of damaging the host bodies. The pittance that the Planetary Tourism Agency charged on Earth was irresistible bait for any tourist eager to mix it up with the local population without being discriminated against.

Moy muttered a clumsy excuse in his rudimentary Cetian, stepped out of the way of the gray-garbed Cetians, and watched them. One of his favorite pastimes now was guessing the original race of the Body Spares customers by looking at how their "horses" moved. This was a group of seven, and they all walked holding hands. Though the way they walked would have been the envy of the most graceful human ballet dancer, they were clumsy compared to regular Cetians. And they gestured a lot. A lot. They were talking almost more in gestures than by vocalizing.

Aldebaran polyps, most likely. Their sign language gave them away. Moy watched them hopefully. Unfortunately, they were headed away from the plaza and from his performance. They were probably very rich. Their super-resistant anatomies adapted perfectly well to any biosphere, so taking Cetian bodies was just an expensive whim.

Someday he'd visit Aldebaran, too, he promised himself. Of course, it would have to be when he was very rich. Nobody but a polyp, or someone occupying the body of a polyp, could survive the tremendous pressures under the oceans of that world.

What would it be like to weigh nearly a ton, have hundreds of tentacles and one giant muscular foot, and move slowly across the bottom of the ocean? If nothing else, a very interesting experience. . .

Sigh. He'd probably never find out. More than likely there was some regulation or other stipulating that members of "inferior" races, as humans were considered, could not occupy the bodies of beings from species with full galactic rights.

No matter how much money he managed to amass, there'd be something he could never shake. His original sin: being human. . . And most of the universe would be out of bounds for him forever.

The idea was so depressing that for a second he seriously considered skipping his own act. Leaving it all and returning to Earth. He'd be poor forever, but at least he'd be among his equals.

Probably during the Union Day carnival they'd hardly even notice he was gone, and there wouldn't be many consequences. . .

But at almost the same moment he remembered how he had gotten monumentally drunk barely a month before on a distillation of native algae that seemed acceptably similar to white wine from Earth. And how, thinking that being drunk was a perfectly acceptable excuse for skipping out on one of his two weekly performances, he had remained nonchalantly asleep in his tiny accommodations.

Three hours after his act was supposed to begin, two Colossaurs, next to whom Ettubrute had looked like a cream puff, woke him by bashing down the partition wall enclosing his room. He didn't dare put up more than verbal resistance (they obviously did not understand Planetary, and they weren't carrying translators) while they dragged him someplace that looked too much like a jail not to be one. There they literally threw him in head-first. It was all but a miracle he didn't break his neck when he hit the floor.

A mere thirty hours later his agent deigned to show up, and Moy kept his mouth closed and hung his head while he got one of the harshest reprimands of his life before being set free. Along the way, he found out that Cetians considered breaking a promise an extremely serious offense. Whether you had an excuse or not. And that's how they'd seen it when he skipped out on a show he had previously agreed upon. He was stunned when Ettubrute revealed the size of the fine he'd had to pay (which, of course, would come out of his honoraria) to free him... And even more so when he learned that if he did it again, the punishment might even include being expelled from Tau Ceti as an undesirable alien—and having everything he'd earned on the planet confiscated.

Obviously, being an alien was an enviable position only on Earth. Everywhere else in the galaxy it was as good as being garbage. Especially if you were an alien who didn't belong to one of the powerful races like the grodos or the Auyars. Not even ignorance of the local law absolved you from obeying it.

"*Dura lex, sed lex,*" Moy uttered solemnly as he returned resolutely to his tent. The law is harsh, but it's the law. He couldn't let himself suffer artist's block, the way things were. He'd act. "The show must go on," he whispered. Though what he really felt like doing was shouting "Shit!" at the top of his voice.

He didn't, because he couldn't remember how to say it in Latin just then... And because of the harsh blow that his respect for the lovely dead language had suffered when he found out that greatest living expert in the language of Virgil wasn't a human, but a segmented guzoid from Regulus who needed a voice synthesizer to be able to recite the Eclogues. Plus the blow to his already shaken human pride.

He looked up at the city clock, a gigantic holographic image that floated above the tallest buildings in Ningando like a long and oddly colorful cloud. There should still be a few minutes before it was time to start the show.

With those Cetian clocks, there was no way to be sure. The image had no numbers or hands: just one long bar that kept changing colors, section by section, as time went by.

At first Moy refused to believe the clock meant much beyond its decorative function, like any analogue dial on Earth. He smiled skeptically whenever he asked some Cetian for the time and the Cetian, after giving him a look of scornful superiority, glanced up and told him to the second. They must have other, hidden clocks—that was just for show.

But he soon learned he was wrong.

The natives of Tau Ceti had extremely sharp senses. Visually, every inhabitant of Ningando could differentiate ten or twelve shades of red that the most subtle human painters or illustrators would have thought identical. Any Cetian would make a human musician with so-called "perfect pitch" look ridiculous. The Cetians could distinguish not merely eighths but hundredths of a tone—a fact that made their language especially complex, since the intensity and modulation of the message often contained as much information as the message itself.

All this had been a further blow to Moy's human pride. As if it weren't enough to feel you were practically invisible when you were walking around among crowds of gorgeous and tremendously sexually attractive Cetians who were completely ignoring you, from that moment on he had to remain silent when any xenoid critic smugly observed that terrestrial arts were pitifully primitive and crude. Especially if the critic was a Cetian.

To a race with such subtle senses, even the *Mona Lisa* or *Guernica* must be little more than pathetically composed splotches of primary colors. Like practically all figurative art... No wonder almost all their art was purely abstract, coldly mathematical. Who wants reflections of reality when you can't help but be aware that that's all they are, mere reflections, always imperfect, falling sadly short.

"Too bad for them, poor people," Moy muttered sarcastically as he reached his platform, and he felt better.

Perfection was a two-edged sword. Those beautiful humanoids would never be able to enjoy the simple pleasures of an outline drawing, the joyful distortion of forms in a caricature, the vibrant colors of expressionism.

Moy had even begun to suspect (and it was no small consolation) that he was the only living being in Ningando capable of appreciating the city's harmonious orgy of colors and forms in all its magnificence. For its inhabitants, the city must be a collection of hopelessly crude attempts to achieve an impossible aesthetic ideal. The fate of the Cetians deserved more pity than envy: they were so perfectly well equipped to quest for beauty that they'd never find anything lovely enough to satisfy them entirely.

Even Colossaurs, not well known for their artistic abilities, their vision limited to black and white, must be more familiar with aesthetic pleasure than the sophisticated Cetians...

"Speak of the devil and his carapace will appear," Moy muttered with amusement when he caught sight of a reddish bulk approaching the platform from the other direction.

Ettubrute's massive frame cut a path through the motley Cetian multitude like a red-hot knife through butter. Not even in the carnivalesque confusion of a Union Day could he possibly be mistaken for a Cetian in disguise. It wasn't the carapace, or the volume of his arms and legs, which afterall could be imitated by fake limbs—it was, rather, a certain gracefulness, rough and indefinite, but very much there. Powerful, curt, very unlike the fluid elegance of the Cetians' gestures.

Besides, for a native it would have been in very poor taste to dress up as a Colossaur. They employed Colossaurs as guards or police officers, jobs that they considered base and dirty. But they despised them. For all Cetians, Ettubrute or any other member of his race was the epitome of vulgarity, bad taste, and boorishness. Coarse, unmannered louts, exhibitionists who disdained even the basic civilized courtesy of wearing clothes, determined at all costs to display the rough crimson surface of their armored plates.

Though when push came to shove, for a Cetian, a Colossaur was always preferable to a human, Moy reminded himself, with biting irony. Better the honest lout than the crooked savage...

Moy also knew that, beneath the Cetians' outer guise of refinement, the Colossaurs' brute power and vigorous, elemental culture exercised a strange fascination over the decadent sophisticates. Ettubrute had once taken him to a pornography screening (completely underground, of course) featuring several of his fellow beings. Nine out of ten in the audience were natives of Tau Ceti. Moy later learned that this sort of holorecording was the second currency of trade between Colossa and the Cetians. And, though Moy hadn't found the show very appealing (it made him think of two battle tanks ineffectually attempting to make love), the Cetians got fired up. They screamed throughout the show, touching each other in a veritable collective frenzy that Moy found much more attractive than the main feature. Beautiful bodies twisting and writhing lewdly, trying in vain to imitate the Colossaurs' formidable body language...

"Chill," he told himself, feeling the onset of an erection. He smiled, shaking his head. He had turned into a total deviant. But nothing odd about that... The truth was, his sex life over the past several months had been anything but normal. Even for an Earthling who had grown accustomed, almost from childhood, to the idea of sex with any more-or-less humanoid (sometimes not even that) arriving from the depths of the galaxy.

His ideas about what constituted pornography and/or obscenity had changed a lot during these months of touring. Though he still laughed at jokes that were more or less about hybrid sex (such as the classic: "The Embassy of Aldebaran on Earth emphatically protests the public screening of holofilms on the cellular fission and budding of Pacific corals, considering them decidedly pornographic and therefore detrimental to the morals and good taste of its tourists visiting the planet. . ."), he already understood what Freud had expressed many years before: When it comes to sex, totem and taboo are very relative matters.

Fortunately for him. . .

Sex was a price that, though not explicitly listed in the clauses of his contract with Ettubrute, he always knew he would have to pay. Not just his occasional "relaxation sessions" with the Colossaur (which he had almost come to enjoy) but other things as well.

Such as a particularly humiliating party at the home of some rich collector of native arts who wanted to find out whether what they said about the animalistic nature of humans was true. Or being looked up and down, naked as a newborn, by a circle of inscrutable guzoids who had bought one of his works. . .

"Occupational hazards," Moy muttered. Well, if he ever got tired of his performances at least he had a good shot at making it as a freelance social worker. Sure, the profession was strictly off-limits to males on Earth. . . but, as you might expect, there was a black market that kept growing larger and larger. And more dangerous. . .

"Ready? Prepare self. Soon now." Ettubrute's hoarse voice brought him back to the present. "Not looking good. . ." The Colossaur sounded worried, and his tiny pig eyes scrutinized Moy's face closely from the depths of their armored sockets.

"No problem, Bruiser. It'll all come off fine, like usual," Moy sighed, giving his agent's red armor-plated back a friendly punch. "Go to the console. These guys are obsessively punctual. . ."

When the Colossaur was at the controls, Moy furtively poked his head through the folds of synplast at the entrance to the tent and scanned the scene.

There sat his audience. Dozens and dozens of Cetians, wearing all sorts of costumes, all in animated conversation, patiently waiting for yet another Union Day show to begin. Some had seen it before and were coming back to enjoy it again. Others, excited by their friends' descriptions or by the holovision ads (they'd better have been; those spots had cost an arm and a leg), had come with some skepticism to see if there was any truth in what they'd heard. Or, more likely, hoping to get a laugh out of the bumbling attempts at making art by a race as inferior as the humans.

Moy felt the familiar sensation of heartburn filling his esophagus. All a bunch of carrion vultures, disguised as birds of paradise. Beautiful, colorful plumes, but under their fine clothes, hungry birds of prey. And he was for dinner.

He was set. He'd gotten into just the right mood for doing his performance. The emptiness was eating away at him. And the rage, and the envy, and the pride.

He sighed. Wearily lifting a hand, he gave Ettubrute the signal. At once the powerful fan mussed his short hair. He walked out.

Then the charges went off.

The amount of explosives had been calculated to the milligram. The four synplast walls that formed the tent went up in a cloud of atomized particles, which the jet of air from the fan scattered in a kind of reverse snowfall.

A bit too much explosive, and the shock could hurt the audience. A bit less, and the synplast fragments would have been too large for to handle, and they might have even wounded the spectators.

Ettubrute really knew his business.

Moy cleared his throat to begin his discussion of theory, improvising on a set of basic ideas on each occasion, playing off the audience's emotional state. He let his eyes wander over the sea of expensive costumes, and. . .

Surprise. There, with her father, was Kandria, more beautiful than ever. Her presence pleased him and intrigued him: How had she gotten to Ningando? Had she been so successful with her Multisymphonies?

Or was she, maybe, searching for him?

Hope rang in his heart like a bell.

She saw him and waved respectfully. She smiled.

Her father, the cold humanoid, also saw him but didn't move a muscle.

Strangely embarrassed by the girl's admiring gaze, Moy hated going back to performing while she watched. He felt like a trained circus animal, like a pitiful buffoon. Again he thought of canceling the performance.

This was all a farce. He was no artist, just a poor mercenary. . .

The silence stretched out. The courteous Cetians sat. Moy remembered how huge the fine would be if he didn't perform, and, plucking up his courage, he began.

It would all just look like another pause for effect. . .

"Praised be Union Day, and long life and prosperity to Ningando and its people." He had practiced the phrase a thousand times, even using the hypnopedia to help him memorize it. A couple of sentences in the native language, without translators, were just the ticket to win over any audience from the get-go.

"But you must forgive me if I feel distressed in the midst of so much good cheer. I am so sad—because art is dead." Ettubrute had just turned on his cybernetic translator. As always, Moy wondered whether a dead device could really catch and reproduce all the fine emotional and aesthetic nuances of his speech. He imagined not, but he had no other choice than to hope it would manage anyway—partially, at least.

"Art is dead. It was killed by holoprojections, by cybersystem chromatic designs, by musical harmonization programs, by virtual dance simulations, by all the technological paraphernalia whose only aim seems to be to eliminate the need not only for the artist's skills, but even for the artist's presence." He was bending theatrically lower and lower, as if defeated by the circumstances. This was the sign for Ettubrute to start the activation sequence for all systems.

"But the artist refuses to be ignored! I refuse to fall into oblivion!" He lurched forward with a savage expression, and the Cetians drew back slightly.

Moy suppressed a smile: they were getting what they'd come for. The human savage. The elemental madman. The brilliant naïf, all subconscious, no processing.

"The artist cannot die. Because an artist enjoys the immortality of Prometheus. Because he dies in each of his works. Because he puts a piece of his life into each thing he creates. Because every bit of material that sprouts, transformed, from his hands is another piece of time that he has snatched from implacable entropy." And Moy turned around to face the machine that was beginning to deploy.

As always, he was momentarily enraptured by the inexorable, lethal beauty of the device he had designed himself. Straightening up and growing like the hood of a colossal cobra or the ominous shadow of a dragon, the mechanical joints slid silently, one over the next. Until the archetypal figure of a cross had formed. Rising threateningly and enormous over the human's silhouette. As if waiting.

Moy turned back to face the audience.

Too bad they wouldn't get the Christian reference...

"The artist can and must die—in, through, and for his art. The artist is obliged to deconstruct himself in his art." He noted with the usual satisfaction that the translator hesitated briefly at the word "deconstruct."

Deconstruction. He could have included the term in the cyber-glossary. . . but he liked to know that he, a simple human, a child of one of the least sophisticated cultures in the galaxy, could make his masters' most advanced technology waver.

"The artist is a booster antenna. A funnel. He captures and guzzles the world's pain and pours it out into his art," and he took the apparently casual step backward that was the arranged signal.

The machine, like a carnivorous plastometal flower, leaned down and trapped him.

The Cetians stiffened with fright when the links and fasteners surrounded the human's body and limbs like the tentacles of a giant polyp. Then they lifted him several yards above the stage without visible effort.

"The artist's works are his clones, his children. They are his lacerated flesh and blood, his message. His anguished cry to a world that no longer hears any voice but that of pain and blood!" Moy howled heartrendingly.

The first five bleeders clamped onto his neck, thighs, and forearms, locating his veins with millimetric precision. Moy felt the shock of pain, masked almost immediately by the analgesics coating the needles. He winced; well, no one's perfect. Can't make an omelet without breaking a few eggs, or do his performance without feeling some pain.

The negative pressure regulators worked properly, and five streams of scarlet liquid shot out in precise arcs. First sprinkling the stage, then falling into tiny crystal vessels that sprang from the machine, until they were filled. Then the bleeding stopped.

Moy made a fist with his right hand.

"He can deny his hand, try to exchange it for mechanical fakery. But no device can equal the fertile pain this hand feels when it holds a brush and creates." He tensed and took a deep breath. Another dose of analgesics was injected into his system.

The semicircular blade sprang, swift and well-aimed as an axe blow, cutting the hand off and tossing it through the air. Another mechanism caught it before it could land. It connected electrodes to the convulsing nerves of the hand and put a brush in its fingers.

The hand, writhing, drew meaningless lines across the canvas that formed the stage, dancing in uncontrolled paroxysms. More and more slowly, until at last it remained motionless.

As usual, the spectacle drew murmurs from the well-mannered public. But Moy knew that the magic was already working. The audience was his. His slaves. He had them in his grip. He could do what he wanted with them.

"The fragile, transitory body is not what makes the difference. Who cares about the hand that drew the line, if the genius that drove it lives on in the line itself?"

Feeling the subtle creeping sensation inside the coarse fabric of his trouser leg, Moy relaxed his sphincter to allow the nanomanipulators to penetrate him. He recited a yoga mantra to stave off nausea while the delicate mechanisms snaked up through the curves of his intestine.

"Often, faced with the seeming perfection of the art, no one cares whether it was drawn by hand, claw, tentacle, or pincer. Some believe that art is art, whether made by a Da Vinci, by a Sciagluk, or by a computer." Viewers waved their heads from side to side in agreement.

Moy hated the abstract, frigid compositions of Morffel Sciagluk. Nothing but a three-dimensional imitator of Mondrian, in his opinion. He only mentioned him for practical reasons: few of these Cetians knew the first thing about Leonardo. Or his *Last Supper*, or the *Mona Lisa*.

Through the veil of the analgesic drug, he felt the diffuse pain of the nanomanipulators penetrating him through arteries and capillaries, moving among muscles and tendons. Mobile fibers one molecule wide, spinning their web inside the edifice of his body. When the tickling reached his left arm, he gulped. The wave of analgesics that flooded his nervous system convinced him that Ettubrute was on the ball, that he could continue to the next step without risk.

"But only flesh and blood, mind and manipulating organ, can give birth to art. And if that exact conjunction does not exist—no art is possible." He relaxed, waiting.

As always, the explosion surprised him as much as the audience. Though there was hardly any pain.

The meticulously measured collection of volatile molecules in his left arm transformed into an explosion, spraying bones, tendons, and fingers into a spectacular bloody cloud. By a calculated manipulation of force fields, the heap of remains that had once been an arm floated in the air for a few seconds without spreading. Until Ettubrute turned off the antigrav effect. Then they fell to the stage, amid the fervent applause of the enthusiastic spectators.

Taking advantage of the pause, Moy sought out the mestizo girl's eyes. They were filled with admiration—and horror. Good. Now she was as much his as the rest of them. Or more so.

He strained his ear to try and figure out whether Ettubrute had already turned on the mechanical womb. It wasn't really necessary yet; they had the best model on the market, and the synthesizing process was very quick. But it was always a relief to know that if something, anything, unexpected happened, then. . .

He pushed the thought from his mind and continued.

"Art is self-mutilation. It is the deliberate extraction of our most secret innards: our dreams."

The razor-thin blade of a semicircular pendulum (a reference to the Edgar Allan Poe story, which they would never catch) swung three times before opening the artist's abdominal cavity with surgical exactitude. The bleeders automatically reversed their function, and not one drop of blood clouded the view of the organs.

In anticipation, the nanomanipulators had injected different colorings into each organ, and Moy's guts were a living symphony of exposed and pulsing colors. The analgesic drug circulated through his veins, preventing him from losing consciousness or going mad from sheer agony before the climactic moment. But the sensation of lying open, defenseless, strangely empty, was not something that derived from pain. And it was incredibly uncomfortable.

"Dreams are the intangible substance that gives life, depth, and sentient volume to a work of art. What projects it beyond its narrow material frame." Moy closed his glottis, concentrating on breathing through his nose.

The pressurized hydrogen was injected into his intestine. The loops of the intestine, left clean by the nanos, inflated. Ghostly, semi-transparent, rising from their place like the spirals of a horrendous larval snake. A surprising play of light glowed from within them, thanks to the gas.

"Although the light of art is always ephemeral, that light is the artist's breath of life, his soul, which expires in each work of art."

A nano punctured an intestinal loop and the superinflammable gas escaped with an audible hiss. Then the spark triggered flames, and for an instant Moy's body was engulfed in a burning cloud.

Only for one second. Any more would have been dangerous; it might have burnt his skin and flesh. The volume of hydrogen was calculated to the cubic centimeter.

"And every critic, every exegesis, every interpretation of a work of art is a self-reflection, a journey to the inner self of the person who gave birth to it and clothed it in the flesh and skin of concepts." Whenever he got to this point, Moy always regretted not being a woman. With a shredded uterus, this part of the monologue would have been much more powerful.

Even so, the vision was pretty stunning.

The knives of the nanoskinners sliced his epidermis, and the strips of skin fluttered in the wind like a macabre fringe. Bloodless. The surface capillaries were nearly empty; the bleeders were working at full capacity, concentrating the vital fluid in his essential organs.

Moy felt dizzy and nearly fainted. But the neurostimulant circulating through his system instantly revived him. He smiled, pleased. Ettubrute was one hundred percent alert to his slightest vital signs. And he now heard the dull rumble of the mechanical womb doing its job. Everything was going fine. As always.

"Behind the flesh and blood of emotions, the skeleton of theories and grand schemes is laid bare, the subtle framework of sex and power in mixed substrates."

In perfect synchrony, both of the artist's legs—first the muscles, sliced from within, then the bones, breaking with an audible crack—fell onto the stage. There they kicked convulsively for several seconds before falling still.

A few liters of blood flowed from the cut femoral arteries, streaming over the strangely empty trouser legs. Then the nanos stopped the flow. This wasn't a mistake, but another well-calculated and inconsequential effect. With his body reduced practically to head and trunk, Moy simply did not need so much fluid. Besides, it might overwhelm the bleeders.

Moy followed a Tibetan breathing pattern.

Pain does not exist. Pain is an illusion.

I exist. I am real.

"What's art without the hidden alphabet of sex?" he howled.

At that cry, the nanos cut away the bloodied rag to which his trousers had been reduced, and his sex stood erect, as if defying death. Not from artificially high blood pressure in the corpora cavernosa, nor from a timely dose of hormones. Moy was aroused, as always. It was the old irony. Eros and Thanatos.

The proud exhibition only lasted a couple of seconds.

Moy relaxed. Now, the most difficult part. . .

The erect phallus exploded in a cascade of blue liquid. The nanos dissected the testicles from within and made them fall with a dull thud onto the stage.

When the effects of the analgesic overcame the pain and emptiness in his mutilated groin, Moy breathed more calmly. The worst was over now. The rest would be more impressive than painful.

Kandria was watching him in genuine adoration. He had to take advantage of this mood of the girl's. They were going to have a great time together, after all...

"It is the artist's sacrifice, his spirit, that makes his work soar with creativity." Moy gulped.

The artificial oxygenation system was set in motion, swapping out oxygen for carbon dioxide in his red blood cells without the mediation of his lungs. The nanos penetrated his bronchial tubes, and more hydrogen was injected into his pulmonary tissue. The pendulum again laid him open, this time at the thorax, and his swollen respiratory organs rose like balloons.

They lifted his tortured body even higher, as if fighting to break his chains. At last they did so, and he floated freely above the plaza.

More applause, now almost frenzied.

Scornfully, Moy thought they not only knew nothing about human anatomy, they seemed to know nothing of basic physics either. It was totally obvious that the volume of air displaced by his lungs was insufficient to lift his body—even without arms or legs. Only the antigrav field, carefully managed by Ettubrute, made this extraordinary spectacle possible.

He gulped again. With no air in his lungs, only careful pumping by the pneumatic nanomachine attached to his larynx allowed him to keep talking. And he knew how ridiculous he would look if it failed.

"But always, inevitably, after the last brushstroke the artist falls back to hard reality!" Moy closed his eyes, and the chill of another dose of analgesics relieved his veins.

The lungs exploded with another burst of flame, and his body plummeted from up high. Below, the machine awaited him, deploying spikes and ridges, like the jaws of some terrible shark.

Poe's other terror: the pit. A skillful intertextuality, wasted on all these xenoids, completely ignorant of human culture.

Even so, the audience shrieked.

The fall looked accidental, but it was meticulously managed by the antigrav fields. Several spikes impaled the remains of the artist's body. One ran through an ear. Another went in through his cheek and came out through an eye socket, popping out his right eye.

"Looking at the external surfaces of this world of illusions is not what matters most to an artist! There's much more than that!" Moy roared, and he felt his veins relax with the last, huge dose of analgesics. Prelude to the end.

He smiled.

His left eye burst from the pressure, splattering vitreous and aqueous humor, one tinted green, the other purple. Then it dangled from the optic nerve like a faded flower.

"The essence, what no machine can imitate, is the artist's absorption into the universal, the final annulment of the ego that he suffers in creating art!" Moy relaxed entirely.

"*Alea iacta est*," he thought, the die is cast, and greeted the darkness.

The nanos that penetrated his brain suddenly cut the supply of blood and glucose to its neurons, hitting his major synapses with well-calculated electrical shocks. Moy sweetly lost consciousness.

Clinically, he was already dead, though his heart continued to beat. No one in the audience had realized that what the machine was displaying to them was a cadaver. It was essential for the final act. No analgesic drug could even lessen the supreme pain of that finale.

The pneumatic nanomachine injected air at high pressure into Moy's larynx, modulating the horrific posthumous scream that made the vocal cords vibrate until they broke.

Prelude to apotheosis.

The explosive went off in his heart, and a fraction of a second later, the one in the corpus callosum of his brain.

The two most important organs in the body flew in pieces. The spikes and ridges of the machine fell upon the remains like hungry hyenas. They danced their frenzied choreography, mincing the remnants of the body like the teeth of some gigantic cannibal. And when there was nothing left to cut, they rose, oscillating menacingly, as if looking for their next victim.

Moy's recorded voice, reverberated deeply: "The world is the machine. Devouring art, it devours its creator. It thirsts for blood, pain, and art—and there are always new artists yearning to become its food. This is life, and this is history. This is the great cycle."

And the machine folded up, slowly, deliberately. The lights came on and the applause exploded, more fervent than ever.

Most of the audience left. Whispering, overwhelmed, looking eager to go back outside, back to reality.

Kandria waited longer. With tear-filled eyes, she exchanged views, brightly at first, then forcefully, with her agent-father. She wanted to see Moy and congratulate him—it had simply been perfect.

The Centaurian saw no need to overpraise the competition. Besides, this Moy wasn't suitable company. They might establish an emotional bond that could distract her from her artistic path. And he was her father, and she owed him obedience...

They argued until Kandria, furiously disengaging from the Centaurian, ran into the crowd without a backward look. Her father-agent smiled: this was just another form of respect.

He calmly followed her. Outside, his large purple eyes met the beady eyes of Ettubrute, and the two agents exchanged knowing looks and a shrug of the shoulders.

Yes, human artists were very difficult. Whether it was your child or your lover-friend... You had to be tough for their own good.

The art dealers and collectors, Cetians and members of other races, flocked to the platform like flies to the scent of a fresh cadaver. The Colossaur, cold and professional, responded to their offers and organized an auction, quickly and efficiently.

The great canvas that served as stage, plastered with Moy's limbs and viscera, was sprayed with epoxy resin by an automated mechanism. The fast-drying substance formed a thin, transparent layer that would protect the work from time and putrefaction.

After a short bidding war with two grodos, an Auyar bought it for seventy thousand credits, cash. He then offered half a million credits for the machine, but Ettubrute was unshakeable. No, it wasn't for sale. He wouldn't even listen to proposals.

The Auyar made another offer. Magnificent. . .

Ettubrute's little eyes shone with greed.

Well, he'd have to confer with the artist. . .

A hologram of Moy taken at the start of the performance, with a succinct biography in the Cetian syllabic alphabet, was projected in the space above the platform. The audience members who still remained, as if reluctant to leave, applauded once more. For fifteen credits, anyone interested could have a copy of the documentary. For 150, a holorecording of the entire performance.

There were more than fifty buyers. The show was a resounding success.

Moy, of course, only found out an hour later, once the autocloning was complete and his new body was available. Ettubrute, solicitous, gave him the whole story as he helped him from the mechanical womb hidden under the platform.

Despite the news, Moy felt no better. He coughed repeatedly to clear the mucilaginous pseudoamniotic fluid from his lungs. His hair and body felt disgustingly sticky, and he had a horrible taste in his mouth. All his muscles were shaking. He urgently needed to shower, to eat. . . and to sleep.

These cloned rebirths were wearing him out more and more.

"Having sold very well. Your debt being paying off," the Colossaur encouraged. "Having very interesting Auyar offer. They pay much."

"Forget about it. I'm not going to Auya. I don't trust guys who don't show their faces, and I like my memory too much to let them erase it." Moy shook his head, blinking to improve his vision. In spite of high-speed cloning, this business of changing bodies twice a week had its disadvantages. It always took you at least six hours to get totally used to your new anatomy.

"Not being on Auya, being here in Ningando," the Colossaur persisted. "For Auyar diplomatic staff. The erasing of memory being only. . . partial. Lasting one month the contract. Eight thousand credits per performance. . . not counting profits from selling canvas at end."

Moy whistled: that was nearly five times what he usually earned. The Auyars were loaded, for sure.

"Well, that changes everything," he smiled. "With those kinds of earnings, we could both retire. You told him yes, of course, we'd love to do it, I imagine, Bruiser?" He playfully slapped his pectoral plate.

"There being one detail," Ettubrute clarifies, almost timidly. "Requesting daily performances, and double performances weekends, or being no contract."

"Shit on a spaceship," Moy muttered, gulping as he mentally calculated as quick as he could. That made nine times a week. Thirty-six deaths and resurrections in a month. At eight thousand per, plus the canvasses—it was a tempting offer. But all those auto-clonings. . .

All that discomfort, half the time adapting to a new body. . . plus the chance of brain damage from abusing the process, which wasn't trivial.

On the other hand—he'd be able to return to Earth a potentate, make whatever art he wanted without worrying whether it sold or not.

Two scales, one balance.

And the scales weighed practically the same. Hard to decide.

Without really knowing why, he thought of Jowe. Jowe never would have ended up in a situation like this, but... he wished he knew what Jowe would have done in his place.

"You think it's worth it, Bruiser?" He looked at Ettubrute.

The Colossaur stared at him in turn, then shrugged. "I not risking anything. Being your life. Deciding you. Thinking that getting better price possible from Auyar? Being hard bargainers they..."

"I'll try, but eight thousand's pretty good," Moy sighed. "Hey... Did you see that girl... you know, Kandria? The mestizo girl, human and Centaurian? She didn't wait for me?"

Ettubrute looked at him slowly, for a long time. "No," he finally grunted, shifting his gaze. "Leaving almost right away. Arguing with father-agent about possibility her doing something similar. Differing opinions."

"Oh! So she's a plagiarist," Moy said, and something broke inside him. Suddenly the world looked and tasted like ash. "Alright... I think I'll take their offer, Bruiser."

The Colossaur lay his enormous paw delicately on his shoulder. "Moy..." It was the first time in months that he had pronounced his name. "You... you... being able taking it... so often?"

"I'll get used to it," Moy replied nonchalantly, but as if from a great distance. Like a robot. "Know something, Bruiser? Life's a piece of shit. We ought to plan something special if those Auyars are going to pay so well. Before that mestizo chick and others like her start copying me. I'll be the first, ahead of my time. That has to be made clear. All the rest are just following the path I blazed."

"Perhaps," the Colossaur mused. "What having in mind?"

"Something more... spectacular." Moy was talking, feeling like his mouth didn't belong to him. "Maybe use acids. Or poisons. Or nanocharges to send teeth flying through my cheeks, one by one..."

He clicked his tongue. "You might try to think up something yourself, Bruiser! You know as much about human anatomy as I do, I'm sure. . . Oh, and you know something else, Bruiser? I think I told you one time, I had this friend on Earth, a guy named Jowe. . . A brilliant kid. Well, I just had a great idea: with all that money, when I go back, I'm going to find him, wherever he is. . . You'll help me, won't you, Bruiser? When it comes right down to it, you and I are in this together. . ."

The Colossaur stopped walking for a moment, while Moy kept going.

Ettubrute watched him move on, away. The artist was still talking. Excited, gesticulating, not realizing he was alone. Cutting a path through the crowd of Cetians, who stared at him in surprise. Some pointed, shaking their heads reproachfully. Others, who had possibly witnessed his performance, made way for him with respect.

"Yes. . . When it comes right down to it, you and I are in this together, Moy," the Colossaur whispered, so low that the artist, walking far ahead, never noticed that he had used perfectly correct Planetary syntax.

Nor, of course, that his agent's tiny pig eyes had a suspiciously moist sheen. . .

November 15, 1993

The World Human Parliament

Xenoid tourists who want to learn all about the political history of Earth always get the same tour: First they view the ruins of the Acropolis in Athens and the Roman Forum, then their guides take them to Geneva, proud seat of the World Human Parliament.

The visit invariably takes place in two stages over two days.

First day, a Sunday, they are brought to the large building where they tour the immense, empty halls. This allows them to appreciate the walls and floors of fine marble (a material found only on Earth), the gigantic holoscreens, the comfortable ergonomic desks decked out with sophisticated computer voting terminals. Visitors can also admire walls adorned with frescos by great contemporary Earth artists—allegorical representations of Truth, Justice, Virtue, and the other eternal themes of every democracy.

The next day, a Monday, the xenoids return with their guides to watch representatives and parliamentarians in plenary session. They attend their heated debates, listen to their passionate arguments, watch the voting process with great interest, taking long holovideos of the hotbed of human passions that constitutes any governmental body.

Their guides then wearily explain the principle of representative democracy, by which each city sends its favorite sons to Parliament so they can all come to common agreement on which decisions are best for the whole planet.

This explanation typically satisfies ninety percent of the tourists.

As for the other, more curious ten percent, who keep on asking how Parliament can be sure Planetary Security will carry out any regulations they pass, how the people who elected them can remove them if they don't fulfill their promises, and other fundamental questions, the guides take them outside the gigantic edifice and show them something.

A simple Planetary Tourism Agency sales kiosk, mobbed by all the other tourists trying to buy reminders of their stay on Earth.

Smiling wistfully, as if they are letting down their hair, the guides mention the fact that this one simple kiosk takes in almost as much money in one day as the entire monthly budget of the World Human Parliament.

Then the interested tourists stop asking questions. They've understood who really rules the planet. And they march off, content, back to taking holovideos.

The Champions

We are the champions.

The best on Earth.

The defenders of human pride in the sporting arena.

The public knows it. They have confidence in us.

We know it because their raucous cheers rock the fuselage of our aerobus like thunderbolts when they detect us in the sky. Our vehicle, painted in the colors of Earth, descends from the high-velocity lane and heads along the wide avenue toward the stadium, gliding a few scant yards above the heads of the fervent crowd.

They worship us. We're their idols. If we win today, we'll be even more than that. Practically their gods.

"What a sea of people. The pilot's going to get us killed," grumbles Gopal, our coach, looking down through a hatch. He can't help it. These ceremonial pre-game entrances always make him jittery. But the rest of the team, including me, really enjoy it. It's a beautiful tradition, and what would Earth be if we gave up our traditions, too?

Our pilot is used to crowds, and he confidently drives the aerobus above the ocean of humanity. Doesn't even glance down.

I do. The thousands of faces, wild with hope, thousands of hands shooting me the V for Victory, gives me strength before each game.

Today I'll need it more than ever. This is going to be the toughest Voxl game of my life. My gateway to fame if I do well. My path to becoming a has-been, a nothing, if I fail.

I'm going to go out there and give it my all.

Everybody else on the team knows how important today is, too. Each in his own way is focused on a single idea: winning. Nobody wants to think about a loss. . .

Losing would mean eternal shame. Maybe the end of our careers, maybe no Voxl team would ever want to give us another contract. . .

Just thinking about it brings bad luck.

But no. Victory is ours. It has to be. Today, we're not just the best Voxl players on Earth right now; we're the best in years. We are the champions, and this might be the year.

Never before have six humans this good at Voxl played together on the same team.

Mvamba, tall and skinny as a basketball player, is kneeling in front of a miniature folding altar. Praying in his deep Bantu dialect to a tribal fetish, carved from a piece of wood as dark as his skin.

Sometimes it really does seem to help if you believe in a personal, intimate little god who watches over you, pray to a protective spirit or a guardian angel. Not even two years ago Mvamba was a regular guy driving broken-down old aerobuses around Sydney. Just one more African immigrant, left stateless after the xenos sank their whole continent in Contact times. A scout from the local team, the Black Hands, saw him throw a rock at a mugger and decided to give the kid a tryout. His career rocketed straight to the top: center forward for the Black Hands, offensive back for the Melbourne Skulls. . . and now, his big shot. A chance only one in ten thousand will get: defending the colors of the whole Earth. A rookie couldn't ask for more. Most likely, he's giving thanks to his fetish for his good luck.

Here, watching Mvanda's prayer with a smirk, is Arno Korvalden, the Danish defensive back. The Blond Hulk. A committed atheist and the burliest guy on the team at 412 pounds and six feet nine inches. Also the oldest hand. He was playing with the Copenhagen Berserkers back when I was still swiping credit cards in the outer ring of the Havana astroport. Sportswriters have been speculating about his retirement for some time. But the Great Dane keeps on playing, and right now he's the best defender on the planet. Not that he cares much how Earth does; Arno is a pragmatic guy, a mercenary who only responds to the scent of money. Gopal only got him to play with us by promising him a huge bonus, which he'll make win or lose. Anybody else and there'd be doubts about how well he'd play, but the Blond Hulk is a man of his word. And, simply put, he only knows how to give one hundred percent. Obviously he'll do his very best.

Yukio Kawabata is here and not here. Though his body is present, the Zen Buddhist trance he's been in for nearly an hour has probably sent his spirit back to the imperial Edo of his samurai ancestors. From the way he plays it, Voxl is obviously just a modern equivalent of Bushido for him. Yukio is an idealist through and through. He can afford that luxury; he's rich enough already. His family owns a nice block of shares in the Planetary Tourism Agency. That's why he doesn't care how much he makes or whether he wins or loses. He plays well, better than anyone else; that's his obsession. And he's a terrific right center, with reflexes and fast legs that are the envy of lots of professionals in the League.

The League. . .

The League is like Mecca and Valhalla put together for any Voxl player. The League is where teams of every race meet and compete. The armored, incredibly agile insectoid grodos versus the polyps of Aldebaran, slow to move on their wide, muscular single feet, but with hundreds of whip-fast tentacles to make up for their speed. The hulking, red-carapaced Colossaurs versus the rapid, svelte Cetians.

The League means astronomical salaries, unimaginable bonuses, the ability to travel anywhere in the galaxy. And an entourage of publicists trying to get you to use their expensive, sophisticated gear. Being a player in the League is almost better than being a god.

The League is the dream of every human player. It's only there that Colossaur, human, and polyp can play on the same side, no difference, no racism. At least in theory.

Jonathan, our veteran player, has told us the story a thousand times. He was there, at the top. But then he fell. He's never told us how or why, and we've never asked him. The first rule of group life: respect everybody else's secrets if you want to have a private life of your own. That's the only way the team can eat, travel, sleep, and play, always together, without killing each other. Follow that rule, and you avoid the unnecessary expense of psychologists and counselors. Ignore it—and they'll still be a useless expense, because they won't prevent or even delay the inevitable explosion of violence.

Jonathan must be busy with his medical monitor, as he is before every game. He keeps obsessive track of his blood pressure, pulse, erythrogram, temperature, and the hormone levels in his blood. I get the impression he's taking it too far. His expulsion from the League must have broken something inside the complex machinery of his mind. But who cares, so long as he plays as well as he does. And his fixation on keeping in top physical condition has brought about the miracle that maybe even he no longer believed possible: At the age of forty-two, he's been given a second chance. After eight years, three of them without setting foot on a Voxl court, he's made it. He's the only human who'll have played for Team Earth twice. If he doesn't make it now, I don't know what's going to happen to him. And I don't want to be around when it does.

The situation of the Slovsky twins is totally different. They're only eighteen, and they've been playing practically since before they learned to walk. The sons of Konrad Slovsky, the famous coach, Jan and Lev were already famous when they were kids, before I ever touched a voxl. This is their first year as pros, and they don't look nervous. They are two bundles of muscles and sinew trained to perfection. And as if that weren't enough, the two of them play together with the sort of perfect coordination I've only seen in holovideos of Cetian clone teams.

They're all engrossed in their holographic simulator. Sometimes I feel sorry for them. They never talk about women or holofilms or even drugs. Maybe it was their father's fault: he's nearly turned them into robots, superspecialized Voxl-playing machines. If something or someone stopped them from playing, it would be like keeping them from breathing. Their life is about getting better and better at it. For them, no training is ever hard enough. If Gopal ever wakes up with the unlikely idea of going a little bit easier on the team, Jan and Lev will probably protest and accuse him of treason against Earth or something like that.

Monomania seems to be an essential condition for becoming a good Voxl player. At least if you're human.

Sometimes I wonder whether I'm still me. Whether I haven't gone crazy, sacrificing my whole life to this game...

Sometimes I also wonder what I'm doing here.

But much more often I'm amazed at myself. At how far I've come, starting from as far down as I did. In five years, from petty street pickpocket to high-performance athlete. From failure to triumph. From anonymity to fame.

If my mother could see me now. Her always telling me I was a bum, a lowlife criminal, no good for anything but Body Spares. And my father. I hardly remember him; lost in space with his homemade starship, trying to make an unlawful escape. Running away from poverty when I was just two...

Or María Elena, the first girl I made love with. At sixteen I was more scared than she was, and she was eleven. She was running away from boarding school to be with me. Where could she be now? Probably drowning in the swamp of social work. An orphan girl doesn't have too many options. At least her physique should help her: she was always pretty, and you could tell she was going to have a great body. She was already practically a little woman at eleven: tall, slim, coalblack hair, cinnamon skin, jet-black eyes.

My mother, who kept telling me about my future in Body Spares, was the one who ended up there because of a fight with her neighbors. She always had a bad temper, and in the end the cheap rum had made it worse. By month two she was dead; an Auyar picked her to be his "horse." But thanks to the measly enough death benefit I got from the Planetary Tourism Agency, I was able to buy my first set of Voxl gear, second-hand but functional. And I started playing.

It was an all or nothing bet. Like my whole life has been. An orphan boy doesn't have too many options. . .

Yes, I've been lucky. But I need to keep on being lucky.

I kiss my cross with the image of the Virgin of Caridad del Cobre, blessed by Cardinal Manuel Castro himself. When he gave it to me a week ago, he said I was the pride of his diocese and my people's hope.

Protect me, dear Virgin. Keep my rebounds on target and my throws perfect. Free me from all wounds and give victory to your most faithful son: me, Daniel Menéndez. You, who can do everything. . .

The pilot drives the aerobus languidly. We pass between two walls of floating hologram ads, grazing them. We could have flown straight through them without trouble, but that would have meant dealing with a hailstorm of complaints from the advertising companies. Not even Earth's heroes are above commercial laws.

Past the titanic holoposters, there it is. All ours.

There's supposedly room for three quarters of a million people in the Metacolosseum of New Rome. Six levels. Sixty gigantic holoscreens. Enough airconditioning for a mid-sized orbital city. Entrances large enough to let in small asteroids.

Today it's full to bursting. The tickets for this game are always sold out nearly a year in advance.

We float through the main entrance, above the sea of people, dotted here and there with silvery bubbles. The force fields of the prime box seating of the richest and most paranoid xenoids. Other extraterrestrials, more confident about their tourist immunity, prefer to risk getting their data cards lifted in order to enjoy the jubilant atmosphere of the human throng. The authentic local color. The incomparable emotion of being one more person in the audience at the

Voxl game of the year—Voxl, the galactic sport, as the reporters and advertisers like to say.

We set down on one of the two empty towers that lead straight to the playing court. We all look at the other tower and think the same thought: who will our opponents be this time?

We've faced players from every race in the simulations. We know the strong points and weaknesses of every species, their tricks, their skills. . . but not even the best holograph can be more than a pale reflection of reality.

As soon as the landing gear of the aerobus touches down, the hemisphere of the force field closes above us, hiding us from the public and the public from us. Gopal is the first to leap down, and half a minute later I've got the whole team lined up in front of him.

Our old coach stalks back and forth in front of us, his hands behind his back and a scowl on his face. He looks more like an old general than ever. Finally he stops and sighs. Here comes the speech. I think, with a cynical sense of relief, that it'll be his last.

"Players!" he booms, and now he's more like a drill sergeant, because no general would howl like that. His voice sounds too loud for his long, gaunt body.

"I'm not going to tell you all what you already know. I'm not going to remind you how much is riding on your victory, today, right here. I just want you to think about one thing: that we're humans. The sons of Earth. . ."

"AND PROUD OF IT!" we scream, as he has taught us.

"Good." His smile fills our hearts with something ineffable. "Do you all know what it means to be the pride of Earth? It means that, just this once, it doesn't matter if you were playing on opposite teams in the World Championship six months ago. Or if the countries where you were born have hated each other to death since before Contact. Now we're all one thing: humans. And they're all xenoids. The enemy. It's us against them. It them or us. And nothing else matters."

He let out a deep sigh. "As for the rest, I hope you already know it after six grueling months of training. And if you haven't learned it, may Allah help us." We all smiled at the joke, added to break the tension.

Jonathan glances at me and winks. Meaning, "The old man says the same thing every year." Probably true, but I can't laugh. As team captain, it's up to me to set an example.

"Forget defense. We're playing to win. As the game develops I'll be giving you instructions," Gopal adds, and his olive Hindustani skin looks pale with exhaustion. "But don't forget that you'll have the last word, because. . ."

"WE ARE THE CHAMPIONS!" The battle cry fills our hearts with faith, and Gopal grins like an old gargoyle.

"Yeah. . . What I was about to say, though, was that you're the sorriest troop of monkeys I've ever seen set foot on a Voxl court. But, sure," he winks at us, and for a fraction of a second he's nearly Mohamed Gopal, the Delhi Wonder, once more, the first human to play in the League, "now you'll get your chance to prove me wrong."

Jubilant, confident, laughing, we race off to our changing rooms. Each has his own, the door marked with his name. As always, Mvamba comes in last. He doesn't know how to read. He waits until everyone's there so he'll know which is his by simple elimination. Well, some skills aren't strictly necessary for being a good Voxl player.

And you really don't need to be able to read in today's world. Computers talk, so do credit cards. . . Even so, the African's illiteracy is a secret between Jonathan, himself, and me. We especially promised him that Arno Korvaldsen would never find out. The Blond Hulk made such cruel fun of the Slovsky twins for not knowing who Julius Caesar was, if he ever learned about this he'd make Mvamba the target of his taunts for months. And ridicule is practically the only thing the former aerobus driver fears. He's so shy. . .

It isn't easy to live and play as a team. Not for anybody, especially not for the captain. My position brings lots of responsibility and not much credit. Everybody's always waiting to see me make a mistake or forget something, from the coach to the substitute player. Meanwhile, the only praise I get is winning. The eighteen points on our scoreboard. It's only then, without needing anyone to tell me, that I think I've really done a good job. Never perfect, though. No such thing as a perfect game in Voxl.

The second I slide the door open, the antigrav field lifts me into my room. They say that League stadiums have internal teletransport booths and that none of the spectators come out to watch live games because they all prefer to see it on holovision.

Bah. They say so many things about the League... Here on Earth, the holonet broadcasts the games, too. Sure, there are lots of details that you can appreciate better, replays from different angles, in slow motion or infrared... But it can't be the same as being right here in the Metacolosseum, roaring at every move the teams make. If it were, why would so many xenoids be coming here instead of watching it from the comfort of their hotel rooms?

I start gearing up. The ceremony is as ancient as Voxl itself. Some two thousand years old, from the time the Centaurians started playing it on their frigid world, long before they came into contact with other intelligent races.

Gopal helps me on with each piece of the uniform, just as personal servomechs are doing in each of the other teammembers' changing rooms. Helping the captain dress is an ancient privilege for the coach... and our last chance to exchange views.

"Careful with Mvamba's leg, it's still weak from his latest defracturing treatment," he whispers while helping me pull the medical monitoring and feedback lining over my bare skin. It's a complex device that will oversee my physical status, second by second.

My metabolic stress levels and any fractures, sprains, or dislocations will be logged by the system. It will also ensure my heart doesn't explode while the device administers the hormone and stimulant dosages I'll need to bear up under all the stresses and strains of the game.

"You think the twins will make it through to the end of the match?" I ask, bringing up an old point of contention: for me, despite their undeniable physical conditioning, they could still use a little battle hardening.

Gopal nods confidently. But he whistles a catchy tune from Delhi that I've heard him hum other times when he's nervous and doesn't want anyone to know.

He's not positive they'll hold up either. I'll keep that in mind.

Over the inner lining he places the shock-absorbing coverall that will protect me from the effects of the force field suit, the outermost layer of my armor.

"Keep an eye on Arno," Gopal is still counseling when he begins placing the field generators on me. "Sometimes he forgets he's on defense and he tries to win the game all by himself."

I nod. I'll keep an eye on Arno.

When I turn the suit on, an impenetrable force field surrounds me. A calculated diffraction effect makes it glow in the glorious pink and blue of Team Earth. And the number 1 that identifies me as captain, under the triangle logo of Planetary Transports Inc., our official sponsor. May the Virgin protect them a thousand times.

Competitive gear for a first-class Voxl player is incredibly expensive. Factor in the strict technoscientific quarantine to which Earth is subject, which means that practically every piece of gear has to be purchased from the Centaurian corporation that hold nearly exclusive manufacturing rights throughout the galaxy, plus the fact that the training equipment, special diets, and all the rest practically double those costs, and you start to realize that the guys at Planetary Transports are true patriots. That they're highly committed. And that they're likely to boil us alive if we don't validate their investment by giving a good performance they can use as advertising.

For a quarter of what they've invested in feeding me, monitoring my medical condition, training me, and suiting me up, my father could have bought himself a first-class ticket and gotten off this planet safe and sound.

I'm going to dedicate this match to you, Papa. . . wherever you are. If you weren't pulverized by an asteroid or recycled by the gypsy junk-hunters, maybe you're still tumbling along out there, frozen for all eternity. All I know for sure is that you didn't make it. Sorry, old man. A few more years and I would've taken you on a trip. Of course, you had no way of knowing that, or patience enough to wait for the miracle. . .

And you, Mama, forgive me. . . I always talked back to you, telling you that your sharp tongue and bad temper would get you sent off to Body Spares. But I hated being right.

Body Spares. Spare me.

At press conferences there's always some reporter, dumb as a rock, or maybe just misinformed, who asks the classic question. As if it were the most baffling riddle in the world: why don't we just use the bodies of "horses" specially designed for Voxl, instead of putting our own bodies at risk?

At first I'd go off into long explanations. Now I just look at them and smile. Idiots.

The punishing training sessions and the huge doses of synthetic hormones and drugs we subject ourselves to, at the risk of destroying our metabolisms forever, are no fun, true enough. But there's no other way.

Completely suited up, with the suit turned on but my helmet not yet connected, I stand up and take a long look at myself in the mirror. Six foot three, 230 pounds of pure muscle. Not uniformly distributed, the way it would be on any average bodybuilder, but beautifully concentrated, almost sixty percent in the legs. Each of my thighs is thicker than my waist. My calf muscles are as big around as my head.

In normal gravity I can jump five feet eleven inches straight up without even flexing my legs. I have quicker reflexes than a hysterical wildcat. I can drop a coin, roll to the floor, and catch it in my mouth before it hits. A Voxl player's body is the most precious equipment he possesses—and the hardest to acquire.

An anatomy like this has to be carefully cultivated, sometimes for years. Years of training each reflex, each muscle, to reach perfection. I wouldn't trade even the strongest body straight from a Body Spares booth for my own. Not even the body of a twelve-foot Colossaur. I wouldn't know how to handle it like I do this one. It wouldn't respond to me in the same way.

Only one in ten thousand humans has in his genes the potential to become a Voxl star. Only one in five million has what it takes to become, someday, a member of Team Earth. The champions.

Having this muscle power so concentrated in your legs can be a bit much, even a pain, in everyday life, it's true. But we're Voxl players because—among other things—we aren't multimillionaires. If we could use one body to train and play in and another the rest of the time, we'd simply have no need to play. And we wouldn't. Except Yukio, maybe.

But for now, even he doesn't have enough money to afford the luxury of using a body that isn't his own.

It's true, since there's two sides to every coin, that some unlucky players rent out their bodies to Body Spares for pretty good money. Their main clients are xenoid ex-players curious to see what the body of another species feels like. For them, it comes out pretty cheap.

But even those bodies, compared to ours, are like twentieth-century helicopters next to a late-model aerobus. . .

While I'm thinking all this and looking at myself in the mirror with satisfaction, Gopal places the captain's vocoder between my teeth. Like my teammates', mine is a combination of dental guard and laryngophone. It allows me to communicate with the rest of the team and to activate or deactivate the field shield by flicking a special switch with my tongue.

My vocoder also has two other tongue controls: one to talk with Gopal without the rest of the team overhearing us; the other, more important one lets me stop the game clock whenever one of my players gets hurt or if we want to go into a strategy huddle.

Just as I'm finished getting dressed, the warning bell rings: time to head for the court. Off the court, with my suit turned off, each step I take is as ponderous as a graceful tyrannosaur's. I climb onto the antigrav field, which now whisks me straight to the place where we'll meet our challenge.

We still don't know whom we'll be facing.

In the World Championship and in League play, you always know your opponents beforehand: their favorite formations, even the clinical histories and psychological profiles of each player. And based on all this information you draw up a strategy.

But not in this match.

The League team that will be playing us won't find out far in advance, either. Maybe it's only now, as their ship is already entering the suborbital trajectory for Earth's troposphere, that their coach will be informing them of the League's irrevocable choice: they are the ones who will be testing their strength this year against Team Earth...

We walk out onto the court.

Or, better said, we enter into it. Voxl is played inside an enclosed rectangular hall, measuring about twenty-five feet high by fifty wide by one hundred long. That is, one by two by four *arns* by the standard Centaurian measure.

The walls of the playing court are still transparent in both directions, so we can see the crowd going wild outside. Lots of them with their faces painted half pink, half blue, waving huge flags with Earth silhouetted against a backdrop of stars. We can make out the convulsive movements of their mouths and their necks strained from yelling.

But we can't hear them. It's completely soundproof inside here. And when the game begins, the polarized walls will turn opaque for looking out. Nothing must distract the players of the galactic sport.

"They're saying, 'Go Earth, pink and blue, we're gonna stomp all over you!' and 'Earth, Earth, Earth is hot, the xenoids, they ain't diddly squat!' " Jonathan's voice comes over our headphones, letting us know what's up. He can lip read. He taught deaf kids for three years after they kicked him out of the League. A crappy job, but it beats starving to death or sinking into male social work, super-dangerous and illegal.

He chatters incessantly. Seems nervous. He's normally quiet as the grave before a match. I'll keep an eye on him. I don't want him to fall to pieces right now...

Suddenly Jonathan points up, and Mvamba does the same. No need for them to say anything. It's almost telepathic, the way we can tell the entire stadium has fallen silent.

The League players have arrived.

The ship is black. Blacker than black. So dark it gleams in the setting sun like an immense and ominous beetle. It docks at the empty tower, the visiting team's, and the dome of the court immediately hides it from us.

Even so, we've had time to notice that the ship is at least ten times the size of our aerobus. They must have onboard changing rooms. As usual, the League team will come down ready to play.

I look at my men for the last time before the decisive moment. Mvamba. Arno. Yukio. Jonathan. The Slovskys. And me. Humans all. To the xenoids, we're trash. Members of the most backward, despised, subjugated, and humiliated race in the galaxy. Relentlessly crushed in our crude primitivity by technologies so advanced they seem like magic to us. By economic powers so massive they could pay their weight in gold for every Earthling and even for the whole planet itself without much effort.

By destructive forces so extreme they could wipe the entire solar system from the galaxy.

Humans, like ninety-nine percent of the audience.

For them and for us, this is our only chance for revenge. The only occasion when, once a year, we can face off with them, the proud, domineering xenoids, on nearly equal terms.

It doesn't matter that no human team has ever managed to beat a League team in Voxl.

We are their hope, their demand for justice, their favorite sons, their thirst for revenge. We have to win.

We're going to win. Because we are the champions.

Because we have all the anger, if not all the strength.

So, if any justice exists in the universe, victory will be ours.

We all feel the same way. Even though no words are spoken. . .

We see the mouths in the crowd distended in a silent scream of infinite hatred. And before turning around, we already know that behind our backs the League team is walking onto the court. We wheel about in unison to face them. To see them, to gauge them, to meet them.

My eyes and all my teammates' eyes scrutinize them avidly. Gathering data, imagining likely strategies, weighing possible strengths and theoretical weaknesses. They must be doing the same with us.

Voxl teams are limited by weight, not by the number of players. No more than 1,263 pounds, exactly six Centaurian *paks*.

Our team weighs that much on the nose. Jonathan, our sub, matches the 201 suited-up pounds of Yukio, our lightest player. There'll be six of us on the field, and we haven't left a single gram of advantage to our opponents.

There are just four of them; they're betting on strength.

Their defensive back is a Colossaur who's been surgically stripped of the bony plates of his natural armor. Under his still-unplugged, transparent suit, his skin is a strange pale pink instead of reddish-brown. A real giant of his race; must weigh about 650 pounds.

Clever trick, that amputation: on the field, where we all wear the same armor, the thick natural carapace of a native of Colossa would merely be dead weight. So he gains mobility and keeps 650 pounds of muscle, plus the added advantage of a very strong tail.

I seem to see the Colossaur's tiny sunken eyes smiling as he scans our lineup. Not even the Blond Hulk, with his 412 pounds, could meet him in a direct hit, and the dirty scum feels safe. He knows we'll have to spend most of our time trying to avoid him.

Before dismay can chill my team's spirits, I tell them over the vocoder, "Forget about running away from the ogre. We're going to control him. In pairs—I don't want any heroes. You listening, Copenhagen? Anyway, he's not much for legwork. . . We'll beat him on the rebounds. Mvamba, you'll help the Hulk check that shelled mollusk. And if he looks too big, look at him with one eye closed and he'll seem smaller."

Their laughter tells me everything's going well. It's very important, if you want to be a good captain, to toss in a joke at the right time. It raises morale.

Apart from the Colossaur, there are the Cetians. Two handsome specimens. Identical as raindrops. Like they're clones. Worthy opponents for the Warsaw twins. If Jan and Lev manage to check them, they'll have graduated to manhood.

The Slovskys are heftier than the slim pair of xenoids, who must not even reach two hundred pounds each. Probably their equals in coordination. But speed is another kettle of fish. The natives of Tau Ceti aren't just as beautiful as angels, they're also as nimble and slippery as eels, more than any other humanoid. They're almost a match for the insectoid grodos, the fastest beings in the galaxy in spite of their armored chitin exoskeletons.

Well, at least they didn't bring any grodos. There's no way to remove the weight of their shells without killing them. . .

But what really has me worried is their fourth player. There's a look of disgust on Gopal's face. The twins' jaws have dropped. With a peremptory gesture I order them to keep quiet. None of the other players seem to have recognized him.

It's Tamon Kowalsky, the former captain of the Warsaw Hussars who led them to championships three years in a row. And the captain of Team Earth five years ago. Jan and Lev grew up in the shadow of his legend. Their father was his coach. . .

Now he's a traitor. A sepoy. A turncoat mercenary who sold out to the League and is playing against his own race, against his own planet. He has a credit tattoo over his right eyebrow, which speaks for itself about the privileged economic status he's achieved. But it's a sure bet he's a social pariah, a lonely outcast.

He probably has enough in his account to buy the whole Metacolosseum and maybe half of New Rome, but it doesn't look like the money has made him happy. Behind his wild mustache, his face has the same sour look as ever—or worse.

He's superfit. About 240 pounds, a little more than my current weight. Can I take him on? I've seen him play with the Hussars. He was already fast then, and nobody was better than him at picking up rebounds. Since he joined the League he must have gotten tons better. I'm going to need Yukio with me just to neutralize him.

My guys are looking curiously at Kowalsky. Dangerous.

I'd better tell them who it is.

"That's Tamon Kowalsky, from the Hussars. Samurai, you and I will take that renegade. Banzai?" I ask. The Japanese looks at me, and his eyes blaze. Bushido does not forgive betrayal.

"Banzai. Domo arigato, Daniel-san," he replies, half-joking. We studied Japanese together, but of course he speaks it much better. Genetic predisposition, maybe. Ever since they instituted Planetary as the common language for all Earth, historical languages are just a hobby for a few nostalgics.

The bell rings and we approach our opponents to give the traditional Centaurian greeting: the slightest of contacts between the tips of our fingers, our arms held out straight. A paranoid race, those Centaurians, I always think at these moments.

Returning, we energize our suits while the polarized transparent walls go opaque to hide us from the audience. Gopal returns to his room, and we remain there, waiting. Watching, all our muscles taut, for the voxl to materialize.

These seconds drag by like centuries.

The voxl is not a ball but a spherical concentration of force fields. It has mass, though not much, and it bounces off the walls. . . But that's where any comparison with a basketball ends.

There are two very curious characteristics of the way it interacts with the force fields of the six court surfaces. The first is that it gains speed instead of losing momentum every time it bounces. As if the walls had an elasticity coefficient greater than one. It takes just five or six rebounds for the voxl to move at such a high velocity that not even our hypertrained reflexes can really follow it.

The second peculiarity is that, like all force fields, it is extremely slippery. Which means that the angle of its bounce will be almost entirely unpredictable. Even when it strikes perpendicular to the wall, ceiling, or floor, you can bet the voxl will almost always shoot off at an angle of at least five or ten degrees of deviation—and at a higher speed.

The only things that slow the voxl down (and not by much) are the force fields of our suits, which have the opposite polarity. But it is so slick that it doesn't make much sense to try to catch it directly. It's impossible to hold; all that will happen is that it will fly off slowly in the direction you least want it to go.

Batting it produces similar effects. You might as well wrap it up with a bow and hand it to the opposing team: it will tumble off in any direction at all, the more slowly the harder you hit it.

The surest way to control this willful object is to use soft, almost tender strokes to change its direction and velocity. With lots of practice and at least as much good luck, you can almost get it to go where you want.

As if all this didn't make Voxl difficult enough, our suits also pick up velocity when they bounce against floors, walls, and ceilings, though not as terribly quickly as the ungraspable voxl. Largely because at the outset of the game, the gravity in the court is turned down to 0.67 g, the normal value for Centaurians, and that slows the action down a bit.

You can see why one journalist said that a Voxl match, especially a match played by novices, looks a lot like a madman's notion of how planets move through the solar system.

The scoring system isn't very rational, either, at first glance. The match ends when one team accumulates eighteen points. But the points don't accumulate one at a time. No, that would have been way too easy and too boring for the sadistic Centaurians.

The first goal, by either team, is worth six points. The second and third are five each. Fourth, fifth, and sixth, four points. The seventh and eighth goals are worth three. After that, if neither team has won yet, the remaining goals are worth one point each, with a win requiring a two-point margin.

Games rarely go into single points. The system is conceived so that the stronger team, the one that can prove its superiority and dominate the first four goals, will leave the other team on the field in the shortest time possible. Or, as they used to say where I come from, "Adiós, Lolita de mi vida!"

Nor is it very easy to score a goal. The Mayas may have thought that it was nearly impossible to propel the rubber ball on their *tlachtli*, using only their knees, hips, and elbows, through the high stone hoop barely wider than the ball itself, but if they'd seen Voxl they would have thought their game was child's play.

There are only a handful of rules. You can touch the voxl with any part of your body, but there is no hoop or goal posts or anything of the sort. You make a goal by sending the voxl on a triple rebound between two opposite walls (including floor and ceiling) without any interference from the opposing side after the last touch from the player who sets it in motion.

And doing that, again, is anything but easy.

When you also take into account the fact that the concept of fouling or rough play doesn't exist in Voxl, you'll have a better understanding of the true purpose of the forcefield armor suits. First and foremost, they keep the players' backbones from being shattered into a thousand pieces half a minute into the match. The suits have the curious and highly useful property of possessing a large moment of inertia. In addition to their tendency to act like a compact mass whenever hit by an external impact. That is, when a 650-pound Colossaur falls on top of you going a hundred miles an hour, you won't be inexorably pulverized; instead, you will "merely" be sent flying slowly in the opposite direction...

Even so, injuries happen all the time. And that's where the sub comes in, to take the place of the wounded guy while the medical monitor fixes his sprain, dislocation, or broken bone with its orthopedic machinery, making him good as new with a nice dose of custom drugs and regenerative synthetic hormones.

The bell rings again. It's coming. Any moment now...

There it is!

The size of a human head and tinted a vivid green, the voxl materializes against the immaculate white of the court. The League team uniforms are magenta blurs, racing to capture it. We're bolts of pink-and-blue lightning, out to stop them. Bursts of color, putting the spectators' visual agility to the test as they try to decipher the tangled web of our nearly supersonic movements.

Mvamba picks up speed by bouncing off the Great Dane's stomach. Kowalsky and the two Cetians use the Colossaur's huge shoulders to do the same. The Slovsky twins flank the walls. Yukio bounces off of me, and I set off spinning across the floor almost frictionlessly, aiming to sweep opponents aside and intercept the voxl.

The Colossaur smashes into Mvamba, rolls over him, and keeps going. Mvamba is swept aside like a feather, spinning erratically. Arno tries to cut off the ogre from Colossa, but is unable to contain him. Bad. Oh, better: the Slovsky twins run into the Cetian clones and dominate them. Yukio gains control, and the first bounce is ours...

But Kowalsky jumps and avoids my sweep. He goes after Yukio, runs into him, uses the momentum to get off the ground. Very bad. He reaches the voxl after its second bounce and sends it sideways. One bounce, two... One of the Slovskys (I can never tell them apart) intercepts and dominates it. Our bounces. One, two... The Colossaur steps in. Arno tries to stop him, but a half turn and a twist neutralize him, and the third bounce is ruined. He's strong, this Colossa kid.

Now he's dominating. One, two... I'll stop this...

But here comes Tamon Kowalsky, slipping between Yukio and me and separating us. Very talented... Three.

First goal goes to the League: six to zero!

They're good, they're the best damned players I've ever met. I call time and coach my players.

"Now it's their serve. Dangerous," I warn them over the audio system. "Arno, you underestimated the Colossaur. You're no match for his strength, one on one. Yukio and Mvamba, take care of that ogre. Play him for speed. And you, Great Dane, neutralize that renegade. As if your life depended on it, Korvaldsen. Twins, good play, guys—keep doing that, but don't get cocky. Those clones are real treacherous."

Voxl on the visitors' side. It touches the floor, shoots off. One of the Cetians controls it, a Slovsky intercepts. But doesn't dominate, lets it get away. The Colossaur, confused by Yukio and Mvamba. Arno corrals Kowalsky against the ceiling. Here's my chance.

I jump in and capture it. Dominate it, and here goes the bounce: one, two. . . My guards forgot about the Colossaur's tail. It flicks me aside with a skillful backslap and I mess up my own goal.

Now it's a Cetian with the voxl. Kowalsky blocks me, but the Slovskys jump in. One bounce. . . The twins are fast, they snatch it before the second rebound.

They block the Colossaur's back and pass it to Yukio, who makes a breakaway. He's our lightest player, our swiftest. One, two, thr— Kowalsky blocks it at the last second, goes into a secret pass, and now the Colossaur has it. He's too slow, he'll have to pass it to one of the others. Arno?

The Blond Hulk gets there on time, sets his weight and inertia against the giant xenoid's, and spoils his pass. Voxl out of control. Jan Slovsky traps it at low velocity, bounces against the ceiling. He's magnificent. How did he capture it?

I stop one of the Cetians. This is going well. The Slovskys: one, two, thr— Kowalsky, again! The worst thing is, the twins are following the same playbook their father created for that renegade when he was captain of the Hussars. That won't work.

Now he rebounds, evading Mvamba. This Tamon is a thorn in my side. Lev Slovsky joins in, his brother supporting him from behind: the renegade can't escape the pair of them. They're like one mind in two bodies. . . Shit, he tricked them! He wasn't trying for a goal. He passes to a Cetian who's not guarded. I try to get there, but. . . Floor, ceiling. . . Yeah, I have time. . .

Ohhh. . . The Colossaur hurls Mvamba, blocking my way. Floor again: that's three. Hell and damnation.

SECOND GOAL TO THE LEAGUE: ELEVEN TO ZERO!

I call time again.

"Captain, I suggest you switch tactics." Gopal's voice is cold. He only calls me "captain" when he thinks I'm not doing it right. But what more does he want? "Be creative: they're expecting twins against clones and for you to go for the goal. Kowalsky is the real danger; have the Slovskys stop him, and leave the clones to the African and the samurai. Your skill against the Colossaur's brute strength, and that leaves Arno free to go for the triple rebound. He can do it."

"We'll see," I reply, a little skeptical. It's a risky formation, but it might work. I'm not sure I can handle the Colossaur. Nearly three times my weight, and besides, that tail. . . But, nothing ventured, nothing gained. End of time out.

There's the voxl, on their side. They head out, intending to hold to the strategy that's already given them an eleven-point lead. They hesitate for an instant when they notice our changed lineup. What were you expecting, weirdos? Humans must be the only animals who will trip over the same rock twice—but never three times.

The twins completely cancel out Kowalsky on the second rebound. Good for their morale: seeing that they can take on their idol. Mvamba and Yukio are keeping pace with the clones, the voxl is left unguarded, and the Colossaur can't decide between the Dane and me. . . Perfect, he's going for the one with more body weight.

Arno doesn't even try to keep the voxl; he passes it to me, and the ogre pivots and comes after me. He's not going to have enough time. Kowalsky tries desperately to get out the trap. But the Slovskys have learned their lessons well; they're impenetrable.

Sheesh, this Colossaur is fast for his size. He's almost on top of me already. Now, the surprise: when the magenta mound reaches me, I pass to Arno. Who's totally free. The Colossaur is on top of me. . . I curl into a ball to protect myself, while I glimpse Arno out of the corner of my eye controlling handily. This is going to be a rude awakening.

One, two... pain. The impact twists my back, something seems to break. I scream. Darkness. And from far away, over my headphones, my team shouts victory.

Black, everything black and hot.

GOAL FOR EARTH!!! FIVE TO ELEVEN!

TIME OUT: DANIEL MENÉNDEZ, CAPTAIN OF TEAM EARTH, OUT FOR INJURIES. SUBSTITUTE JONATHAN HENDERSON JOINS PLAY.

"That was a brave play. Even suicidal, I'd say. Like trying to stop a charging bison. You were lucky to get out of there alive," Gopal's voice comes across the void.

He's proud of me, old man...

I emerge from unconsciousness for good when he claps me on the shoulder. The electrodes of the medical monitor are tickling me. I can't feel my legs, but that's nothing new.

"Four?" I ask with a smile. My mouth feels woolly.

"Not that bad, just three broken vertebrae. I told you, you were lucky to get out alive. A couple of minutes in the defracturing machine and back into the game with you. You still have a good induced regeneration quotient. It would take Arno twice as long to recuperate—he's really abused his body."

"I take pretty good care," I sigh, relieved, trying to sit up and watch the holoimage of the game that's monopolizing the former Delhi Wonder's attention. But I can't manage. It hurts too much. "What are they doing now?"

"Arno's leading them, they're trying to do the trident," Gopal explains, lost in thought. It isn't so easy to take in the whole picture of the game from outside. "Don't wriggle so much. Now you're getting a hundred milligrams of regidrine. Daniel, that play turned out well, but we can't repeat it. I have to protect them." He looks away from the hologram and smiles at me. "You're the best captain I've ever had. None of the others would have sacrificed like that for a goal. Facing down the Colossaur by yourself was crazy."

"But it worked," I smile. That's it; it's on his conscience, since he's the one who suggested it to me. "And it was my decision, not your fault."

"Obstinate as ever. The first time I saw you, I knew you were the sort who'd never stop till you made it," he says, not listening to me. "Oh, Daniel, if the rest of the team had your heart. . ." He watches the holoimage and clicks his tongue, disgusted. "Look, they made them fall for the old shell trick. . . Mvamba still has lots to learn. Nobody's going to keep them from letting the League score another goal." He looks at me and sighs. "Ready, champ?"

"Let's go," I answer; I'm ready. I can feel my toes again.

He helps me suit up a second time. "This time, try leaving the Colossaur unguarded. . . If you can block his passes, all his strength won't do him any good. Good luck, champ!" he sends me off with a pat on the back.

I return to the court as the announcement comes:

THE LEAGUE SCORES THE FOURTH GOAL OF THE GAME. SCOREBOARD: FIFTEEN TO FIVE. THE CAPTAIN OF TEAM EARTH IS BACK. SUBSTITUTE LEAVES THE COURT.

Yes, Gopal was right: once they let them form the shell, they could kiss that fourth goal goodbye.

I gather the team around me.

"Hey, let's not let it get us down. We can do better, am I right? Gopal thinks we should leave the de-shelled giant unguarded." Skeptical whistles. "You're right, it's crazy. So let's just pretend to do it," I crack my knuckles enthusiastically. "At the moment of truth, let's have the twins against the Colossaur, Mvamba and Arno against the

Cetians, I'll take on Kowalsky, which leaves Yukio free to score. And, heads up, a little bird told me that if the shell worked for them last time, they'll most likely try the cross next. That's what the Hussars always did, remember?" Confident laughter.

That's my team.

Like I'm a fortune-teller. They try to fake us out by starting off with the trident (copycats!), but then they form the cross. Kowalsky up the side, one of the clones up the middle, the other on the other wing, the Colossaur bringing up the rear.

Mvamba and Arno play against the Cetians, the twins pretend to be confused and leave the Colossaur behind, unguarded. Kowalsky shoots forward and here he comes, handling the voxl. He's going to pass it, he can't resist the temptation. Now!

The switch-up. The Slovskys stop the magenta mound practically cold; I'll never get tired of saying it, those kids have talent. Arno squashes the ex-captain of the Hussars into a corner (I'll have to kiss him for that steamroller move). I control one clone, Mvamba mixes it up with the other, and now Yukio has the voxl.

My samurai feints behind the Colossaur's back (yes, he's already cut free, a couple of two hundred-pound humans can't hold 650 pounds of xenoid for long) and gets one bounce. . . Mvamba and the twins in a scrum with the giant, while I'm practically doing somersaults to block the clones. Kowalsky gets away from Arno (too slow and heavy to hold him) and rushes over, but Yukio screams "Banzai!" and wraps him in the serpent's embrace. The voxl moves on its own, from inertia. Two. . . The third rebound is completed right in front of the Colossaur's nose. Timed to the fraction of a second. I'd give half a million credits (if I had them) for his helmet to go suddenly transparent. A look of surprise, of rage, of both?

How do you like that, Gopal? In the end, we did leave him unguarded.

EARTH SCORES THE FIFTH GOAL OF THE GAME! NINE TO
FIFTEEN!

We scream like crazy and hug in a frenzy. The magentas look at us
without moving. They must be burning with anger.

Kowalsky comes over and turns off his helmet. His broad whis-
kers stick sweatily to his cheeks. He smiles. No fury, all pro. "Hey,
kids, chill—it's just a game." He comes even closer and whispers to
me, "But put a move on, mestizo," he nearly spits the insult in my ear.
"Win or lose, I make more in one day than you do in a year. I'm in
the League, get it? Something you can only dream of. Don't forget: I
already made it to the top."

I don't answer, and he turns his helmet back on.

A crude psychological trick, insulting me. Yes, I'm mestizo—my
skin is the color of café con leche, I can't deny it. In pure logic, it
would be stupid of me to feel insulted by what he said. But there was
such contempt in his words. . .

Something is burning inside me.

Want the voxl, renegade? We'll give it to you, but good. Let's see if
the guys in the League know how to lose.

I call my team over.

"Okay, they're asking for it. Let's drive them crazy with the
tunnel. We'll start by pretending to lose control right away, at the
serve, and throw them off guard. And we're going to erase those
six points they're up on us. Because, what are we?" I shout this
last question.

"THE CHAMPIONS!" they reply in unison.

Nothing in the universe can stop us now.

I pretend to mess up my control of the voxl and send it flying away
from me at an odd angle, gaining velocity. They fall for it like fools, all
chasing after it.

So Yukio easily reaches the other end of the court. And when a Cetian goes after the rebound, the line already has the field split down the middle. Arno crushes the clone, whose pass to Kowalsky goes wide. Lev Slovsky takes it, and there you have the tunnel effect: Slovsky—Mvamba—me. And Yukio, protected behind the wall of bodies, open for the goal. One, two. . . The Cetians crash into Jan Slovsky and me, Kowalsky tangles with Mvamba, and. . . What are they doing? But Arno isn't even part of the play! The Colossaur is rushing at him full speed! Shit, no. . .!

"ARRGGHH!" The Blond Hulk's scream of pain blasts through the headphones. He didn't have time to turn off his vocoder. . .

SIXTH GOAL FOR EARTH!!! THIRTEEN TO FIFTEEN! DEFENSIVE BACK ARNO KORVALDSEN INJURED. HE LEAVES THE COURT. SUBSTITUTE JONATHAN HENDERSON TAKES HIS PLACE. BOTH TEAMS PAST THE TEN POINT MARK, PAUSE FOR HALF-TIME.

The paramedics cart off Arno Korvaldsen, mercifully unconscious. His enormous back twisted into an impossible knot, his limbs convulsing. The doctor looks at me and shakes his head. He won't get over this.

Sons of bitches, giving us the goal so they can take out our defensive back. It's a diabolical strategy. Jonathan doesn't have the weight it takes to be an effective substitute for the Blond Hulk. We'll have to reconfigure the whole squad.

The Slovkys, helmets already off, look on in astonishment as they carry the Dane off the court. Apparently they believed he was simply indestructible. They're deeply shocked—and so am I. Injuries in Voxl are as common as sweat. But ones as serious as this are pretty rare.

The magenta but unmistakably human silhouette of Kowalsky comes up to me. He turns off his helmet, smiling sarcastically.

"Poor old Dane, he hurt his widdle backsy. They shouldn't let the elderly play with us, the best guys in the League, no matter how big they are. Sometime unfortunate accidents happen. . . This is Voxl, mestizo. Let's see how well you do now without your defensive back, Latino." He turns his helmet back on and leaves.

I didn't look at him. Didn't say anything to him. Didn't break his neck, like I'd really love to do. He plays for the League, and when the game clock is stopped, he's as untouchable as a god. Like all xenoids.

The last time a human Voxl player responded to a Centaurian's insults and stuck four inches of steel between his ribs, the xenoids sprayed the entire Melbourne Astrodome with mushroom gas. Only five thousand people were killed, crushed in the panic to get out, but two hundred thousand humans were condemned to a slow, horrible death, watching their lungs rot for the next ten years, until the end came. There are worse things than mere death. . .

And the worst part is, the Centaurian didn't even die from the stabbing. There's no justice in this world.

Gopal comes over, his expression inscrutable, and whispers, "It isn't worth regenerating that body. Multiple head injuries, eight vertebrae pulverized, six broken ribs. Worst of all, brain dead. They'll have to autoclone him—his insurance will cover the expenses. When was the last time he recorded his consciousness?"

I sigh. "Arno was a meticulous guy. Right before the match. How long will it take?" I finally ask.

"An hour, I think. . ." Gopal shrugs. "Mechanical wombs are getting faster all the time. And it's been a long time since I saw anything like this. . ."

Yes. . . When you play Voxl, you know it could happen to you at any moment. At first it's very scary, but after a while you get used to the idea. When all is said and done, if your insurance covers it, and the worst is never going to happen to you. . . And then, all of a sudden, it happens near you. Very near. And you realize that you're never going to get completely over the fear of dying. Because it's horrible. It always will be, even if the darkness only lasts for a while. Even if resurrection is guaranteed.

Arno won't see how this game ends.

I call the team. I can see in their faces that they already know.

"An hour," I tell them anyway. "You know already. He'll wake up plenty of pounds lighter, he'll have to get his new body ready all over again, more hormones, more training, special diets and all that... A Voxl player's body doesn't just depend on his genes. It'll be at least half a year before he can play again. So I really want, as a gift when he wakes up, for us to be able to tell him, 'Arno, we won. We did it for you, Great Dane.' What do you think?"

We shout.

We are the champions.

Of course we'll win!

Full of faith, we run to the hydromassage tank.

We've already reached a point no human Voxl team has gotten to in decades of matches against League players. Thirteen to fifteen. The last time a Team Earth got past the ten point mark against xenoids was twenty-six years ago, captained by the Delhi Wonder—our very own Mohamed Gopal.

All the executives of Planetary Transports Inc. must be patting themselves on the back for sponsoring us. In exchange for their large and risky investment, now they have exclusive rights to the five minutes of half-time advertising in the game of the millennium. Worth billions.

Like all the other annual Voxl matches between humans and xenoids, this one is broadcast via holovision to the five continents of Earth, to all the worlds that comprise the League, and even to those colonies that have their own orbital hyperantennas. At this moment, more than four fifths of the entire human population must be in front of their holoscreens, praying to their gods for our victory.

And probably a good fifth of the entire galaxy is paying attention to the outcome of the game, though, of course, more out of curiosity than because they're fans.

We're going to show them that Earth is more than a tourist trap.

Though, without Arno, we'll be walking a tightrope.

"Remember the Chinese box?" I ask the team while the vibrations of water massage our overexcited muscles. "It hasn't been used in a long time. . . They might not be taking it into account."

"Staking the whole match on a coin toss is too risky," Jonathan hesitated. His hands are shaking. He sure goes all or nothing. "I don't know. . . If we score, we'll only have sixteen. But if they stop us, counterattack, and score, we lose everything. We should be cautious. . ."

"Screw cautious!" Mvamba sits bolt upright, sending water splashing everywhere. His eyes shine with the determination of youth. His ebony body, like a beautiful statue, is still trembling from the emotions of the game. "I say let's do it!"

"Let's do it. For the Blond Hulk," the twins say in unison, square jaws jutted forward.

Yukio, narrowing his lips, nods in agreement.

Jonathan raises his hands, gives up, nods with them.

This is my team.

I look at them, proud. They're as much mine as they are Gopal's. First-class human beings. Faces of steel, pure determination. Faces like those of the agents on the Planetary Security recruitment hol-oposters. Earth's soldiers. Faces like that of the stone-jawed worker whose enormous hologram is floating now over the Metacolosseum, broadcasting his message, "If you have to send a package, there's nothing like Planetary Transports Inc. It'll get there safe, it'll get there today, any day."

As he says it, he crudely hugs the topheavy blonde smiling at his side, an image brimming with subliminal messages of virility and patriotism.

Except the face of this worker, and those of the Planetary Security agents, are just computer-generated forms. My team is real.

That's the difference.

The League guys must think they've demoralized us by taking out Arno. Think we'll start playing defense. Which is what we ought to do, by any logical criteria.

They can't expect us to attack. Especially not to run a play as suicidal as the Chinese box.

Maybe it'll work. Maybe it'll surprise them.

And all these years of taking synthetic steroids for breakfast, lunch, and dinner to transform my metabolism completely, of consuming stress relief drugs and neurostimulants that have driven me all but crazy, haven't been in vain.

And all the aches on rainy days, reminders of the hundred fractures I've accumulated and the two autoclonings I'd prefer to forget, haven't been in vain.

And all the time I've gone without having an erection that wasn't electronically induced, without a normal girlfriend, without any friends or family other than one Voxl team or another, hasn't been in vain.

Maybe everything will turn out okay. And then this will all have been just an investment. Risky but intelligent, in the end.

A sort of long-term deposit, so I'll have a pile I can count on later for a secure old age without deprivation.

So I won't end up, like so many others, joining the ranks of ruined former Voxl players. Dragging around the withered, useless remains of my oversized thighs amid moans of pain. Pining for a roof over my head and a plate of food, forced to rent out myself for a pittance to Body Spares, or falling into the underground male social work network to get by for a couple more days.

I watch Jonathan from the corner of my eye. He's still trembling, and rightly so. He's practically an old man, and he hardly knows how to do anything but play Voxl. If he doesn't make it now, he'll never get a second chance. The end of his playing career is near. . . terribly near.

Today he'll be a hero or nothing. Shameful failure or total triumph. He'll be playing the most difficult position for a welterweight like him: subbing the defensive back. I know he'll go out there and give it his last drop of sweat, his last gram of effort.

I look at Mvamba. Calm. At his age, barely at the start of his sports career and already a member of the Team Earth that hit double digits against League players, he'll be showered with contracts. For him, old age is still a faraway menace. And compared with the Sydney where he grew up, that inferno of violence and filth, every day of his current life is a paradise. Whatever might happen, he's already won, and he knows it.

The fact that he still wants to bet it all on the Chinese box, risking serious injury, speaks well of the fetish worshipper. He has great heart, this African ex-aerobus driver.

But maybe at the last minute his survival instinct will make him hold back. . . I'll trust him ninety percent. Not a hundred.

Yukio is inscrutable as ever. He never joins in. He belongs and doesn't belong to the team. When we go out on the town as a group, he prefers to head off on his own. I don't feel he's totally mine. If he didn't play so well, I'd distrust him. What's a superrich shareholder in the Planetary Tourism Agency doing here, sweating blood and risking his life with the scum of the Earth that we are? Playing for playing's sake—I don't get it. For honor? What honor do we humans have left?

What, other than survival at all costs, does a race that has been defeated and humiliated on every front have left?

The days of samurais and warrior glory are long gone. Contact came and changed everything. Now, Yukio Kawabata, the pathetic descendent of the feudal lords of Japan, is trying to wrap his nakedness and frustration in the tattered cloth that does such a poor job of covering us: dignity.

Ha. A human Voxl player, dignified? Like a passionate Centaurian, an educated rat, or a kind grodo. Absurdities. And if Yukio believes in them, he's a dumb idealist.

But in the long run, it's his business. Dumb or not, something tells me I can trust him absolutely. He's made from the same material as the kamikaze pilots in World War II. Even when they knew the Japanese Empire had lost, they flew to their deaths in the face of Yankee artillery fire, shouting "Banzai!" in their explosive-filled Zeros.

Yukio would have been one of them, if he had lived then. He won't fail me.

And the Slovskys? I watch their faces, flushed from debating the plays they'd made. Jan and Lev, nearly indistinguishable. Their cheeks still covered with peachfuzz, not a shadow of a beard. They're kids. And at the same time, they're like thousand-year-old men who've seen it all before and have lost interest in everything. Robots specially programmed to play Voxl, that's how they've chosen to appear. But, I wonder, what lies beneath?

Do they hate the tyrannical father, the coach who forced them onto the court almost before they learned to talk? Do they hate me for making them face off against their idol, Tamon Kowalsky? Or do they love me for giving them a chance to play, though on opposite sides, with the beloved captain of their Warsaw Hussars?

But beyond the game, what are they? Or is it just that they aren't anything else? They seem happy, arguing about Voxl all the time. Breathing Voxl. Sunk knee-deep in the shit of Voxl and enjoying it more than anyone. What was that old saying my mother always told me when I was a kid?

For a man who dies doing what he likes, even death tastes like heaven.

Lies. Heaven, shit. For the Slovskys, like for all the rest of us, death and defeat are going to taste like shit.

I can count on them to the very end, too. Deep down, their supposed lack of interest in everything but the game is just a mask to hide their infinite shyness and clumsiness outside the Voxl universe. Their shame at knowing they're just humans. They aren't so different.

We are the champions.

The best of the best.

The salt of the Earth.

We're going to wash away the shame of Contact. Take revenge for that xenoid humiliation on the only field where we're almost equals.

Inside the cuboid court, it doesn't matter how many planet-sized battleships we humans can put into orbit, or how many millions of credits we can call our own in infobanks around the galaxy.

Or does it?

Because, can't this League team count on medical monitors a thousand times better than ours? Simulators and training systems we can't even imagine?

Sports equality is a pipe dream.

Otherwise. . . why hasn't any Team Earth *ever* won a match?

Until today.

Today is different. I can feel it in the air. Today. . . who knows.

Because we are the champions.

The best sextet of humans who ever rebounded off a Voxl field.

The great human hope.

The secret weapon of revenge—closer now than ever.

END OF HALF-TIME COMMERCIALS. TEAMS, TAKE THE FIELD.

The pink-and-blues and the magentas are returning to the fray.

"Let's see how well you move now, little Latino," is Kowalsky's whispered insult, his idea of a greeting before he turns on his helmet.

Sure, renegade. Let's see how you handle it. Let's see if the cunning in your human brain is a match for all six of ours. There's a good reason why the League team wanted at least one *Homo sapiens* in their lineup. The Centaurians invented the game. . . but we're the most creative now. And everybody in the galaxy knows it—that's why they record all our World Championships and study them, to steal our strategies.

Sure, Kowalsky. You're going to see how well I move now. Let's see if playing in the League has taught you any new tricks—or just made you forget most of what you used to know.

It's our serve. "Chinese box," I remind my guys over the vocoder.

There's the voxl, red now instead of green. Second half. How long has it been since a human team saw this color in a match against League players?

Dear Virgin, do not forsake me at this decisive hour.

Yukio diverts it without letting it touch the ground. A nicely controlled play. The Cetian clones take off to catch it.

Jonathan risks a collision with their full force and stops the voxl cold before the Cetians arrive. We wait. Kowalsky hesitates, then finally sends the Colossaur after us.

Now.

I rebound off Mvamba and wrap myself around the voxl. I can't hold it, but it's stuck in the cage I've formed with my limbs, head, and body. I'm defenseless; now everything depends on my team.

The Colossaur reaches me and I tense up—but the Slovskys shunt him aside before he can do me any damage. Well, what happens next is useful to us. His slight contact is making me float up slowly, and I suddenly arch my back, propelling the voxl against the ceiling.

First bounce.

As if in slow motion, Jonathan reaches it and wraps around it. I join the Slovskys: we have to immobilize 650 pounds of Colossaur! Mvamba stops one Cetian and the slippery Yukio gets Kowalsky and the other Cetian entangled. Jonathan reaches the floor, still wrapped around the voxl, which he frees almost tenderly.

Second bounce.

Jonathan took a big risk by squeezing the voxl with all his strength against the wall. Now it shoots off—fortunately, in the perfect direction. Back at the ceiling. God exists, He is here with us, and He guides our voxl. Thank you, sweet Virgin.

The Colossaur makes an all-out effort to reach it, sweeping the twins aside, but I pin his tail between my back and the wall. One second, two. . . He's wriggling away, he's too strong. And there's hardly any friction between the force fields of our suits. The magenta mound reaches out with his tridactyl hand and. . .

Too late!

Third rebound!

This one was for you, Arno. . .

SEVENTH GOAL SCORED BY EARTH!!! EARTH TAKES THE LEAD ON THE SCOREBOARD! SIXTEEN TO FIFTEEN! EARTH, EARTH, EARTH!

See now how well I move, renegade?

I can almost feel the court shaking. Out there, the Metacolosseum of New Rome must bursting with joy. Collective hysteria.

In here, we are the champions, and we're going to win.

Going to take revenge for Earth's humiliation, forever.

Going to earn a place in glory.

The next goal decides it all.

Our serve.

We salute Centaurian-style, with our fingers tips, arms outstretched.

And go on the attack.

For the first time in a quarter of a century, Earth is winning.

Mvamba—Yukio. The Slovskys show off with a swift bounce off the demoralized Colossaur's chest, and they keep control. The court is ours.

Kowalsky tries to snatch it and fails, but the Cetians act in coordination and steal the rebound that Jonathan was about to capture. . .

There's no escape: Mvamba steals from them and passes to me. I've got it: one, two. . . The Colossaur sweeps the Slovskys aside and messes up the play. He dominates. The twins neutralize him again but now the voxl is Kowalsky's. The clones block me doggedly.

I slip away from the Cetians and thumb my nose at Tamon Kowalsky. The twins are controlling the Colossaur.

Tension. It's a battle for the deciding goal.

Muscle fatigue. Adrenaline pulses into my blood.

Virgin of Caridad del Cobre, give us this goal.

The Cetians take Yukio out of circulation, hurling him into Mvamba. It doesn't matter, he'll get over it. I dodge the charging rhinoceros of a Colossaur and make a long pass to Jonathan.

He catches it between his legs and goes for the bounce: one, two. . .

An unguarded Cetian intercepts it and rebounds off the other one.

Kowalsky hems me in.

One bounce, two. . .

Sweet Virgin, don't abandon me now!

Yukio still dazed. Mvamba moves in, but erratically. He hasn't entirely recovered. . .

My soul freezes when I see there won't be enough time.

Now something is burning inside me. It can't end like this!

I shout over the vocoder: "Revenge! Everybody on Kowalsky!"

. . .and three.

EIGHTH AND FINAL GOAL, FOR THE LEAGUE. EIGHTEEN TO FIFTEEN. LEAGUE WINS. LEAGUE CAPTAIN TAMON KOWALSKY INJURED.

And we lose.

But it was too much for the Warsaw Hussars' old captain. Jonathan, Mvamba, the Slovskys, and me, piling on him.

When they turn off the field and gravity goes back up from 0.67 g to our normal terrestrial 1.0 g, Tamon Kowalsky lies sprawled across the floor of the court, looking like a broken doll. The paramedics take him away without even turning off his suit. They only take off his helmet, which rolls across the floor.

"That's Voxl, schmuck," Jonathan mumbles, dealing it a splendid kick, angry tears in his eyes. "That's for Arno—and don't you ever insult a human player again."

I look at him, astonished. How could he have known?

He shrugs, a stricken look on his face, and points to his vocoder. It isn't the official model at all—it's had a lot more than "slight modifications."

"Sorry, Daniel," he whispers. "Electronics is another hobby of mine. I thought if I knew what you and Gopal were saying I could play better. I placed a microphone in your helmet. . ."

"Forget about it, doesn't matter anymore." I pat him on the back, trying to seem nonchalant. "Hey. . . so, what are you going to do now?"

He smiles and shrugs again. "Well, I'll manage somehow. I can always go back to teaching deaf kids. See you around—someday, I hope. Take care, captain."

He leaves. A good guy, that Jonathan. Too bad.

Brooding, I take a few steps and pick up Kowalsky's dented helmet. Disconnected, it's as transparent as mine. Practically identical. No magenta, no pink-and-blue.

Maybe I shouldn't have given that last order. . .

In the end, we're not just humans, we're equals.

Well, it's not so serious, either. In half an hour he'll be recovered and celebrating another win with the Colossaur and the Cetians.

I wonder if he'll still be their captain off court. . . They must have other rules in the League. Most likely, when it comes to salaries and privileges, he's at the back of the magenta pack.

Mercenaries always pay a price.

He chose. Better a lion's tail than a rat's head. A full stomach without honor before hunger with dignity.

I look up. The walls are transparent again. I can see the crowds leaving the titanic stadium. Silent, hushed. Like every other year. But in twelve months they'll be back anyway, the same crowds, hoping again for a miracle.

Why did you abandon us, Virgin?

We lost.

I'm having trouble getting used to the thought. I feel so empty I can't even be depressed. Or cry, or scream. . .

Maybe next year they'll let me be part of another Team Earth. Not as captain, of course, but something's better than nothing. . . After all, with me leading, we almost beat the League.

"Stop thinking about it." Gopal's voice, and his hand on my shoulder, startle me. "Every game, somebody's got to lose. It's tough when it happens to you, sure. . . but there's a little compensation sometimes."

"Experience?" I suggest, cynically. And immediately want to take it back. I don't mean to hurt him.

"No. Experience is what we get when we don't get what we want," he shakes his head. "I'm talking about. . . a whole other level of benefits." His voice is trembling slightly. "Daniel, I want to introduce you to an important person. He's very interested in meeting you. Over there. . ."

I turn around reluctantly. I'm not in the mood for rich, bejeweled fans, keen to console me and tell me that we'll have better luck next time. . .

Surprise. He's decked out in jewelry and he's most likely a fan (what else would he be doing here?). But he's no human.

Eight legs. Cold, multifaceted eyes. It's a grodo.

"Modigliani is a scout for the League," Gopal explains in a mischievous tone, behind which I think I can detect a little. . . sorrow? Envy?

I stare gaping at the insectoid. I still can't believe it. . . This is too good to be happening to me. . .

"Mr. Modigliani, I am. . .," I stammer, extending my hand to him. I would happily cover his grey chitin carapace with kisses.

Thank you, sweet Virgin, for hearing my prayers.

"Skip the mister," the electronic voice crackles from a translator-synthesizer on the insectoid's chest. He ignores my proffered hand, which I withdraw. "Just Modigliani. You know, Danny, you've got a tactical sense that I've rarely seen in any player."

"Umm. . . Thanks, mis. . . Modigliani. . ."

"Well, now you've met, and since I can see you understand each other, I'll leave you alone," Gopal remarks, squeezing my shoulder. "I'm so happy you have a good future to look forward to." He leans forward and whispers in my ear, "Don't sell yourself cheap. Don't accept his first offer." And again, out loud, "See you around. . . Danny." There's a slight mocking tone in the way he says it.

He's never called me anything but Daniel. Or "captain."

I watch him. He walks away, whistling. To be forgotten. He has no future to look forward to. After ten years as a player and fifteen coaching the ever-losing Team Earth, his fifteen minutes are up. Mohamed Gopal, the Delhi Wonder, is retiring for good.

I wonder what he'll live from now. For him, as for the Slovskys, Voxl is everything.

I'll call him some day. . . For now, I have more urgent business to attend to. I turn my attention back to the grodo.

"Modigliani. . . You picked a very nice name. Do you know who he. . ."

"No, and I don't care. We just like Earth names with four syllables. There's a music to them." The grodo gesticulates bluntly with two of his chitinous legs and places another pair on one of my shoulders, forcing me to walk at his pace. He's as tall as me, and thinner, but much stronger. "Okay, Danny, I like to get straight to the point. I followed the match closely. I was interested in Arno Korvaldsen and you. We'll make him the same offer when he finishes autocloning. But he's not young, and if he's lucky he'll last one more season. As for you. . ." He paused.

I have my heart in my mouth. Let it not be a pittance, sweet Virgin. You know I'll have to take it, no matter what. . .

"Three seasons with the Betelgeuse Draks. . ."—tell me how much, you repulsive bug, I don't care if you're listening in on me with your telepathy, I'll beg all the forgiveness I need later on but for now, just tell me how much already—"for half a million credits a season. Medical expenses and training costs included, same goes for accidental death insurance. What do you think?"

What do I think? A swindle, that's what I think. I hope you're listening in on my brain this time. The Colossaur and the Cetian clones who played against us today must make ten times that much. It would be interesting to know how much Kowalsky, their captain, makes. Maybe less than me. . .

It doesn't matter what I think, Modigliani, because I have to think it's fine. I don't have any other options. I'm going to accept, you know I'm going to accept, I know that you know that I know. So stop pretending.

After all, I can consider myself lucky.

"Perfect," I articulate at last, my mouth feeling full of clay. "When do I start?"

"Soon as you pick up your gear. My ship is leaving from the New Rome astroport in two hours. Look for it, its name is Velvet. I'll expect to see you onboard." Modigliani walks and pivots. "I'm going to see Korvaldsen. . ."

"And the others?" I still dare ask him, before he's too far away.

"Oh, yes. . . The others," he says unenthusiastically. "Not interested. Too old, one of them. Too green, the rest. Those twins, however—maybe next year."

A terrible scream at my back. I turn. A long gleam of burnished steel stained with blood spins across the floor of the court. The commotion of paramedics rushing to the scene. No point even looking. I know perfectly well what it is.

Seppuku. . .

Yukio, theatrical as ever. He swore he'd commit harakiri if they beat us. Dignity as light opera, honor as prop. As if he didn't know that, worst case, his family would autoclone him. These samurais and their cult of blood. . .

I'm more worried about Jonathan. And Gopal. They're perfectly capable of walking out of here calm as can be, and then, far away, jumping into a tank of acid. To leave no traces.

Poor guys. . .

I feel sorry for them, but life goes on. Some rise, some fall. Each to his own problems. I'm not the captain of Team Earth anymore.

Dear Virgin, I'll light you a candle at least as big around as my thigh. For all you've done and will do for me.

And when Arno wakes up, we'll go buy three cases of beer each. And find us a good pair of social workers, doesn't matter how much they charge. Because this is worth celebrating.

It isn't every day you have this sort of luck: a contract with the League. Now, to travel all over the galaxy. To live.

Now I'm really going to play.

I'm sure Arno thinks the same, he's so pragmatic.

The pride of Earth, the hope of humans, the revenge of the oppressed. . .

Screw that.

No we *are* the champions.

On the best paid team.

The only one that's really worthwhile.
My mother would be proud of me—I'm sure of it.

November 23, 1995

The Sacred Tigers

The Ussuri or Amur tiger, *Panthera tigris altaica*, is the largest feline on Earth. And, after the polar bear, the most powerful living terrestrial carnivore.

It is a tiger subspecies adapted to the cold taiga, its dense fur nearly white with pale brown stripes. It can weigh as much as 650 pounds and measure some ten feet from nose to tail tip.

A beautiful animal that had almost no natural enemies, it was the indisputable king of the taiga—until the advent of man.

Hunters and herders from the Yakut, Buryat, and other Siberian ethnic groups, who had no weapons but their bone arrows and spears, respected and admired the tiger as the ruler of beasts. To their shamans it was a sacred animal, both tutelary deity and demon, and the highest proof a man could give of his bravery was to hunt one alone.

Then the white man arrived with firearms and money and alcohol. The fur hunters.

Attracted by the high prices fetched by the valuable black-and-white coats of their gods, hired guns from all over the world joined the semicivilized sons of those very Siberian tribes that so revered the Amur tiger to decimate their numbers, never very large to begin with. Directors of zoos, in whose cages the immense felines played such an important role and attracted such large crowds, took care of the rest. No protective legislation could prevent the disaster.

By the turn of the twenty-first century, the fifty-four remaining Ussuri tigers were living in captivity in various zoos and private parks across the planet. Each was worth hundreds of thousands of dollars.

Then came Contact...

As part of their plan for restoring the ecology, the xenoids skillfully crossbred and cloned the fifty-four survivors, and in a matter of twenty years the population of Siberian tigers had grown to several thousand. Though their genetic diversity had diminished somewhat, the subspecies could be considered rescued.

Nonetheless, *P. t. altaica* continues to be categorized as a "protected species." Each specimen is carefully tagged at birth with a locator-transmitter that allows the appropriate department in Planetary Security to track its location and health status second by second, monitoring them with dedicated satellites.

Pity the human who dares hunt one of these priceless white tigers. The minimum penalty, if extenuating circumstances such as self-defense or something along those lines can be proved, is two years in Body Spares.

Local reindeer herders have learned to tolerate the overpopulated great cats' constant depredations as a necessary evil. They try to keep their herds away from the areas where tigers prowl, but in any case they always expect a certain loss margin in the heads of cattle that will inevitably be taken as prey.

Hunters in the region avoid the tigers like the devil; regardless of how desperate they get, regardless of how few animals they have taken, they never shoot them. They even keep a close eye on their snares and traps to save any cubs that may have accidentally gotten caught in one.

Once more, though in a very different sense, the great cats are sacred to the sons of the taiga.

For the Ussuri tigers, life is easy and comfortable now. Domesticated reindeer are easier to bring down than their wild cousins or the giant elks. They reproduce unafraid that wolves or bears, decimated by hunters, could wreak havoc on their litters of cubs. No one hunts or harasses them. . .

Most of the time.

Three or four times a year, men from Planetary Security land on the taiga en masse. They serve as bodyguards to some visiting xenoid VIP, almost always a grodo or an Auyar who previously expressed a desire for some relaxation. And who paid a generous sum for the right to get it...

And what better entertainment than hunting the largest feline on the planet? Exciting, primitive, and... utterly exclusive.

The hunting party is organized with mathematical precision, with beaters, spotters, and tall hunting platforms from which the xenoids may fire their projectile or energy guns at their leisure, free from any risk that the desperate cats might leap high enough to reach them.

Generally, the tigers shot by each visitor number in the dozens, though it is said that some grodo or other who was an exceptionally good shot once managed to rack up a hundred kills.

Sometimes, if the top brass of Planetary Security, or of the Planetary Tourism Agency itself, deign to join the fun, by the end of the hunt the feline carcasses carpet the frozen ground so thickly that the snow, packed hard by the huge paws of the tigers as they tried to escape, is more red than white.

Occasionally guests from other worlds will capture a live cub and take it home with them on their hyperships, like some exotic striped souvenir of their trip to Earth.

They always leave loaded down with pelts, after the beast's carcasses have been quickly and skillfully skinned by the experts from Planetary Security (who in the process recuperate the locator-transmitters). The rest of the pelts, either entire or reduced to handicrafts, along with the claws, teeth, and bones, become "luxury items" to be sold for steep prices in exclusive boutiques to the wealthiest xenoid tourists. Or they are exported to other worlds, to the same end.

When the humans who control the planet and the visitors who control the galaxy leave the site of the hunt, the wolves and birds of prey feast grandly on the formless skinned bodies of the dethroned kings of the taiga.

The shamans of the local tribes also rummage patiently through the trampled snow, recovering every fragment of skin, every hair, every tooth, every precious remain of their fallen gods, to use in making their time-honored protective amulets.

They jabber in their ancient tongues, which they still insist on speaking in addition to Unified Planetary, caressing the remains of the hunted cats. No one knows what they say. . .

But there are tears in their eyes and rage in the movements of their wrinkled hands when they drive their knives into the snow, and when they look to the sky, as if they are waiting for something. . .

The Rules of the Game

Raindrops? Come on, kid, run!

Damn these cloudbursts!

So crazy, it's salty as seawater. . . And these Kevlar uniforms weigh a ton when they're soaked.

Hurry up, inside!

Whew, out of breath. . . I can't run like I used to. Good thing we're inside now. And the night started out so pretty—you could even see the stars. With all these Auyar suborbital propulsion experiments, the atmosphere of this planet's gone haywire. It's as likely to rain as to hail. And always briny. Only thing left is snow in the middle of summer.

Wow, looks like a real gullywasher. Too bad we aren't baby cucumbers, we'd make some fine pickles. Close the door and take your helmet off, like me. Make yourself at home, you know. . .

What? So, we won't be able to control the perimeter?

Kid, use your gray cells, don't make me change my mind about you. Who'd go patrolling when it's cats and dogs out there? Looking for what?

Anyway, our only job is guarding this place—not the perimeter. If some cannibal cult was crazy enough to go swimming in this downpour and they decided to enjoy their menu right in front of our noses, it's their problem, I'm staying put. Our responsibility stops at the electric fence around this place.

It's a nasty job, you don't have to tell me. The only worse job to pull is ship patrol—running around up there, chasing those idiots who try escaping the planet in their homemade rockets. Getting bored to death like an oyster out of water, that's all you can do up there in orbit.

Though at least now and then they save some suicidal maniac from freezing solid up there in space. But this guard duty we pulled here makes about as much sense as searching for deposits of ice in the desert...

Nothing ever happens here in the Body Spares depository. There's nothing to steal, and you can't find anything much quieter than a body in suspended animation, human or not. Maybe just an actual corpse.

Truth is, keeping night watch here is a pretty stupid anachronism. A leftover from back when they didn't really understand xenoid metabolism yet, and the boys upstairs were scared that some restless tourist might crawl out of his tank and cause problems zombying around out there while his mind was in another body.

The good part is, shifts here are two hours shorter than normal. Just to make sure we don't commit suicide out of pure boredom... Especially in this rain. We can't even watch people walking by.

Not having anything to do always makes me jittery...

Play cards? Sonny, you know as well as I do regulations say we can't gamble on duty. Maybe some other time. I love hearts. And poker? Forget about it...

But it occurs to me right now all of a sudden that everything happens for a reason. That's right, Markus—that's your name, right?—I think we're gonna find this salty rain as good as holy water. It's gonna give us a little time to relax. I've been meaning to talk with you for quite a while...

Don't tense up. Just a little talk between partners, not another exam. Basic training's over. I just want to talk, one Planetary Security guy to another. Man to man. Forget that I'm a sergeant for now, doesn't matter.

Truth is, right now we practically are the same rank. You're a rookie agent, and I'm a sergeant in the doghouse...

No, it's no secret, and it doesn't bother me, I'll tell you what happened: a stupid minor incident. This over-sensitive social worker, at the astroport a couple of weeks ago. Girl named Buca. . . Her face was smeared with that waterproof makeup they all use now, like a mask. I guess it helps them all look the same. And the xenoids love it.

I swear I tried to be nice to the little slut. I thought it was what she needed; she looked so nervous after one of those suicidal Xenophobe Union maniacs started a shootout. Though we neutralized him right away. And one of my agents got a little rude with her. I tried to fix things up—and, see what you get. Seems the girl didn't like my style. And she complained to headquarters.

Happens every day. Normal procedure is, you file the complaint and that's that. But some grodo had picked this Buca for incubation, so I was screwed. Complaints from the xenoid big fish always cause a stink in the corps—and that's never good for us little guys. Something you'd better start learning now. Result? Sergeant Romualdo gets a full month of street patrols, night patrol every third night, and a cut in salary.

Hope nothing like this ever happens to you.

Though, if my nose isn't mistaken, you'll go far. Think that's funny? Whatever. Sergeant Romualdo Concepción Pérez rarely goes wrong in his predictions. I see a very promising career here waiting for you in Planetary Security. As clear as I see your face right now. I'd even dare to bet that, if you put nose to the grindstone a little, you'll make NCO at least in a couple of years.

Me? Been sergeant twelve years now. But don't think I envy you for that. In this life, everybody gets as far as they're gonna get. I have no complaints, sergeant's fine with me. When it comes right down to it, though I've picked up some culture, I'm still a poor ignoramus who has a hard time reading.

But you, with the schooling you've got. . . IQ of 148, and you can tell you're educated. Mind if I ask you a question? Just out of curiosity, why didn't you finish your degree in fission engineering, if you were already in your fifth year and you just had two more to go?

Oh, sure, financial problems. Can I guess? Your parents were paying for college, and all of a sudden business slowed down for them. . . Oh, an aerobus accident? Sorry, kid. . . Guess you'd rather not talk about it. . .

Lots of guys go into Planetary Security for the same reason. As unpopular as the corps is, it's one of the few places that's always posting new jobs. And compared with the crumbs you get paid for any other job on this planet, our 350 credits a month isn't so bad, is it? Especially when you think that they don't require prior experience or training. Everything you need they teach you in the Academy, eh?

How do I know what you studied? Come on, kid, I just read your file. . . Sure, it's supposedly private, only officers know the access code and blah blah blah. . . but being practically an oldtimer in the district gives you certain privileges, even on the computer.

Illegal? No, I wouldn't go so far as to say illegal. Just. . . unconventional. If we're going to be partners, it's only logical I oughta be a little curious about your bio, right?

Besides, I don't know what you have to be ashamed of, your record's impeccable.

I could tell from the start, you were good material. I've been observing you for days, and I like what I see: enthusiastic kid, a little impulsive, only natural at your age. Twenty-four, right? But you think before you act. In this line of work, that's the key thing.

Besides, I've come to like you, though you're pretty quiet. Or maybe that's why. Listen before you talk. I hate those smart-alecky cadets who graduate from the Academy and think right away they know everything because they've had a few practice hours on the simulators. The best school, the only school that really matters, is the street. Here in the daily grind, this is where you truly learn. Your whole life long. Tell me if it isn't true: you never graduate from the street, and you never finish learning all its rules.

The rules of the Great Game.

Yep, Markus. . . .. Life is a Great Game, and an agent has to know its rules like the back of his hand. . . especially if he hopes to advance his career, like I suppose you do. To be a winner, not a loser.

You don't catch where I'm going? Oh, kid, come on. . .

I'm gonna tell you a little story to help you understand. You like stories? Good thing.

When I was a rookie agent like you, I also served with an old sergeant, like me now. I remember him like it was yesterday. Aniceto Echevarría was his name. A good guy, generous, brave. The wackos from the Xenophobe Union wiped him out, and to avenge him we spilled a lot of blood. Whoever we wanted.

How time flies. It's been a long time since then, yeah. . .

Well, turns out poor Aniceto was crazy about raising fish. He read lots of stuff about it and he was always talking about exotic species of saltwater fish and freshwater fish, artificial food, live bait, temperatures, the pH of the water. . . And about his "little collection," as he called it, with more love in his voice than some parents show when they talk about their own kids.

One day, two weeks into partnering with him on street patrol, he invited me over to his house, and. . . Stop thinking those nasty thoughts, Markus: Aniceto was all man. Me too. So wipe that little smirk off your face or I'll get angry.

Ok, that's better.

It was a tiny one bedroom, but beautiful. Nice furniture, full of appliances, but no glitz or ostentation. What especially caught my eye was how many huge fish tanks he had everywhere. His "little collection" was almost better equipped than the Great Aquarium of New Miami, believe me. With aerators, a gas recycling system. . . the works. And he had so many fish—and what fish! No lie, old Aniceto had managed to put maybe half a million credits worth of fish behind those glass walls.

And when, dazzled by all that beauty, I asked naively how he could support such an expensive hobby on a sergeant's pay, he just smiled. He stroked his mustache and showed me something I'll never forget.

At the bottom of one of his saltwater fish tanks he had this huge thing. It looked like a flower with a thick stalk and semitransparent reddish petals that swayed in the gentle current of the water. A beautiful underwater flower. . .

But it was a voracious animal. What I had thought were petals turned out to be tentacles that could release a powerful toxin. In the middle was its mouth, always hungry.

What? It's called an anemone? Well, if you say so. . . I'm a simple ignorant sergeant. What do I know about critters.

Aniceto told me to keep an eye on the anemo-thingy. It was beautiful. Really beautiful. And I thought it was even more beautiful when a mid-sized fish swam by and got caught by its lethal tentacles, torn to shreds, and gulped down in a matter of seconds. There was an innocent cruelty in that act.

The best part is that earlier, lots of other much smaller fish had been swimming around it, and nothing had happened to them.

I called Sergeant Aniceto over to show him, amazed. But he just glanced at the deal and told me, "Keep on looking. Look very closely now, Romualdo."

And that was when I realized, Markus, that this wonderful, deadly creature was now surrounded by other little fish. Red, blue, and violet, painted like clowns. They were nibbling at the remains of the bigger fish that had gotten stuck in the tentacles, and they seemed immune to the terrible toxin. Now and then they would corner some unlucky little animal that had lost its way in the forest of tentacles, and they would devour it. The huge beast let them do it. Afterward they even hid out among the poisonous tentacles.

Oh. . . symbiosis, you say? Okay, then, symbiosis.

So Aniceto put his arm around me and said, "That poisonous animal is the Law. Or all of Planetary Security, if you prefer. It's like a blind net, but it has a mind. It doesn't care about the tiny fish, so it lets them be. Same with the really big fish, which are so strong they might cause problems. It's just the mid-sized fish that are food. Those, it attacks."

"And those painted clowns, what are they?" I asked, amused by what I thought was his two-bit philosophy.

"They're us," replied the old sergeant. "We help make sure the Law is carried out, that Planetary Security works. Make sure the garbage doesn't accumulate and clog the net or strangle the hungry beast. In exchange, we prosper in its powerful shadow, with impunity. The monster recognizes us and identifies us by our uniforms. That's how things work in this world. Do you get it, Romualdo?"

You bet I got it, Markus. So well, I've never forgotten it.

Do you get it now?

We lost a great actor when you decided to enter the Academy, kid! You're blushing like a virgin overhearing guys talking about an orgy. But you don't have to pretend you're naïve or innocent around me: If you still haven't figured out, at the age of twenty-five, that the salary Planetary Security pays us, big as it might seem, isn't enough even to pay for the wax we use to shine our service boots, I'm gonna start thinking you cheated on your IQ test.

You aren't that big an idiot, I don't think.

Oh, I know—something else has you worried. You're afraid of the bloodhounds from Internal Affairs, eh? Prudent kid. I know all the symptoms: the twitchy eyes, the constant glancing around, like a trapped cat. . .

But tell me honestly: do I look like an undercover Internal?

And I assure you there aren't any hidden microphones or nano-cameras. We're totally safe from indiscreet eyes and ears. Why do you think I insisted on going inside? The rain wasn't really all that bad. . .

It's because electronic recording gizmos don't work here. The science guy from headquarters can explain it better. Something to do with the electromagnetic pulse they need to keep some of the weird types in anabiosis. Like the polyps from Aldebaran.

That's exactly why we're talking in here. I like to look out for myself, too.

Oh, and the guys from Internal Affairs... Don't believe everything you hear about them. They aren't so mean as they're made out to be. We're in the same boat, all of us. Even they need a present for the girlfriend now and then, or something extra for their kid's registration in the University, and then they come to us. Coworker to coworker, get it?

Of course, if you go overboard and try to become a millionaire in one month, you'll stick out like a bonfire on a dark night. Then they won't have any choice but go after you like hunting dogs. That's their job—keeping up appearances, maintaining the façade. It has to look like the system is working perfectly.

Don't look like that, son. It's about time you figure out, once and for all, that the whole business of Protect and Serve, the thin wall between Earth and Chaos, and all that stuff they made you learn by heart in the Academy—it's pure veneer. Working for Planetary Security isn't what you imagined it was, Markus. Believe me, not your instructors.

I was already patrolling this city when they were still playing with their robot nannies. The devil knows as much as he does because he's old, not because he's the devil. Forget your hypnopedia articles about the agent's duties, paths of glory, keepers of public order, and on and on. That's all cosmetic, to impress the civilian sheep who pay our salaries with their taxes.

This is drudgework. Breaking your back and risking your skin day after day for a bunch of civilian ingrates who'll never see you as their savior, but their enemy. Never as the sheepdog guarding the herd, just another wolf, and that's how they treat us. They despise us, they exclude us... Why do you think we almost always marry women who are also in the corps?

All that for poverty wages and a pension that's not worth shit—if you even make it to retirement age.

I bet you're wondering, if this is such a nasty life, why are there still any agents? Why hasn't everybody in Planetary Security thrown away their vibrobadges and said the hell with it? Why is it still so hard to get into the Academy and why do all the young people fight to make it? I mean, it must've been pretty hard even for you with your big IQ, eh?

Fact is, maybe the salary doesn't go far enough, but the uniform gives you certain opportunities. . . I prefer to call them "unadvertised rights." Sheer justice. There has to be some sort of benefit in it for you, when it's your hide on the line when one of those drugged-up wack jobs from the Xenophobe Union for Earthling Liberation tries to make mincemeat of a grodo just because he's been scared of bugs since he was a kid.

Corruption, you say? Oh, Markus, that's a real big word, real ugly.

I can see you and me have a serious problem with terminology. I'd rather call it compensation. But if you insist, sure. Corruption. Call a spade a spade.

But don't start trembling at the sound of those three syllables. Cor-rup-tion. And not just here in Planetary Security; it's practically the official sport of this planet. All those officials who pretend to be so pure, who love to give holonet interviews where they spout off diatribes against the "intolerable venality" of our corps—they take in tons more than we do, and for less risk. Criticizing your neighbor for being dirty is still the best method for concealing the dirt you're covered in yourself. So forget about them and live your own life, son.

That's how it is.

But at the same time, you shouldn't think that you're a god because you have a gun on your hip and a vibrobadge ID. And you can't let people get away with anything just because there's some money in it. You'd make a huge mess of things, and it would end up costing you.

We're the ones who keep order—even if it isn't the same order the Manual talks about. But it's a lot different from chaos, is that clear? And a lot better. Chaos is bad for everyone, even the Mafia and the Yakuza, the biggest fish. That old saying about "good fishing in troubled waters" is bunk. Nobody comes out ahead when things are messed up.

That's why there are rules that everybody follows. To keep the system working, Markus. And that's what I've been trying to explain to you from the beginning. . . Sorry if all that about Aniceto's aquarium sounded like a shaggy dog story.

At least it's a good story, isn't it?

I'm not very good with words. I could never have made a good instructor sergeant. Luckily I prefer to be on the street. I'm more used to using my electroclub and my minimachine gun than my tongue. And that's even after all the education I've gotten since I joined the force.

Look, to get to the point. . . This is all about what happened the other day. When we were patrolling around Little Havana and that small-time pickpocket snatched the Cetian lady's purse. You had fast reflexes and you were very fast when you ran after him through the middle of that crowd. Perfect, that's what's expected of you. . . And your legs are a lot younger than mine.

You caught him and returned the purse to that xenoid lady, all dolled up in phosphorescent flowers. Just like you're supposed to do. And her? All she can do is say, "Thanks, officer, these Earthlings are awful"—as if you're a Colossaur, not a human. And not a single credit. Bad luck—tourists are almost always more grateful. But that's work.

The bad part is, afterwards, you acted like a total idiot. You wasted time and money, and you created unnecessary problems.

In spite of all the signs I was making, you announced publicly that you were going to drag the poor kid down to headquarters. Even worse, you actually did it. You didn't care about his tears, you didn't care that he said he was on Ahimasa's list, you entered him into the computer. Just like the Manual says.

Now the little thief has his arm tattooed with the ultraviolet marker, and there's no way to mistake him for anyone else. I bet you feel proud about what you did? Branding a juvenile delinquent, making it easier to follow him and keep him from committing more crimes in the future. What a model public servant. You even think you were generous with him, dropping the charges. Because if you had reported him, he would have ended up with a couple of months in Body Spares, right?

Well, let me tell you what you really did. You condemned him to death... Unless he's brave enough to amputate that piece of flesh from his arm by himself. That's the only way he'll get rid of that tattoo.

And I'd like to imagine you did it out of ignorance. Because if I thought you had done it on purpose... Better not even mention what might have become of you by now. Here in Planetary Security, the worst sin you can commit is to lack esprit de corps. Break the rules and you're automatically out of the game.

Markus, in case you didn't know it, those kids from the gutter are worth their weight in gold for certain "jobs." Not especially legal ones, of course. Since they were never registered by their parents or families, they don't have Social Security numbers, which makes them unidentifiable citizens. That means they can get in anywhere without being detected.

That's why they're allowed to live. Too bad their bosses pay them chicken feed, which is why they have to risk small-time robberies on their own account. A street orphan's life is tough. Only one out of a hundred reaches the age of fourteen.

When some xenoid who's paying more attention than average discovers that one is lifting her purse, and she calls for help, that's where you step in. The whole "Stop that thief!" scene: you chase him down, catch him, return the purse to the extraterrestrial, just like the

Manual says, and they either give you a tip or they don't... But then you throw out your instructions, and you ask the kid who his boss is.

A street kid's master is always ready to pay. Ahimasa would've paid you a handsome sum for you not to tattoo his boy. A nice bargain, and everybody's happy—even the kid. He might get a bit of a whipping, more for his clumsiness that for the purse-snatching itself, but at least he'd still be alive and still have a job.

If it troubles your sense of morality for the kid to get off without being punished for stealing, I assure you that the beating Ahimasa would have given him when we turned him over would have taken away his appetite for robbery for quite a while. The guys in the Yakuza are heavy-handed, and they don't hold back with the neurowhip. If that boy ever tried it again, he'd be a lot more careful not to let his victim detect him.

Instead, what do they have now? Just a registered kid who's worth nothing and who knows too much. Ahimasa will have to rid himself of him as quick as possible.

So, all on account of you, because you followed the regulations just as they're laid out in the Manual and you don't know the rules of the game, we now have a businessman—maybe not a totally legal one, but honest after his own fashion—who's forced to contract a hit-man to get rid of a poor kid. A kid who, for all we know, he might have even come to like. And a minor, a runaway, scared to death, who'll be very lucky to escape with his life. A waste of time, credits, and human resources, and so much trouble...

That's not how things are done, Markus.

Have you seen how many people greet me when we're making our rounds? Some of them were kids like him, years ago—and I'm sure that every night, before they go to sleep, they still give thanks to God and the Virgin that I was the one who first caught them. I feel proud to be a member of Planetary Security every time I recognize one of them... They're alive and they've grown into men thanks to me.

That's what it means to be generous and to serve the public interest, Markus.

Do you understand the difference?

So you see, things are always more complex that they seem. The stuff they told you in the Academy, that there's a war between our forces and crime that's being fought on the streets across this planet—forget it, right now. There aren't two sides. We're equals. All fish swimming in the same water. The only thing that makes us seem different is this uniform.

You're an educated kid, Markus, so I imagine you must have heard of Jean-Jacques Rousseau and his social contract.

Well, there's another social contract at work on Earth today, and we're the guardians of it. Since nobody could survive if they followed all the laws, we're the ones in charge of turning a blind eye to the minor infractions that are necessary to stay alive—so long as the violators don't question the system itself too much.

Every seemingly honest citizen is breaking the law, one way or another. You yourself: sincerely, have you always paid your taxes properly and on time? You never rigged an energy meter? Aha, you see?

We make sure that the narrow margin of illegality we all live in is kept under control. Kept at a level acceptable to everyone. No serial killings or xenophobic terrorism, but everything else? Illegal gambling, soft drugs, unincorporated services, small-time pickpockets, minor robberies. . . Those aren't the enemy, the others are. The xenoids, you understand?

How did you insult agents when you were little? What did you yell at them? "Buglickers," am I right? Servants of the extraterrestrials, that's what you thought we were. Don't deny it. . .

In a way, those people from other planets pay our salaries so we'll keep the peace in their tourist and finance paradise. And they could care less whether we kill each other, or eat each other—just as long as we don't bother their sacred inhuman selves.

This planet could be blown to smithereens; if no xenoid gets hurt, it wouldn't even be third-class news in the galaxy. But all it takes is for one stupid tourist to cut a tentacle, and all hell breaks loose.

It's like the story of the boy who was playing with the leash of the organ-grinder's monkey; nothing happened, the monkey didn't react. The boy got bolder, touched the animal, and—*chomp!* He started screaming about how the monkey had bitten him. And what did the owner say? "You asked for it. Play with the leash—but don't touch the monkey."

On this planet, the monkey is anyone from another planet.

Still, you should know that the secret motto of the Planetary Tourism Agency also applies to us: "Take their credits at all costs and by any means."

Which, translated into our slang, means something like: "The tourist is always at fault, and must pay for it." And I'm talking about paying credits, for the record.

It isn't that difficult.

Fortunately, the xenoids who visit us have considerable inherent respect for the Law and its representatives. Maybe things work differently on their worlds, and people in our line of work really do follow their Manuals to the letter there. Though I can't imagine how that could be possible...

Fact is, if you're intelligent, authoritative, and likeable enough, the way they expect public authorities to be, they'll always believe you. That's just what you need. Get them to believe that they were the ones at fault in the aerobus accident where a human with his lights off crashed into their vehicle from behind. Or that they are guilty for being robbed because they were carrying their pile of credit cards in a bag strapped across their bellies, where it's child's play for any pickpocket with a razor to swipe it.

Hit them with every legal technicality. Make them feel guilty. That's the key point. And they'll pay you to get rid of their guilt.

That last bit, most of all.

I'm probably underestimating you. You must know all this already. If you decided to join us, I bet it wasn't out of civic duty or because you were wowed by the guns and the uniforms or the power and the authority you'll represent to your old neighborhood friends and to social workers and girls in general.

Though that's another advantage we have. Kid, if I told you half my sexual experiences, you'd spend half a year masturbating. I've never gotten married. What for? I've got everything I could want and more.

Inexperienced teenage beauties who take to the streets out of poverty, ignorantly wander into the forbidden areas in the astroport, and are willing to do anything if you just won't start a file on them for being illegal underage workers. Hey, Markus, I do mean *anything*. . .

I've deflowered more virgins than a Cetian millionaire.

And the legal ones, the girls who have health insurance and everything, the real sex artists—don't they know how to thank you when you intervene in time and free them from some client with more sadistic tastes than usual.

We protect them, and they pay us back the way they know best. Think of it as an exchange of professional services.

Though that's only one option, obviously. Some prefer hard cash, even if it comes from one of them. But an agent's life is unstable and solitary. . . Patrolling the streets, there's not much chance you'll meet the girl of your dreams. And even less that you'll keep her.

If the only way to get voluntary sex is from paid professionals, I prefer to get it for free at least, and do it with ladies I know and who are grateful and almost friends to me. I feel safer with them than with a social worker who's a stranger. With one of them, you can never be sure she doesn't keep a stiletto under her pillow, waiting for you to fall asleep so she can kill you and rob you.

Of course, that's my taste. You can do whatever you want.

There are some things you can't allow. And if they try to bribe you, to take advantage of your inexperience, I want you to tell me about it right away. I'll take care of those dealer bastards. . .

I've read a bit of history, and I know that in the past they also went after drug dealers. But for all drugs.

How ridiculous. Our system is a lot more rational: you can get whatever you want in the Medical Amusement Centers. Good prices, quality guaranteed, and under the care of trained toxicology experts. It's one of the basic attractions for tourists who can afford it.

That's why guys who deal dirt-cheap, presumably adulterated drugs underground are a discredit to the planet and a threat we can't tolerate. No mercy for them. The guidelines when we catch one of them are hard and clear: take no prisoners. They don't even want that scum in Body Spares. They're almost always addicted to the same junk they sell, and no extraterrestrial in his right mind would want to "mount" a body with such a wasted metabolism.

On the other hand, there are priorities. It goes without saying that if some xenoid perishes under suspicious circumstances, we have to drop all other business and focus on the investigation into the cause of death. And if no guilty party turns up. . . one has to be invented, by hook or by crook. Too much depends on our efficiency in such cases.

Always bear in mind how they wiped Philadelphia off the map: Somebody, probably fighting over a skirt, slit the throat of some Cetian nobody, and the local district guys didn't manage to find out who it was. And the reprisal by the fellows from Tau Ceti: two million humans, evaporated. I doubt you'd like to see the demonstration repeated in another city—with you in it.

There's only one thing more urgent than discovering who killed a xenoid. And that's giving anyone who kills one of our own what they deserve. That's solidarity and esprit de corps. It's comforting to know you'll get your revenge if the worst happens.

But don't look like that, Markus; it isn't all risk and revenge in this job of ours. There's also lots of ways a clever agent can pick up a few extra credits, when he's off duty, pretty safely.

For example, the protection business.

The Yakuza and the Triads monopolize it; they even control most of the freelancers. But if you want to earn every credit that goes into your account through honest labor, and you want to spend your free time doing it, the organized crime guys won't interfere.

Though there are some very good freelancers, lots of retailers think that contracting a Planetary Security agent is the best. It means contracting quality. There's a good reason why we earn our reputation in physical training and gun-handling skills. And just as important, we're permitted to keep and use our guns, even off duty. The Agent's Personal Protection Clause, remember?

That's how it is, Markus: this protection deal has the advantage of not even being illegal. So long as you don't wear your uniform, of course, ha ha! If anything happens, you just state that you were "passing by" and you "fired in self-defense." The Homicide officer who takes the case will know how to exonerate you of any charges. Esprit de corps, get it?

Some expert advice: if you're seriously interested in the protection business, the best thing you can do is spend a few credits on a small initial investment in the Logistics officer at headquarters. He'll give you a Kevlar jacket to protect you, also an unregistered gun. And the price won't be as steep as it might seem, if you stop to think about it. Keep in mind, any shots you fire off duty won't leave a trace on the central computer. To which all our minimachine guns are connected, as they must have told you in the Academy.

The shopkeepers will reward your efforts with a nice, fat bonus. A guard who can fire his gun without a thought is always more effective than one who will reach for it only under extreme circumstances, don't you think?

After the man without the uniform, something about the uniform without the man. And here we're departing from the Law. In case you're ambitious and you really like to gamble.

Every once in a while one of these self-employed businessmen, like our friend Ahimasa, will approach you and offer a considerable sum for the loan of your Kevlar-armored suit. A very considerable sum. Don't hesitate for even a second; give it to him. Without the slightest remorse, and without thinking it makes you an evil traitor to the corps.

There's nothing wrong with agreeing; they rarely use our uniforms for anything but settling inside scores. And if it turns into too big a mess and we have to intervene. . . a Kevlar suit won't guarantee anybody's life when they're up against us. Every reputable hitman knows that the hollow-point bullets we use will blast straight through our own armor. Fortunately, no other weapon on Earth has the necessary firepower.

That's why we're so relentless in going after the arms traffickers who sell masers and rocket-propelled explosives. If gizmos like that started circulating widely in the black market, we'd completely lose control of the situation.

Oh, a couple of details. When you rent out your uniform, never forget two precautions: first, and it's so obvious it's hardly worth saying, remove the ID vibroplate and any corps badges, in case your "clients" get captured. Second, put in a request for a new uniform because your old one was stolen. And make sure the request is backdated to at least three days before you "loaned" it. If they return your suit without any problems, you cancel the request. But if your "clients" are caught or killed, it'll be your best alibi: Another stolen uniform, not your fault, you told them about it in plenty of time, what a pity, there's no decency anymore, somebody from your neighborhood who hates you must've stolen it off the hanger to sell it to those killers, what a coincidence. . .

And don't protest if the service officer charges you a little more for your new Kevlar-armored uniform. He's no fool, and since he hardly has any contact with the outside world, he has to make his extra profit somehow, don't you think?

We all have a right to live.

Oh, about food sellers. . .

Even though you look like the sort who's obsessed with organic vegetables and meat without synthetic hormones and all that old ecological stuff, let me tell you something: It's been years since I've spent practically anything at all on food. My microwave has the immaculate gleam of a machine that never gets used. But I eat breakfast, lunch, and dinner every day like an emperor. Look at the belly I'm starting to get. . . And that's after spending half an hour every day on the jogging simulator.

My secret? Easy. . .

One of the hardest subjects in the Academy was Commercial Hygiene. Was it for you, too? I don't know about you, but I had such a tough time learning the basic regulations about transporting, storing, preparing, and selling foodstuffs. But I have to admit that it turned out to be the most useful subject I took, out of all my preparatory classes. Because, surprise! Hardly any of those regulations are applicable to real life.

It's like everything here on Earth: if food retailers tried to follow to the letter every one of the thousand specifications that the Law demands, they'd go broke. They know it, we know it. . . the Law knows it. There used to be a corps of inspectors who got all the gifts for pretending to have bad eyesight. And the rest of us, twiddling our thumbs and dying of envy. Fortunately, five years ago Amendment 538 gave us total power by turning us into the only control force all over the planet. No more than what we deserved, if you ask me.

So, if you see a grocer selling vegetables that smell like dextrinone, or chickens that are a little swollen from synthetic steroids, and he invites you to breakfast—don't hesitate, accept. Sure, it's a bribe. . . but you can bet he won't set his own table with any of the garbage he sells. Most likely that's stuff he keeps for extraterrestrials, so you won't be harming any humans with your "laissez faire."

And I assure you, in exchange for being tolerant, you'll eat true delicacies. Those are the great pleasures of life, the most basic ones: sex and food. A man has a right to pamper his palate, doesn't he? After all, he isn't some xenoid with a brass gullet.

Yeah, because those bugs don't care whether they're eating crap or caviar so long as the chef swears that it's some exotic Earthling dish. Idiots.

Aside from sybaritic pleasures, my advice is that, if you want to be a father someday, don't sink your teeth into any of the succulent produce you see in the windows, or let yourself be tempted by the cheap, juicy ten-day chicks that look as big and fat as forty-day chickens. They don't do much harm to the metabolisms of the weird guys from other worlds, but those synthetic hormones can really mess up your innards—or your children's, if your wife and you decide to have any in the natural way. Though, personally, I'd invest a few extra credits and get a good custom genetic design. Clean, safe, efficient.

As for the rest, you have to be tough on the retailers and small industrialists who contaminate the environment by dumping their rotting and carcinogenic waste and their untreated sewage straight down the drain. Fine 'em! As often as you have to! So they'll learn once and for all that in the long run it'll be cheaper to install a waste treatment plant than to keep breaking the environmental protection laws.

As you can see, even though I make fun of it, I'm halfway on your ecology and conservation bandwagon. Simple pragmatism: survival instinct, not religious fervor about bugs and flowers.

Earth is our planet, isn't it? Just because the guys from beyond Pluto own it now, it doesn't mean that we don't care anymore, or that we should commit suicide by drowning in our own shit. Not to mention, that would also mean losing the tourism that still barely keeps us afloat, which depends so much on our virgin forests and all that. . .

What else. . .

Oh, yeah. Practically the most important thing: They must have talked to you about staff rotation in the Academy. Three months here on patrol, three in Deterrent Force, three in Homicide, and so on and so forth. A cute little system that one of the big bosses must've dreamed up—with the idea, I guess, of preventing the poor agents and regular old sergeants from feeling too tempted to fall into the horrendous venial sin of corruption. . . No doubt the moron thought he was an absolute genius for coming up with that.

But don't let it get you down. Every law has its loophole: we've come up with our own system. They never rotate an entire department all at once, so when it's time for us to separate and you know what your new post is going to be, I'll personally tell you who makes the rules over there. . . And he'll give you the instructions, the contacts, everything you'll need to take over from the agent you're replacing, in every sense.

Understood? Yep, Markus, you're a smart boy, just like I thought. Quick on your feet. And you smile. I'm glad you like these proposals. As you see, belonging to the glorious Planetary Security force isn't as bad as lots of people think.

A few more bits of advice. Sorry if I'm starting to sound pedantic. I'm getting old, and not having kids of my own has made me feel a little paternal towards young rookies like you who don't know anything about life yet. Besides, I really do like you.

Get used to improvising. Forget the Manual. There's no system of rules that can cover every possibility. Every day, an agent runs into situations that don't fit the standards.

For example, if you're patrolling a dark street and you find a minicontainer with two kilos of telecrack in it, and there aren't any witnesses. . . Or if some cloned Cetian damsel is impressed by how tight you wear your uniform trousers and wants to know what your favorite brand of sex lubricant is. . . The decision is up to you.

I have a personal rule: Never let a child, a woman, or an addict down. You can always go a little bit out of your way for your neighbor, don't you think, Markus?

Of course, if you attract some Colossaur's attention, I recommend that you start coming up with excuses faster than an aide in the diplomatic corps. They say even their vaginas are armored.

Not to mention the acetic acid that the guzoids of Regulus secrete. . . I wouldn't wish that on my worst enemy.

Ha. The stories I could tell you. . .

You don't know how lucky you were to join Planetary Security when you did. A few years ago, an agent who refused too often might end up in suspended animation, inside one of these tanks. The xenoids practically owned us, and they didn't like any kind of refusal.

Now we have certain rights.

And we've fought good and hard to get them, I swear. Ten years ago, saying "Planetary Security agent" was the same as saying "piece of garbage." We had to show those stuckup xenoids there was no way they could control Earth without us. At least not without wiping out three quarters of the population.

Out of curiosity, where were you born, Markus? Right here in New Miami? Thought so. A smart urban kid. I'm a clever country boy. From a little hamlet on the bank of a river off in the boondocks, between the hills and the jungle: Baracuyá del Jiquí. They still haven't figured out that we're in the twenty-first century yet. They're still living in the nineteenth there.

Every time it rains a little, the Jiquí River bursts its banks; the main street, which is the one and only street in my town, turns into a lake, and you have to get around by raft instead of on foot. We didn't have access to the holonet in my house—not even electricity. We carried our water in buckets from the river.

I didn't see my first aerobus till I was ten. Up until that moment, my highest ambition when it came to transportation was to have my own horse. My mother and father didn't have many entertainment alternatives or any idea what contraceptives were, so they had fifteen kids—nine sons, six daughters. Ten of us survived. Seven boys, three girls. At the age of forty-three, my mother looked seventy.

I wasn't old enough for them to take seriously, or young enough for them to pamper. I got the worst of both worlds, being in the middle. My older brothers beat me because they were stronger, and I had to take care of the little ones because they were younger.

By the time I was I was ten, I realized I wouldn't inherit so much as the dust from the little bit of land my father farmed. I wasn't too fond of spending the whole day glued to the field, anyway. What I most wanted was to live in a real city, not die making scratches in the Earth. And since I was always pretty dense, and not even good at sports despite this big old body, the only way I could figure to make my dream come true and get out of there was the uniform. So as soon as I turned sixteen, I ran away from home, with my little bundle of clothes and my one pair of shoes. I listened to those holoposters that promise you heaven and Earth, and I enlisted in the Planetary Security corps. I would have done it sooner if I could've fooled them and pretended I was older than I was. Even though I looked twenty, they'd only have to run the numbers to figure out I wasn't even eighteen yet.

Ah, Baracuyá del Jiquí. Sometimes I get nostalgic and wonder what my brothers and sisters are up to. Whether they ever got married, whether I have nieces and nephews, whether they got beaten to death by the Earth. Whether Mama and Papa are still alive. They must be really old. I never went back, never even sent them a holovideo. It was hard, but I told myself, "Romualdo Concepción Pérez, not one step back, not even to get a running start." And I stuck to it.

Most of the old guard in Planetary Security came from places like my village—or worse. Our boss, Colonel Kharman, is from the Dayaks on Borneo. A tribe that still lives in primitive communities, bones through their noses, shrinking the heads of their dead enemies.

Back then, no wimp from the big city would want to wear this uniform or put on this badge. Well, not today, either—you're the exception, not the rule. Your little city friends think anything's better than being a "fink," as some imbeciles still call us.

Did I have a hard time at the Academy? You bet I did. I had to learn how to use the sanitary facilities, the computer terminals... how to fight, like it or not. That's something I had in my blood. If I hadn't learned to defend myself, to dish it out and to take it without crying, almost before I learned how to walk, my four older brothers would have beaten me to a pulp. Or my father would have beaten the stuffing out me for being a wimp and a crybaby.

Back then, we only took one year of preparatory classes, and then they set us loose on the streets. There was real urgency. If we survived the first three months, it's because we were good students. If we were left by the wayside... Well, the xenoids from the Selection Committee had millions of applicants to fill any vacancy in the corps.

At first, with no friends or acquaintances, without the slightest idea how things worked here in the cities, we tried to follow the Manual to the letter. Bringing the full weight of the law down equally on anyone who broke it, not taking anything into account. For anybody.

As for me, nobody was going to send me back to Baracuyá del Jiquí for going easy on a civilian. They might be as poor as me and as desperate as me—but if it was them or me, it was going to be them. Same with strikes. If you had to give a good dose of electroclub to a bunch of uranium miners who were asking for better antiradiation suits instead of working, you let 'em have it. They might be as wretched as us... but that's why they were paying me, dressing me, and letting me live here. And in this life everything has its price.

Pickpockets, pushers, the Mafia, Triads, Yakuza? To me, they were all the same shit. Tough on everybody. Those were brutal times.

It was in those days that the legend of a street war between crime and us was born. Because they didn't pull punches. For every Yakuza we sent to Body Spares, his friends rubbed out one agent. Till things started to even out.

It's only now I realize how stupid I was. If it hadn't been for that lesson old Aniceto taught me with the fish-eating critter in the aquarium in his apartment, I'd probably be dead now. Like lots of guys who graduated with me but who weren't lucky enough to meet someone who could explain the rules of the game to them.

I can't complain, for sure. I've made out like a prince.

When I'd already been working on the street for a couple of years, and the Yakuza and the Mafia knew who I was and looked out for me like I was pure gold, Amendment 456 came out and made everybody in Planetary Security an automatic citizen of the city where he worked. Me, Romualdo Concepción Pérez, born in Baracuyá del Jiquí. . . a citizen of New Miami!

I felt on top of the world. A couple months later, I made sergeant, they assigned me my own tiny apartment, and I moved out of the common dorm. That's how I've lived all these years.

Why haven't I moved up in the ranks? I'm going to let you in on a secret, Markus. Take it or leave it. The sergeant is like the keystone in the arch. Come on, son, I can't believe a kid with your education doesn't that—the keystone, the stone that holds all the others in place. The one that goes right in the middle. The one that's most secure.

Who gets it when some spoiled xenoid complains? The lowest-ranking agent. And who has to put his head on the chopping block when they kill some idiot tourist and the xenoids make human heads roll to calm their people? The top brass. And who are the obvious targets for the wack jobs from the Xenophobe Front, every time it they get the bright idea of orchestrating one of their little campaigns against the "finks and buglickers"? The officers. Not one of the guys who started out with me is still around. Oh, sure, some of them were intelligent types who rose like cream: lieutenants, captains, majors, colonels. One of them even made general. And where are they now? Retired without honor on half pensions, in prison, shot dead, begging on the same streets they used to rule over, or recycled like compost in the organoponics. The machinery swallowed them up.

Keep me a sergeant. Not too high, not too lowly.

Avarice broke the moneybag, Markus. Keep it small-scale, personal, and you can control things, and there isn't too much danger of being turned in.

When the racket gets big-time, Yakuza-style, you start getting competition. Sharks bigger than you want a piece of the action. . . and there's always some xenoid organization that has more power and will break your back.

If you knew how many times I've seen a syndicate rise up in Planetary Security, just to fall under the extraterrestrial boot, with these eyes destined for the recycler!

Meanwhile, a good old sergeant has plenty of authority. He's the one who passes the orders down, the oil that lubricates the machinery. He's guaranteed his piece of the pie, and nobody messes with him. I never get mixed up in the big operations, especially if I'm not asked to. Live and let live, that's my motto, Markus. Things'll go better for you, too, if you live by that rule.

Sometimes you have to play the heavy, that's true. And it hurts. Man, does it hurt.

A few months back I had to arrest this young kid, and I still can't get it out of my mind. A freelance protector—at least, that's what he thought. Truth is, he was too naïve for that racket. His name was Jowe, and he was also an artist. I saw his paintings. . . Maybe they were good, but I didn't like them. They were real strange, and I don't understand all that stuff.

Well, seems like this little painter had forgotten to pay the Yakuza his monthly dues, because he had stopped charging this social worker who was living with him. Girl named María Elena.

I can't really remember her face. To me, she looked like any old whore—tall and leggy, like all the rest. I didn't even look at her; I like my women with some flesh on them, it's the xenoids' business if they prefer the bones. This Jowe, though, he looked at her like. . . Markus, I thought I'd done it all, but it broke my heart to have to bring him in. It was like hauling in the son I never had. I even stuck around for the trial, and that was after I'd clocked out for the day. It was over fast, like every trial since the central computer took over judging. He pulled three years in Body Spares. . . He won't make it, I'm certain.

It was practically a hit job. Of course, I didn't haul him in for not paying that debt, but because he was accused of giving money to the Xenophobe Union for Earthling Liberation. Accused by somebody from the Yakuza, it goes without saying. They used us to settle scores with him legally. And the worst part was, it was true. . . Imagine how idealistic, how stupid that poor kid was, wasting the little bit of money he had, sending it to those drugged-out wackos.

When I was hauling him off, he kept staring at that María Elena. Then she ran over, they hugged and kissed and cried and everything. But he was doing it for real, with all his heart. You could tell he really loved her, poor guy. As for her—well, I've seen better acting in our district talent shows.

It was so tough, I still get goosebumps and my eyes still tear up when I remember it. . . I felt like a rat, Markus. Really.

One last thing, this time I'm not talking as sergeant to agent but as a guy with some experience to a green kid. And take advantage now that I'm getting sentimental. Forget about the honor of the corps if things get really ugly. I really mean it.

Better a live coward than a dead hero. He who runs away saves his hide to fight another day, or whatever. There's lots of agents in Planetary Security, but not one of them will give you a new life if you lose yours fighting for a mistaken notion of glory or of taking one for the team. And autocloning is so expensive, it's just for the top brass. Suckers like you and me only die once... and nobody brings us back.

I'm telling you this because the streets have been calm for years, and I know from experience that on this planet there's always calm before the storm. I'm sure the pot's going to start boiling again soon. And even though the electroclub is one of the strongest arguments ever invented, and Molotov cocktails roll off these Kevlar uniforms like water off a duck... details are the devil. An urban riot is serious business. That's where you really realize how much this planet hates us.

One of those street revolts calling for xenoid blood can always be brought under control. We've always been able to control them. Until, every ten or twelve years, suddenly the day comes when the plebs are so desperate they don't give a rat's ass if we shoot them full of holes. Until the day comes when they understand they're so miserable they've got nothing to lose but their messed up shithole lives. And not even that matters much to them if they can trake a few of ours out too. Because it's really the xenoids' fault, but there are never any xenoids around to get bashed; those bugs can sniff out a disturbance better than a mutant bloodhound.

When you see the first riot get out of hand and overwhelm your friends in the antiriot squad, forget about corps solidarity and Greek legends. Run, hide your uniform, find yourself a safe hidey-hole—as far from the city as possible. It happens every ten or twelve years, and it always leads to the same result: Nothing.

The bugs from beyond Pluto show up with the heavy artillery, take their people out of there, and melt the place down. They don't care if us "buglickers" are still here, risking our hides to keep their tourist paradise safe. After all, we're the native cannon fodder. They cut the problem out at the root: they wipe out the whole city, or the whole continent, if things go too far.

Look what they did to Africa in Contact times.

You wouldn't want to see what a place that used to be a city looks like after everything in it is vaporized—just like that, in a couple of seconds. Not many ruins are left, and hardly any human remains. There's no harmful radiation or toxic gas, the soil isn't poisoned, the people who escaped before the disturbances can come back and resume normal lives. If they have anywhere to live. Because otherwise, their only choice is to grit their teeth, bow their heads, swallow their rage, and start working like mules to rebuild their leveled town.

But here and there on the ground, and on some walls that held up, who knows how, there are the shadows left by the volatilized bodies. Like ghosts, motionlessly accusing who knows who. Until the walls are knocked down or repainted.

And nobody cries over them, at least not publicly. The whole thing is forgotten, and life goes on. Until the next explosion.

Once I saw a holovideo about some little animals that look like fat guinea pigs and that live up there in the Artic, eating moss and junk like that. The foxes, the polar bears, the owls, even the Eskimos, all the predators that don't want to starve to death hunt them and eat them by the fistful. But they reproduce, they reproduce. Like guinea pigs, you follow me, Markus? And there's more and more of them—until there's no moss or anything left to eat.

Then they gather, armies of millions and millions of them, and migrate. Like crazy, and nobody can stop them. Not looking for more food or new territory, just looking for the sea. And the wolves, the foxes, all the predators follow them, gobbling them up by the thousands. . . until the fat guinea pigs dive head-first off the coast and swim out to sea. Then the sharks and seagulls keep on eating them, and thousands and thousands more drown. . . until there aren't any left.

And the two or three that didn't migrate go back to reproducing and getting eaten, until ten or fifteen years later the cycle repeats itself. And repeats, and repeats, and repeats.

I'd like to think, only until one day. Though I'm more of a fox or a hawk than one of them. . .

What's that? Lemmings? If you say so. You're the educated one here. Like I said, Sergeant Romualdo never. . .

Click.

"That's enough." Sweating, Colonel Kharman turned off the recording and wiped his forehead with a silk handkerchief. "The rest is half-baked biological and philosophical speculation. It would not interest you, Murfal, Your Excellency.

"Perhaps it would be. . . instructive," the other wondered. His human body moved with the almost imperceptible time lag of a "horse's" movements. Murfal was an Auyar.

"I don't doubt it," Kharman insisted, wiping the sweat from his broad brow. "But we already have more than enough evidence to send that poor devil of a sergeant to Body Spares for the rest of his life. And we know enough about the status and methods of corruption in our corps for us to take appropriate measures. . . I do not know how to thank you enough for your cooperation."

"Rubbish," the Auyar cut him off. "Even you should have realized that the disease has spread too far for home remedies, Colonel. Or perhaps we should investigate you, too?"

Kharman ignored the veiled threat, but started sweating again. It was only after a few seconds had gone by that he was able to ask, in a rather unsteady voice, "Do you. . . have some concrete proposal?"

"Of course." The smile on the body of Murfal's "horse" was like one on a badly built marionette. "Or did you think we supplied you with our huborg prototype just to test it out?"

"I thought that. . .," Kharman began.

"I don't care what you thought," the Auyar again interrupted. "You've already learned that we are capable of building perfect biomechanical replicas of human beings. If we could fool even your sergeant, no Earthling will notice the difference."

"I was very impressed with the way you were able to create an entire backstory for Markus. Parents, education, everything," Kharman observed, still sweating.

"Simply routine. . . But we did not do it as a mere experiment. . ." Murfal took a long pause and smiled once more. "Your Planetary Security is worthless, Colonel Kharman. It is rotten to the foundations—and we do not like that. We need a sound and incorruptible police force that will fully guarantee tourists' safety."

"But. . . they're only human," Kharman tried to argue, wiping his forehead.

"Yes. Regrettably limited, as you all are," the Auyar agreed. "Hence our idea is to replace you with our huborgs."

"All of Planetary Security?" The human high official was terrified and started sweating for the third time. His olive skin had gone almost ashen. "But. . . That's impossible. They are only biomechanisms. . . with flexible programming, of course. . . but they'll have to get orders from someone, be supervised, after all. . . And your tourists won't want to be cared for by biomechanical replicas of humans, no matter how perfect they are."

"They'll never find out," the Auyar shrugged. "Our huborgs can be *more* human than humans. Be everything a xenoid tourist expects from a police force officer, even one belonging to a primitive lower race. But don't worry, Kharman. We'll only replace your street patrol personnel. The higher officials will still be humans, of course. Though also supervised by our technicians. They will work together, for. . . technical reasons. Huborgs can be very delicate sometimes."

"Ah," was all that Colonel Kharman said, beaten.

"It will not be so terrible," Murfal consoled him patronizingly. "And there are still many details in our huborgs' programming that must be perfected. For now we will begin only here, in your district, as a pilot project. It may take a couple of years or longer before the system can be instituted all over Earth. And you cannot deny that we will be saving your planet quite a bit in the matter of salaries. Thanks to which, for example, your own salary could. . . double."

Kharman smiled unenthusiastically and stood up. "Well, Murfal, Your Excellency. . . if everything has been said, I will be going."

"Wait. I want to ask a favor of you," the xenoid stopped him. "I am curious. Do you have any holoimages of this Sergeant Romualdo? I would like to see his face. He is a clever man, it cannot be denied. He was smart enough not to tip his hand until they were inside the Body Spares depository. He knew he couldn't be recorded in there. . ."

"Yes, but he wasn't counting on your huborg prototype's photographic memory," Kharman fawningly reminded him. "He couldn't have known. It precisely reproduced every word that Romualdo uttered." The fingers of the former Dayak colonel from Planetary Security flew across a keyboard, and a holoimage materialized between him and Murfal. "Look. This is Sergeant Romualdo."

The Auyar contemplated the man's features. A leathery face with the melancholy of a man who's seen it all and no longer has faith in anything. The face of a man who knows that if he doesn't take care of the dirty work, somebody else will do it, though no better than he would. Who doesn't enjoy it. . . Who's just doing a painful duty.

"Enough. Turn it off," Murfal sighed, seeming more human than ever. "Colonel. . . Could I ask you for another favor?"

"As you wish, Murfal, Your Excellency," said Kharman, servile but uncomfortable.

"Destroy that recording. I want the secret to remain between you and me. Do not let Internal Affairs take any sort of steps against this Romualdo," the xenoid said absently. "If possible, have him retire *now*. With full honors and a double pension. And I will pay for it, if the paperwork is too complicated. Can you do it?"

"Of course, Your Excellency," Kharman replied, completely dumbfounded. "But... why?"

"Why have I decided to pardon him?" The Auyar stood up with a clumsy gesture. "Because I enjoyed listening to him. Because I like his images: the one of the anemone and the little fish; the one of the child, the organ grinder, and the monkey... And especially the one of the suicidal lemmings. Because, in the final analysis, if Planetary Security is the most venal organization on this terribly corrupt planet, it is not his fault. He said it himself: he never did anything other than follow the rules of the game. The good Sergeant Romualdo did not even invent them. We did. And he had no way of knowing that those rules had begun to change... right now. Goodnight, Colonel Kharman."

"Goodnight, Murfal, Your Excellency," said the former Dayak.

The Auyar halted again on the threshold. "One last minor detail... Do you think it would be very difficult to arrange a visit to that... Baracuyá del Jiquí? Now that I am on Earth already, I would very much like to see it. If what the sergeant said is true, it must be an interesting place. Perhaps I will be lucky. Human settlements as... primitive as that are growing rare, according to what I have read in the tourist guide..."

September 29, 1998

The Majority Shareholder

As soon as they realize that the power actually controlling Earth is the Planetary Tourism Agency, xenoid financiers and investors ask their human hosts why one person isn't in charge of the whole mechanism instead of the cumbersome Board of Shareholders, where nearly two hundred humans argue endlessly among themselves before reaching any agreement.

Upset by the delays that this decision-making process inevitably entails, the xenoids insist every so often that the body should name a single Majority Shareholder with plenary power. One individual, backed by his peers' vote of confidence, who has full authority and responsibility to conclude deals with all non-human investors, discuss budgets and agreements directly, and so forth.

They base this proposal on the fact that the system of representative democracy, which humans always champion, is inevitably more agile than participatory democracy. Though they recognize that it is also less just, to be sure...

The more than two hundred shareholders on the Board always listen with respect to these proposals while glancing at each other with almost imperceptible smiles.

Of course a representative system would save time.

But saving time isn't the key thing here; trust is.

None of them has enough trust in any of the others to think that, were one of them to become the Major Shareholder, he would defend the interests of all in an equitable way... rather than putting his own interests first.

That is the only reason the Planetary Tourism Agency has no Majority Shareholder or anything remotely similar. When the xenoid financiers who call so vociferously for creating the position think it over, they are actually glad that things continue as they do. Some of them even go so far in their change of heart that they speak of "excessive concentration of power"—and propose expanding the two hundred shareholders to four hundred or a thousand.

Earth divided by two hundred is perfectly controllable.

Earth unified under the will of a single man who has the confidence of all the others would be a different matter entirely.

That is why the most important Xenoid Emergency Plan of all, more important even than their general offensive against the infamous Xenophobe Union for Earthling Liberation, is their Karolides Project.

Karolides was a charismatic Greek statesman who came close to unifying the Balkan peninsula in the twentieth century. If he had succeeded, Germany might never have propelled Europe into World War I. But he was assassinated, the Balkans broke up—and ever since, whenever people talk about political fragmentation, the term they most commonly use is "Balkanization."

In the unlikely yet conceivable case that a new Karolides should arise among the shareholders of the Planetary Tourism Agency. . . everyone knows what fate the true masters of the planet have in store for him. And how quickly it would fall.

Politics is implacable.

Divide and rule.

Aptitude Assessment

"Let's get started. . . Identify yourself. Please state your full name."

You might call me an accidental scientist. Despite what they call my "exceptional qualities," I could have died and the world would never have found out if it hadn't been for that lucky incident.

But let me tell you the whole story, since I think we have plenty of time, and the story of what happened that day is worth it. . .

I was fourteen years old when the antigrav balance system of that aerobus accidentally broke down in flight. Right when it was passing over my hometown, Baracuyá del Jiquí, in the Sierra Cristal mountains. . . Well, it's more of a hamlet than a town.

The two professors from the Center for Advanced Physics and Mathematical Studies who were passengers in the vehicle must have been in for a bumpy ride. . . All the pilot could do was make a forced landing, the aerobus wobbling like a drunken duck. But we were in luck: it came to a rest right in front of our house, on the open field where my brothers and I used to play baseball.

I remember it like yesterday. We were all arguing. My brother Romualdo had just run away from home, and without him we were only six boys and three girls. Neither team wanted Giselita, who couldn't hit a watermelon with an ironing board. Or me, either, even though I was an okay player, because they all said my head had some of its stuffing missing. Besides, I was the youngest boy.

By the time the vehicle stopped shuddering my three sisters had already run to hide with my mother in the kitchen. Just the way my father taught them that decent women do when strangers come calling. The three of us boys who were still young, Hermenegildo and

Esbértido and me, ran over and climbed onto the aerobus engine, still hot. We'd seen machines like that before already, but never so close up, and we'd never been able to touch one.

After greeting them and offering them the *bacán, casabe,* and *pru* that they were afraid to even try, my father and my older brothers tried to explain to the pilot—so tall and skinny he looked like a pitchfork— and the two doctors that there weren't any stores or repair shops nearby that carried spare antigrav balancers, and there was no holonet connection or any sort of electronic link to the outside world. And the fastest way to get a message to the slightly larger town of Songo Tres Palmeras was to ride his compadre Robustiano's mare there, because my uncle Segismundo's messenger pigeons were laid up with the pip they had caught after last month's gullywashers. . .

The pilot opened the engine compartment, took a look, spat out fifteen or twenty cusswords, sighed, and said his name was Larsen, and that if that's how things were, well, there wasn't much they could do. Afterwards he did try some casabe and bacán and drank some pru and even the strong coffee, brewed country-style, that my mother gave him without looking him in the eye.

Since he had forgotten to close the engine casing, I got in and started nosing around. It was so pretty, lubricated with a transparent oil that smelled nice, not like the smelly mutton grease my father made me smear over the gears of the little sugar mill and the axles of the ox cart to keep them from sticking. It all looked perfect to me—except for what I later found out was the precious antigrav balance system.

Something about it was terribly off. I'd always been handy with tools, and I loved going around looking things over and fixing them up. And since I was the youngest, it was my job to sharpen the axes, machetes, and plowshares and keep the little mill greased. Without really thinking about it, I set to work on that thing. A bit of wire here, a tiny stick there, a dab of earth over there, a pebble between these two metal clips, and. . .

Yikes! Suddenly the gizmo started bucking like an untamed bronco. Standing in the doorway, Larsen, the pilot, spit out the sip of coffee he had in his mouth, and I got scared and took off running. In one second it was a full-blown chase scene.

But when my father, who was familiar with my habits, started cutting a nice big poplar rod to break over my rump for meddling where I didn't belong, Larsen stopped him.

My father nearly blew his top. Imagine: nobody had ever even raised his voice to him in his own house, and now this gangly city slicker, who wasn't even half his boxing weight, was acting like he knew better than him how he should be treating one of his own sons! It went to his head, and. . . Good thing my mother stepped in and whispered, "Celedonio, just let him talk"—otherwise he would have killed the man then and there.

Larsen spoke. . . and then my father was so proud, he threw down the poplar switch, gave me a hug, and said I was his son, *caray*. Said I'd always been that way, a little strange, but better than anybody with all that mechanical stuff. . .

It turns out I had fixed the antigrav balance system without even realizing it. The best part was, I found out later that in theory no human being could fix one of those units, which only you xenoids were able to manufacture. They were superdurable, built to last, but when one failed you had to chuck it all out and get a new one.

And that was when the two doctors there, with their beards and their wild hair and their crazy eyes, started asking me question after question. They told me that their names were Hermann and Sigimer and that they were astrophysicists.

They asked me about electromagnetism, about the Unified Field Theory, about everything. And I didn't know how to answer any of it. Good thing Hermann had the idea of giving me his laser pen, which had stopped working days earlier—and I fixed it right away, too, with a tiny piece of glass.

Then they both said at once that I had a special gift, that I was a natural genius, a diamond in the rough. And I stood there wide-eyed, not understanding a word of it, thinking they were making fun of me, too, like my brothers... But they started talking with my father and my mother. They went off, talked for a long time, and I could see they were giving my parents money... and finally Mama came back weeping, and she hugged me. She handed me a little suitcase with all my best clothes, six small bars of guava paste, and two big bottles of pru, gave me a kiss, and told me never to forget that they loved me and that they were my mother and father. The old man hugged me, too, and his eyes were wet, but he looked away because men don't cry, and he told me that I would be leaving with those professors and that it would be for the best for everyone. And to be a man and come out on top.

At first I didn't want to, but when Hermann and Sigimer told me I'd be going to the city to see things and machines and learn a lot so I could be like them and serve Earth, I stopped feeling about to cry, and I boarded the aerobus, happy as could be.

And can you believe it? Even though Larsen and the doctors were scared, my repair job on the antigrav balance system held up for the rest of the trip, no problem.

"Is that your real name, please?"

I've never been back to Baracuyá del Jiquí. I do miss the family, but ever since I reached civilization, I've been involved in so many secret projects, they don't even let me go to the corner store to buy pru anymore. My brain is a strategic weapon, they say.

Now, they do get me everything I ask for. If I ask for a bird on the wing, they bring me a bird on the wing.

I did manage to locate Romualdo. He was the brother who'd always been nicest to me. Two years ago, I started to get nostalgic about him and asked for information. Since he'd run away from home, and he'd always talked about going to the city. . .

Well, even though they warned me I'd only be allowed to see him from a distance, in less than a week they gave me his whole dossier and a pile of holovideos that showed him talking. My brother's a sergeant in Planetary Security now. He lives and works in New Miami.

Knowing that, and having the holovideos, was all I needed. Why see him from a distance if he would never know I'd been nearby? Why make myself feel more alone?

And I haven't seen or heard from anyone else in my family.

"What is your current scientific specialty, please?"

Alex Gens Smith, scientist. Terrestrial, human. Height six feet one inch, weight 172 pounds, in case you want to check.

"Are you in frequent contact with your family, please?"

Well, no, but when Hermann and Sigimer brought me to the Center, the people there told me I'd need a more serious-sounding name if I wanted to be a scientist. And they changed it for me. I've been saying it this way for so many years that if anybody shouted "Alesio!" at me now, I wouldn't react.

My real name is Alesio Concepción Pérez de la Iglesia Fernández Olarticochea Vallecillos y Corrales. So, Alex for Alesio, and since Concepción is the same as Genesis, I got Gens for short. And Smith is as common an Anglo name as Pérez is in Spanish, so they're equivalents. Simple transposition of elements.

"Do you have any other sort of stable and/or permanent emotional relationships on Earth, please?"

For the past four years they've kept me busy with an incredibly boring project—military in nature, like almost everything I've done. Well, it was classified, of course, but if you people accept me, I won't be able to keep it a secret.

I work on a principle that a theorist worked out, based on a toy I once built to amuse myself. I'm not very good at formulae or tensor calculus, but I can tell you it has to do with graviton resonator systems.

You know, of course, that the graviton is the elementary particle with the greatest concentration of momentum, making it possible, according to the Unified Field Theory, to convert any magnetic or electrical force into gravitational force. Any child knows that, but I only learned it after I fixed the balance system on that aerobus.

The toy I made was a graviton resonator-based matter miniaturizer. I'd stick any object between the poles of a triphase magnet, supercool it to just above zero degrees Kelvin while bombarding it with positrons in a pulsating ultrasound field, and poof! It would shrink instantly. The effect was caused by overstimulating the mutual attraction between gravitons in the piece of matter. According to the Law of Conservation of Mass, its original mass was unchanged. But it became harder than bicrovan. I had artificially produced hyperdense matter, like the kind in the nuclei of neutron stars. And it was stable; it only returned to its original volume if the process was inverted, at a great expenditure of energy.

The Center people were very excited. They had me create hyperdense projectiles capable of piercing any object, and superarmored plates of compressed cork that were dense as steel. Then it occurred to me to try shrinking things further, and I produced some nano-black holes, very cute. Of course, somebody got the idea into his head of building a weapon that would reduce the enemy to nothingness. They took everything related to black holes, which was what I was really interested in, away from me and gave it to a team of PhDs with a whole mouthful of titles, and they haven't figured out anything after all this time. They told me I had to produce a miniaturizer that would work from a distance. No matter how much I explained to them that it was impossible, because it would violate the inverse square law and relativistic mass-energy conversion, they insisted, warning me that they wouldn't allow me to work on anything else until I did it.

That's another reason I came here—because I'm tired of sitting on my hands, and it makes no sense to waste effort on an impossible project.

But in the meantime, I've been working, in secret of course, on a few other little things. . .

"Alex. . . What is the official reason for your visit to our planet, please?"

No. . . not what you'd really call stable or permanent relationships, I don't. Since my childhood I've been very shy around women. . . It always seemed to me that they talked a lot without saying anything. Like some theorists, for that matter. My mother said that's why I was so good with machines, because they never talk.

But that's not entirely true; when I was working on Artificial Intelligence I got along very nicely with an AI that I called Meniscus.

It all started because we were both getting bored, and we entertained ourselves by competing at mental calculations. . . I always lost on the simple arithmetic problems, but if we went on to topological or phase equations, I walloped Meniscus. Later, when we were on closer terms, we talked about all sorts of things: about life, the mind, what it was like to have sensations and not be just a bunch of electronic impulses inside a circuit box, self-conscious but not really alive.

They erased him three months into the research. They said he wasn't "stable" any more. I've never forgiven them.

I think my problem with women is actually very different. Their scent, the way they have of looking at you, of moving. They make me nervous. They can't be. . . reduced to logical parameters. I know it's the hormones; I even know which hormones, one by one. But it's the synergy of the hormones that throws me off. Even though I understand the effects of each part, I fail to be objective about the resulting whole. I spin out of control, I forget logic.

Of course, I have had experiences. Plenty. But very. . . particular. When I turned eighteen, the psychologists at the Center, who kept me under special monitoring, put me in contact with various. . . professionals.

Social workers, of course. All of them legal, safe, discreet, healthy. Beautiful. The psychologists felt my emotional stability would appreciate an opportunity to replace my theoretical uncertainty with practical experiences.

They were right.

It was great.

Sensorially, a woman is a being of astonishing perfection, who seems to be made for giving and receiving pleasure. The meetings, three times a week, with my new "girlfriends" and their erotic skills propelled me into a period of mental hyperactivity. During that time I produced the invisibility field and outlined the principles of what would later become the silence generator.

I also had a few homosexual experiences. Out of pure scientific curiosity, not genuine inclination. To have a way of judging. How can you say something isn't for you if you've never even tried it?

But it really didn't work well at all. I guess the lessons in machismo that I'd been given as a child were ultimately stronger than any consciousness that it was all simply a matter of prejudices. Young men with waxed bodies, long limbs, smooth gestures, and fluty voices seemed like unnatural caricatures to me. Trying to imitate women and not succeeding. And the others, hairy and muscular, with booming, hypersexed voices, reminded me too much of my father to inspire any erotic notions in me.

I devoted myself fully to the female sex. Time went by. . . And in the end, even though they told me I was a real stud and that they liked me more than any xenoid client, it started to seem. . . insufficient.

It was too easy. Too artificial. I wanted more.

And I thought I knew how to get it.

One of the few times they allowed me to leave the Center, I escaped from the pair of spies they had set to watch me (without my knowledge, or so they thought).

I had taken every precaution. I disguised my body odors so that the mutant bloodhounds couldn't track me. I used interference to make the locator they had implanted subcutaneously in my sternum go haywire. In a word, I disappeared.

I wanted to live life on my own, for a little while at least. I had provided myself a phantom credit card that they couldn't trace, so I had no lack of means. I flew to New Paris, the city of love. I rented a room and got ready to enjoy the *dolce far niente*. And I trusted to luck for finding the woman who would make my heart throb.

But regular women didn't find me attractive. I'm no model of male beauty. . . Of course, I could have had plastic surgery, but I like this face. It reminds me of my family every time I look in the mirror.

After a week of solitude, when I was starting to adjust really well to everyday life, I went back to the pros.

For three nights I spent my money hand over fist, until I was bored once more of sex and of love for sale, and I returned to my inactive solitude.

One night, when I was walking through the recreation of the Latin Quarter, I met Yleka. A woman of emerald and chocolate on the outside, a panther of honey and fire on the inside, as a verse of Valera's puts it. Are you familiar with him? I suppose not. What a pity. Try reading him.

Yleka had been left stranded in Paris by a smooth-talking Centaurian. She didn't have a credit to her name or a roof to sleep under.

I did, and I felt lonelier than ever. . . We slept together. And all the rest. But I didn't tell her I was rich. I wanted to see it matered.

It was a great week. She was tender and funny, and she didn't care that I wasn't very good with anything but objects and machines. That I hardly talked. She talked for us both, and I loved listening to her.

For those seven days she stopped wearing her supertight plastiskin body stocking, and she didn't go out looking for xenoids. She said I was enough. And it wasn't enough for me to spend all day long with her.

I think we each lost several pounds.

Things could have gone on like this a lot longer, I guess. If I had managed to keep my restless brain calm. I tried to continue my work on the silence generator, using homemade tools in my rented room, but it wasn't the same. I missed the labs at the Center and their almost unlimited resources. A habit's a habit.

I think my subconsciousness betrayed me, and I started making mistakes, minor acts of negligence. Leaving a trail. Doing all my shopping at the same store, going to inventor fairs, stuff like that. I wanted them to find me. . . and, of course, they did.

Back at the Center, it wasn't three days before they brought Yleka back to me. But it wasn't the same. The magic was dead. Now that she knew the balance in my bank account, I only interested her as a client. Human, not xenoid, but otherwise identical. Her orgasms seemed fake to me, no matter how passionate they were. Though she insisted that she still loved me. . .

Maybe her coldness was her revenge on me for lying to her. For not being just what I pretended to be. For smashing her illusions of finding happiness with a good, simple man. Even a social worker can have dreams, can't she?

When it was obvious that things weren't working like before, I told her I wouldn't be seeing her any more. It was a mistake. She cried buckets and swore she loved me. But how could I know if she loved me or my credits? I told her that her love was unprovable.

Then she called me a "damned autistic" and an "unfeeling monster." That's the only thing that has always made me angry. Call me a stupid idiot savant, I let it pass. But to say I'm cold and heartless... I used to fight my brothers over less than that until I was out of breath and covered with bruises. Until they also started fighting anyone in our town who said it to me.

I lost control, we argued, I yelled at her... I hit her. Just once, but I felt horrible. If I hadn't restrained myself, I would have kept on beating her. For her own good, I asked the guards to take her away.

I hated her for forcing me to do that.

And my anger made me harangue the people at the Center: it wasn't enough to get her out of my life; I wanted them to destroy her. Not kill her, but harm her badly, forever. Or else I'd never work again.

At first they ignored me.

Then Hermann and Sigimer tried to convince me the nice way.

Later on they used drugs, but it's impossible to force a brain to think if it doesn't want to.

After not touching the machines for two weeks, they gave in. They're capable of doing anything to get what they want. And I knew it, and took advantage. They were only interested in the stuff I could do. And only indirectly, in a secondary fashion, in how I felt. I was one more instrument. Expensive, like a radiotelescope or a synchrophasotron... as such, they had to take care of me and keep me happy.

Another reason why I'm here. I got tired of wearing an invisible inventory number on my forehead...

One week later they showed me holovideos of Yleka. She had already become a human wreck. They had gotten her addicted to telecrack. I felt I had my revenge, but that didn't make me any happier.

I worked and worked. All the years since, I've done nothing but work. Solving very interesting, morbidly fascinating problems in physics and math. To keep from thinking about her.

Every now and then I'd ask for a social worker, and we'd have sex—pure, paid for, and without any implications. Mere gymnastics to relax the body.

One day, months ago, when I was having a few drinks with Lieutenant Dabiel, an officer in Planetary Security's Special Section at the Center and one of the few humans I can call my friend, he told me how easy it had been to get Yleka addicted. How she had received the drug as a blessing... because she only wanted to forget. To forget me.

That was when I knew she had really loved me.

Then I regretted the wrong I had done and wanted to undo it. I secretly ordered to have it checked into... I know that cures exist for any addiction, no matter how powerful, and I was ready to pay any price. What is money good for if not to satisfy your whims?

But Dabiel and his guys informed me that it was too late: Yleka had left with Cauldar, a Cetian who was recruiting workers for a slave brothel in Ningando. And Planetary Security's power and jurisdiction stop at the border of Earth's atmosphere.

So... no. I don't have any stable or permanent emotional relationships. And I never have, actually.

But I'm here to remedy that...

"What is your opinion of the current science policies of the government of Earth, please?"

For years I've been practically an inmate in the Center for Physics and Mathematical Studies.

My work is ninety-nine percent secret in nature, and its results aren't even leaked to the holonet. I don't get published in the science journals and I don't regularly attend conferences or symposia of any sort on the planet, much less off-world. The Special Section of Planetary Security keeps me under a close watch. My life is insured for millions of credits. I'm considered a Planetary Scientific Reserve.

I've never participated in any seminars or courses before, nor have I wished to. As an unknown in my field, I've never been invited before, either.

My trip to this planet of yours to attend the 309th Galactic Conference on Hyperspace Astrophysics is no accident. It came about through a carefully laid but seemingly random plan. The final objective of which was to get to this building and confront this assessment interview. . . and especially its consequences.

I do not wish to return to Earth.

I'm tired of being a puppet. Tired of being alone. Tired of being a freak, of being the precious songbird that is never allowed to leave its cage.

When a delegation of xenoid scientists were visiting the handful of non-secret areas at the Center for Physics and Mathematical Studies, I left my labs with Lieutenant Dabiel's help. I was dressed in a maintenance man's overalls and had disguised my features with some handy plastiflesh makeup, which the lieutenant himself applied to my face. And I was carrying a duster and a water bucket, like a regular janitor.

While the group of scientists from other worlds was listening attentively to the guide's explanations of a device, which I had created myself, for replacing material walls with stable force fields at minimal expense, I struck up a conversation with one of the Cetian physicists.

I already knew that the 309th Conference would be held in Ningando, and my relative command of Cetian allowed me to whisper a few corrections into the Cetian ear of my conversation partner, a tremendous improvement over the arid cybernetic translation that he'd been listening to.

Intrigued and astonished to find such knowledge and such a command of his highly complex language in a simple janitor, the scientist, whose name was Jourkar—you can verify it, if you so desire—was soon engaged in a hypertechnical dialogue with me.

I told you earlier that I generally don't do well with abstractions and theories, but on that occasion the subject was my own device, so...

In under a minute, Jourkar had focused the attention of about three quarters of the delegation on me. Meanwhile, the guide—who didn't recognize me in my janitor's uniform and plastiflesh prosthetics, thank heaven—was probably wondering what sort of dirty jokes the mop monkey was telling the xenoids.

His surprise must have gone through the roof when I risked everything, turned on the device, and gave the scientists a demonstration. Luckily for me, that left him so speechless that nearly a minute went by before he tried notifying his supervisors what was happening over his vocoder. The interference generator in my pocket kept his personal communicator from working, of course.

It was another half a minute before he decided he should run to find some Planetary Security people to inform them of the irregularity. Then, not by mere luck, but by careful planning on Dabiel's part (although we were friends, this cost me a good few thousand credits), a couple more minutes went by before he found them.

That gave me more than enough time to remove my disguise, reveal my real face to the xenoid scientists, and put on the finest demonstration I could.

Once the device was running, in a matter of seconds I constructed a small room that floated half a meter above the floor without touching it. Its walls were pure force fields, not a milligram of matter. And when I concluded my "energy bricklaying" job and stabilized the whole system vibrationally, it was consuming scarcely more energy than a pocket flashlight.

And by fiddling with the topological properties of the Moebius strip and Klein bottle, I even made the space inside my "building" almost twice as large as classical Euclidean geometry would suggest.

Astonished by that display of talent (all modesty apart), Jourkar and the others were of course thrilled to immediately offer me an official invitation to the 309th Conference. And they promised to bring all possible pressure to bear so the appropriate terrestrial organizations would understand how extremely important if was, if they did not want to mar their relations with the rest of the galaxy, to let me attend the event without any hindrance or obstacles.

Then I said goodbye, destroyed my force-field room, tossed the overalls and the duster into the empty bucket, left it in a corner, and got back to my labs. . . twenty seconds before the alarm went off throughout the Center.

Lieutenant Dabiel and several nanocameras (whose existence I had been aware of almost since they were installed, and which I easily had set to record on a closed loop) vouched for the fact that I hadn't left my work desk for a single instant.

They still can't understand what really happened that day.

The heads of the Center understood it even less when the invitation arrived a month later. Jourkar and the others had gone to great pains to keep their promise. The holovideo they sent bore so many priority marks and codes that it wasn't an invitation so much as a virtual command to the government of Earth to allow me to attend the event. . . or take the consequences.

All the Center officials came to interrogate me. Various leaders from Planetary Security, too, and not just from the Special Section.

How had the xenoids learned of my existence and the work I had done, in spite of the curtain of strict secrecy with which they had surrounded me? Needless to say, I knew nothing.

And I continued knowing nothing when they analyzed my brainwaves, curve by curve, while repeating their questions. Neurology isn't one of my fortes, but I had prepared myself far in advance for that test. I found it trivial to construct a brainwave-congruent nanointerferometer and manipulate it with a sublingual control pad to keep them from suspecting anything.

Though they suspected me anyway. Wouldn't you have?

It doesn't make much sense for a human scientist to attend an elite astrophysics event if he won't be able to talk about anything he sees there afterward. . . and in fact, nothing of the sort had ever occurred before in the field of astrophysics. When humans get invited to scientific events outside the solar system, it's usually for sociology, psychology, or, much more often, history.

But the invitation was so imperative, they had to put on their bravest face and grant me permission to travel to Ningando.

Not that they gave up easily. I knew from the outset that I wouldn't be traveling alone, that an entire human delegation would accompany me, though at an astronomical cost.

I arrived with a huge entourage. Seventy percent were secret agents from Planetary Security responsible for keeping an eye on me, who don't understand a word of what's being said here; the other thirty percent are mediocre physicists responsible for explaining it to the agents as best they can, as well as to make sure I don't reveal any of the secrets that they aren't even in on themselves. At least the physicists are thrilled with everything they're seeing, though they don't understand much more than the agents do and they hate acting like scientific policemen. They probably don't even care that their memories will be blocked by your people before you let them return to Earth, and will almost certainly be erased by our Planetary Security when they get home.

All the while I concealed my joy over the successful unfolding of my plan under my habitual mask of bewilderment and confusion in the face of the unknown. It didn't take much effort: ever since I arrived in the astroport I've been completely terrified.

I didn't open my eyes once during the entire trip from the shuttle to the orbiting hypership. I had undertaken the greatest adventure of my life, risking everything. And even though I could change my mind at the last moment, something inside me was whispering, "Alex, there's no turning back now."

When I got to Ningando, I knew I had won. With Jourkar's help, it was easy for me to elude my guards and come here. Now. . . it all depends on you. There. I've laid all my cards on the table.

I don't plan to return to Earth, and that's my final word.

"What induced you to come here and request honorary Cetian citizenship, please?"

First of all, I'd like to make it very clear that I'm not the best suited to testify objectively as to the policies of the terrestrial government toward their scientists. Because I've never been considered a "real scientist." I don't have a degree from any university. Just a few postgraduate diplomas. And the people who gave them to me were almost always more eager to learn from me than to teach me.

They practically considered me an "idiot savant." Are you familiar with the term? Good, good. . . A free electron, unfit to form a part of any think tank or scientific team, because my working methods were far too instinctive and unorthodox. I'm appreciated, I'm well taken care of. . . but I'm not understood or loved. I'm alone. Completely alone, as I tried to explain to you earlier. And the situation no longer seems right to me.

But although I'm more the exception than the rule, I've had enough dealings with "typical" scientists for me to gain a detailed idea of their conflicts and concerns. You may be better able to understand those concerns if I summarize the average career path of a human scientist for you. Though perhaps you already have ninety percent of this information, and your question is more in the line of probing my subjective politics. . .

In that case, I'm sorry to disappoint you. I don't know much about politics. I've never been interested. It isn't. . . scientific.

The terrestrial government—that is, the major human shareholders in the Planetary Tourism Agency, under the guise of the World

Parliament—has the good sense to guarantee a good, free education to ninety-nine percent of the children on the planet. And I do mean ninety-nine percent, not one hundred, because as you can see there are always exceptions. My village of Baracuyá del Jiquí, which has no continuous access to holonet or any other connectivity, must still lie completely outside the World Education System.

According to neurologists and psychologists, my mind's almost complete "virginity" is one of the essential factors that turned me into the freak I am today.

Fine, then; when teenagers finish middle school, they have two choices awaiting them: either they are successful at their aptitude and IQ tests and get into college prep schools, or they fail and end up in tech school. Or they start working, which is what most people have no choice but to do.

For the fortunate few who get into college prep, the state doesn't charge them anything. . . for the time being. But they're racking up a debt that they'll be forced to pay, to the last credit of accumulated interest, in the future.

There are two ways of enrolling in the university: for free. . . if you negotiate a second and even more exhaustive series of exams brilliantly enough. Or by paying and skipping the exams. If the student or the student's family is willing to pay the cost of every class, book, and so on. The privileged few who are able to afford doing this are another matter. Paying automatically gives you certain rights, including the right to choose which career you want to study.

The fact is, the majority of future terrestrial scientists start out among the ranks of those who pass their entrance exams and gain free admission to the university. And when I say the majority, I mean only one out of every hundred college prep graduates.

In practice, only the few who have shown a potential for becoming absolute geniuses have any real possibility of choosing the field of science they will study. The academic fate of the rest depends on a sort of roulette, in which their qualifications play a role. . . but what mainly counts is the medium-term plans of the Planetary Tourism Agency, or of the government, which is the same thing.

It doesn't matter if a young person has been dreaming since childhood of becoming an astrophysicist. If the "needs of Earth" demand x number of sociologists over the next seven years. . . he'll have to study sociology, or drop out of the university.

Naturally, two out of three young people go unsatisfied into specialties that never interested them. If they are interested in learning, better something that nothing, don't you think?

To be sure, it is always possible to change fields.

Though intended for students who discovered halfway through their studies that their subject had no vocational prospects, some thirty percent of students on Earth graduate in something completely different from what they started out studying. And according to conservative statistics, of the other seventy percent, nearly half wish they had. . . but their grades aren't good enough for a transfer request.

The only students who have a right to make such a petition, and only after completing the second year, are those who attain a grade point average of 9.5 or more out of ten. Even so, the deans of each school can turn down a petition for changing specialties at their own discretion, if they feel that the student will be of more use in the specialty he originally started out in.

The deplorable state of the lab equipment in universities on Earth is known throughout the galaxy. We're a third-rate planet. . . Our College of High Energy Physics doesn't even have a small particle accelerator, and future astronomers can only gaze at the stars through vintage two-meter, or at most three-meter, reflecting telescopes. They can't even dream of modular orbiting field reflectors. Much less of off-world field trips.

Our next generation of biologists know such basic techniques as autocloning or body exchange only through crude simulations or well-worn holovideos. Nor do they have access to fauna from other worlds—live specimens are prohibitively expensive. Our geophysicists have fewer opportunities to send probes to the interior of our planet, and they know less about it, than any interested tourist.

Now, medical students do have the luxury of working with real patients from the start. Of course, those patients are humans on Social Assistance, which provides them with free medical care. New medications are also tested on them. Since a human life has so little value, while there's always a need for doctors and new medicines, nobody complains. . . Maybe that's why Earth's doctors and medical system are so famous throughout the galaxy. They don't lack for experience, that's for sure.

Even sociologists are unable to implement real surveys to learn how to use the complicated skewed statistics programs that are fundamental to their science these days. Like everyone else, they work with simulators.

As might be expected, the lack of resources is slightly less grave at private graduate schools and at institutions directly connected with the Scientific Reserve, the places where those who can pay and the especially talented study. . . For the rest, hardly any university on Earth has access to resources other than simulations. And even those are necessarily four or five years behind the models sold everywhere else in the galaxy.

So there is no way for a future scientist to interact with the real world. Indeed, the terrestrial doctrine of higher education could be phrased more or less as follows: "Take these rudiments of theory, then go do your real learning on the fly—and good luck."

Upon graduation the fledgling scientist begins his true odyssey. That is moment when Earth's clever bureaucracy hands him the bill for his "free" education. To settle his debt, he'll have to work for at least five years, not where he wants, but where the government deigns to send him. And the salary over those five years is almost laughable.

If he wants to change postings earlier, at the cost of having his title revoked, he'll have to make a $trong ca$e for it, and even then only after piles of red tape that usually take years to sort out.

For better or for worse, the chaotic state of Earth's economy cannot guarantee placements to more than sixty-five percent of its graduates. More and more young people enter the university every year. And fewer and fewer new graduates find work in their specialties.

There are biologists working as lab technicians in provincial hospitals. Physiochemists as quality inspectors in synthetic food factories. Sociologists underutilized as reporters on some third-rate holonet.

And that's not the worst of it.

Many tour operators, guides, and aerobus drivers decorate their living room walls with the beautiful and useless holograms of their university degrees. Others, even more pragmatic or more cynical, forget about their titles forever, or they set up small enterprises to survive. The "Second-level Scientific Reserve," they're called, and presumably they'll be in demand at some point. . . over the next millennium.

Meanwhile, since you have to make a living somehow and the Planetary Tourism Agency is always hungry for intelligent young people, especially the good-looking ones...

Working in the tourism sector isn't as awful for a scientist as it might seem at first glance. At least you're well-paid, and you come into contact with the genuine source of Earth's wealth: xenoid tourists. Sometimes they learn more about the latest developments in the fields they no longer work in than their colleagues with government positions.

There are even frequent cases of daring to get a title revoked through shady dealings in order to snag a transfer. In order to drop science forever and work in tourism. It's pathetic, but almost a third of the people working for the Planetary Tourism Agency are scientists frustrated in their careers.

"Why Tau Ceti and not Alpha Centauri, please?"

I'm a scientist, more or less. And there was a time when I believed in the future of my planet.

But how can a planet develop in any meaningful way when day after day it throws away its best minds? How absurd does your idealism have to be for you to keep on working as a scientist when you could make so much more as a tourist guide? What sense does it make for a recent graduate to work like a slave in a place he isn't interested in, for five whole years? Surrounded by old men who see his dynamic initiative as a threat and who constantly leave him out of the loop, using his "inexperience" as their excuse? For poverty wages, after seven years of intellectual effort, dreaming of being useful to his planet?

The worst part—and it pains me to say it in this interview, under my special circumstances, but it's true—the worst part is that you xenoids are perfectly well aware of these facts, and you take full advantage of them.

You didn't invent the brain drain, but you perfected and institutionalized it.

It is obvious that a human scientist who refuses to give up on his science will find it much more attractive, most of all economically, to work in any minor branch office of a xenoid enterprise than in most similar terrestrial research centers. He will feel he is making fuller use of his intellect there, will see more of a future. So what if they only allow him partial access to data? At least it's something. . . That smidgen of knowledge is worth its weight in gold to him.

He can travel off planet every now and then. . . even though he can never tell anyone what he saw afterwards. If he works hard and does a good job and shows how exceptional his gray cells are, is even possible—and this is the big dream for many—that they will ask him to emigrate definitively from Earth to work for them.

Do you like old music? No? That's too bad. . . Well, you probably wouldn't be familiar with the songs of Joan Manuel Serrat, anyway. A human, Catalan, twentieth century. . .

I thought not. His nearly forgotten recordings are the best things in my collection. One of the few things I'll regret leaving behind if you accept me. . .

There's a song of his, "Pueblo blanco," that goes. . . No, don't worry! I won't sing it all. I have next to no sense of rhythm or melody. Just one verse:

Run away, gentle folk,
because this earth is sick.
Tomorrow it won't give you
what it wouldn't give before,
and there's nothing to be done.
Take your mule, your lass, your saddle,
follow the road of the Hebrew people. . .

That is, the Exodus. You don't know the Bible either?

Okay, at least. Yes, the Jews, the Promised Land, all that.

When he called it "sick" he was talking about a patch of earth, a piece of ground. But today, speaking of the planet with a capital E, his words have proved prophetic.

This Earth is sick. . .

The days when we thought the future belonged to us are over. Now we're not even masters of our present day, and the glories of the past aren't enough to live on.

Artists, athletes, scientists. . . every human who has some physical or intellectual talent dreams of using it as a ticket from Earth and toward making their way in the galaxy. Even if they have to swallow their pride and drink the bitter potion of exile and humiliation in lands of other races.

Women dream of being beautiful and brazen enough to become social workers and find a xenoid who will take them away from their home world forever. Some men do, too.

And the most desperate ones, the ones who aren't young or beautiful and don't know how to do anything, the ones who see no other way out, take the risk of playing Russian roulette in space. They'd rather face the infinitude of the cosmos in their homemade ships and float, frozen, perhaps in an eternal dream of arriving some day at some other, better, place.

She dreams of him,
He dreams of going far away. . .

That's from the same song. Not the same "him," of course.

The first "him" is you xenoids. The second "him" is us.

What sort of future can a planet have when its residents dream only of ceasing to reside there?

Exodus. Escape. Today that is every human's obsession. Running away, forever if at all possible, from the parched, subjugated, defeated, sterile, sick Earth. And you people, the conquering xenoids, the masters of the galaxy, are the virus behind this sickness.

And still you ask me why I came down with it!

"Why do you think we will find you a suitable candidate for us to confer our honorary citizenship upon, please?"

When a man is going to break with his entire past in order to begin a new life, he has to be very careful in selecting the where, the how, and the when. And small details sometimes take on huge importance.

I picked you for reasons of. . . biological affinity. Neither the Colossaurs nor the grodos are humanoids. My life among them would be much harder than among you people, or the Centaurians. And you are more beautiful, at least. . .

Oh, I have no illusions of being successful with your exquisite representatives of the female sex. I have already told you that I am not considered handsome even among my own people, and I know full well that the only thing that makes me exceptional, my brain, is something that no females of any race place much value on. . . at least, not at first sight.

I actually don't really know why. . . Maybe there was some inherently masochistic element. I was always a pariah, someone apart, who participated in the game but knew he didn't belong there. The moments when I was emotionally happy were the ones when I forgot such a thing. . . temporarily. And, living here in Ningando, amidst so much beauty, I don't think I could ever forget it.

That sounds like a strange reason, I guess. The desire to feel that you are the only unblessed person in paradise. . .

And, also, I won't deny it, I picked you because I'm a hopeless romantic. I suppose there must be thousands of slave brothels in this city, and perhaps hundreds of Cauldars. But I'll check them out, one by one if need be. In spite of it all, I have hopes of finding Yleka, alive. I'm sure she'll remember me. . . Perhaps we'll get a second chance.

Don't you think we deserve it?

"Are you certain that no other Earth scientist has heard of this. . . discovery of yours, please?"

I know perfectly well that the policy on Tau Ceti is not to grant citizenship to every human who comes here begging on his knees for it.

But I believe that you will make an exception for me. . .

I'm aware of the technoscience quarantine laws that have caused terrestrial science and technology to lag so far behind. I fully understand their true purpose, underneath all the altruistic demagoguery:

to knock us out of the competition. To guarantee that we will eternally be a market, not a producer. A buyer, not a seller. Dependent, in a word. To sideline us in the galactic struggle for power.

They don't allow us know the mechanics of controlled thermonuclear fusion, or how antigrav systems work, or the theory of hyperspace flight. . .

Especially that last one. Because. . . can you imagine what would happen to the delicate balance among the races if humans suddenly developed an instantaneous transport system that works across the universe? The chaos that would be unleashed if all the hyperspace shops that xenoids boast were suddenly rendered obsolete?

I have created such a system. Based on classical teletransportation, of course. . . but capable of transferring a virtually infinite mass between two points separated by galactic distances.

It does not require astronomical amounts of energy or special technical knowledge for installation. It does not even need a corresponding piece of equipment at the point of arrival, unlike systems currently in use. Of course you'd need one to return. . . but you could send it by teletransport, too. The system is, pardon my immodesty, simply brilliant. Or brilliantly simple, if you prefer the sound of that.

And if you do not grant me Cetian citizenship, I will publish all the details of my discovery.

Imagine every Earthling building his own galactic teletransport booth, and my race spreading across all your worlds like the plague you've always tried to contain.

I see that you're smiling. . . Perhaps you are thinking that simply wiping my memory clean, or, if worse comes to worst, physically eliminating me will easily put an end to that possibility. Sorry, but I've already thought of that.

At a secret and secure location in my lab at the Center—and at five other sites, just in case—I have left computers with all the data stored in their memory. Each is connected to the holonet. If I return, or if I disappear; if my name or fingerprints or retinal scan show up on any list of passengers to Earth, or if I simply fail to send a specific signal each month, everyone will learn of my invention.

I suppose you could consider this blackmail. But at the same time, don't you think that is more than sufficient reason to declare me suitable for becoming an honorary citizen of Tau Ceti right away?

"Do you consider yourself a mentally sane individual, please?"

My galactic teletransport system is really very simple. But it is based on a very original set of principles and theories, which run diametrically counter to the concepts that advanced science currently employs on Earth. This fact is a logical consequence of my characteristic mental model of reasoning. . .

As I have mentioned, I am one of that odd class of mental freaks that some call "idiot savants," and others, such as Hermann and Sigimer, much more euphemistically call "natural geniuses."

My emotional and social activity is almost entirely atrophied in favor of the disproportionate development of my logic, intuition, and memory skills. I have limitations, of course. For example, you will have noticed that my capacity for abstract thinking is . . . average. Although I have recently been getting better and better at expressing my thoughts in the abstruse system of physical and mathematical formulae that seem to be the lingua franca of science.

I am still more comfortable working with physical objects or analogies than with hypotheses. My mind works better with images than with words or concepts. I'm a born empiricist, not a theorist. That was what allowed me to make my. . . discovery.

Of course, I also have a photographic memory. . . which may have given you the impression that I have much greater facility for social analysis than I actually do. That was purely involuntary; I merely repeated verbatim a few analyses of the situation on Earth that have fallen into my hands by means I would prefer not to mention—but whose points of view I share one hundred percent, though I admit that I would never be able to draw such conclusions on my own.

I'm sorry for the trouble I've no doubt caused you. Constantly drawing on my automatic memory predisposes me towards a bit of logorrhea and incoherence. . . towards digressing and answering questions that I haven't been asked yet, or that I was asked long ago.

My mother always told me that I had all the answers. That my real problem was finding the questions that went with them.

Perhaps that is the dilemma of man and of all intelligent life.

But enough of cheap, sentimental philosophy. With regard to your question, specifically, I think that from a statistical point of view it would be simply impossible for another human being to have reached the same discovery at the same time as me.

Absolutely not.

* * *

"Fine. . . The assessment interview has concluded. Alex Gens Smith, you have been determined suitable for receiving honorary Cetian citizenship. Our colleagues will inform the rest of your delegation of this decision. Your personal belongings will soon be transferred from the accommodations reserved for humans where you have been staying. An official request will be sent to Earth asking to have any personal objects you wish to keep immediately sent to you. Including your recordings of Joanman Uelser Rat. You will be provided with all the information you will have to learn in order to adjust as quickly as possible to life in our society.

"Welcome to Ningando, Alex.

"Forgive my previous coldness. We are no Centaurians, but that is our. . . official attitude in cases such as yours.

"Now, speaking unofficially, I'd like to pass on some information to you that you are obviously unaware of. . . and to ask you a question of a more. . . private nature.

"Your 'discovery' of galactic teletransportation was made eight years ago by us—the xenoids. It is currently in the experimental, pilot project phase. If it hasn't been widely deployed yet, that is because, as you inferred, it will drastically change the entire system of transportation lines across the galaxy, rendering the huge investments of various races in the hyperspace transport fleet useless and obsolete.

"Three years ago, another human physicist, Dr. Dien Lin Chuan of the University of Beijing—perhaps you have heard of him—appeared before our Centaurian colleagues *with the same discovery*. And he filed a request identical to yours. I am authorized to inform you that Dien Ling Chuan is currently a Centaurian citizen with full rights. . .

"My question is: Are you *fully aware* of the fact that this interview has concluded favorably for you *exclusively* because it is in the interest of the races you call xenoid to prevent the species to which you belong from having any chance of technological development?"

* * *

Madness is very relative, don't you think?

An anonymous ancient Arabic poet and philosopher once said, "In this mad world, the greatest madness is to claim to be sane."

I have also heard it said that madness is any behavior or way of thinking that diverges from what is "normal."

My life can't be considered very "normal," I don't think. And every man thinks as he has lived.

So, according to both these views, I must be crazy. . . and I don't care. On the contrary, I'm proud of it.

* * *

"I would like to understand you, Alex, sincerely. You are a very peculiar individual. In all my years of experience here in the Bureau of Human Affairs, I have never met a terrestrial like you.

"Pardon me if my curiosity seems excessive. I am not a government official all the time. I also have my family, my hobbies. . . and one of them is human nature.

"But, tell me, Alex. . . Don't you feel like. . . like a deserter? Like a traitor to your race and to your planet?"

* * *

Yes, I am *fully aware*. . .
But what am I supposed to do about it?
A person has to live, right?

October 1, 1998

Divers

Some sociologists feel that the best sign of a culture's level of civilization is how much distance it puts between itself and its own excrement.

Some ecologists feel that the best sign of a culture's level of civilization is how well it recycles its own excrement.

Some individuals feel that the best sign of a culture's level of civilization is how easily the excrement it produces can be put to good use.

Those people are divers.

There's nothing new about them.

They didn't first appear with Contact.

They seem to have always existed: whether among Sumerians and Egyptians, or among Greeks and Romans, there have always been human beings who live from putting to good use (that is, more or less recycling) the garbage that other human beings produce.

They've also been called ragpickers, junkmen, and by many other names. It is one of the world's oldest professions (or cults, as some term it).

The truth is, they don't make their living from trash but from stuff that is still useful or easily mended, but that other people have thrown away as if it were trash because they don't have the savings mentality, or the right skills, or the time.

All modern civilizations, swept up as they are in the principle of "use it and toss it," squander huge quantities of labor in the form of objects that still almost work. But it's easier and cheaper to manufacture new stuff than fix the old. Even when the new stuff is imported from stars hundreds of light-years away, as is the case for Earth.

Divers, of course, don't see things this way.

Maybe that's why the Earth is now full of divers.

They dive into garbage containers, searching for pieces of wood, bits of rare metals, mechanical parts, cybernetic circuit boards that have stopped working, discarded fragments of robotic systems. Almost everything interests them.

They eat the food and wear the clothes that other, more scrupulous humans throw away. It's good enough for them.

They look like beings from another world: lost in thought, oblivious to the gangs of kids making fun of the way they smell and the rags they wear. Focused on the difficult art of distinguishing between real trash and what can still be used. Some mutter strange chants while their fingers rummage skillfully through the containers, picking out a few things and leaving the rest according to criteria that they alone know. Until they move on, at their slow pace, with all their bags of treasure, to find another goldmine in the guise of a pile of trash, where again they will recover a wealth of wonders.

There are two main types of divers.

The first are those who sell their finds to small-scale raw material recyclers, who are merely divers who've gone into the wholesale business and have therefore climbed up a step on the pyramid of the garbage-heap's dead ecology.

These are the divers who still understand the meaning of money. Sometimes they live in tiny apartments, watch holonet programs on small holoscreens, follow Voxl games. . . They still have one foot in the world, even if they mumble about their past glories and think of an impossible tomorrow. People can still understand them. The work they do, though repulsive and poorly paid, is a job.

The other divers are very different.

They never sell anything to the recyclers. They prefer to keep their finds. And then, in their refuges under bridges or in dark alleys, they assemble, tie, solder, rejoin parts of old computers with bits of rusty old tubing, pieces of rocket casings with upholstery ripped from old aerobuses. They always smile while they work, as if they can see past the discards that they handle so lovingly. They sweat and toil for hours and hours, their eyes gleaming with hope, and at the end they carefully push the results of their efforts aside and start over again on a new assemblage.

No one knows whether they believe they are creating art. Some art dealers have tried to sell these divers' exotic, chaotic contraptions as "installations," but the sophisticated xenoid public finds trash incompatible with the concept of art. End of story.

No one knows whether they believe their strange Frankenstein creatures will work somehow, some day. Or what they might expect them to do. Perhaps be vengeance machines, removing the xenoids from Earth forever and returning it to humans. Or perhaps they would simply destroy all civilization, including human civilization, in order to get rid of all the trash and shame and let some other species—primate or otherwise—start over from scratch. Or maybe they're hoping that their monstrosities will achieve such a major breakthrough for Earth's stunted technology that xenoid domination will fall before man's intellectual dynamism once and for all.

No one knows. . . and very few wish to find out. Or have time for all this. There are much more important things to do. Such as making money. Such as surviving.

And they keep on going, tirelessly joining fragments, muttering their incomprehensible chants, forgotten by the world.

From time to time a very old one disappears. Simply isn't seen around anymore, and it's almost as if he had returned to the bosom of his beloved trash pile. But other, younger ones always come along to take his place. Their skin less wrinkled, their gums more full of teeth, but the same lost stare in their rarely bright eyes.

Older people walk past and sadly shake their heads. Sometimes they stop mischievous kids from beating them and stealing their "treasures," and they mumble, "poor crazy people!" They pretend that they don't see the divers, but they have strange expressions on their faces.

Could it be because they somehow realize the divers possess something that they themselves have already lost forever?

Escape Tunnel

The Crew

Three of them.

An ideal number.

Two men and one woman.

Or, even more precisely, two male humans and one female human.

The female is Friga.

Friga

Friga doesn't much resemble the usual idea of "what a woman should be."

Isn't slender with swaying hips, long legs, and voluptuous breasts.

Doesn't have a heart-shaped mouth, doll-like eyes, and huge ovaries.

Friga has skin as dark as ebony and pearly white teeth. She's six foot two and two hundred pounds of muscles bulked up by the same illegal steroids that atrophied her ovaries to the size of beans after she gave birth.

A jaw like a concrete block, and a legendarily bad temper.

What you call a real butch or virago.

But those who know how she reacts to those words would never risk the consequences.

The last guy who did will never risk anything again. Ever.

Friga isn't a whole-hearted lesbian. It's just that she finds it harder and harder to find a man who would risk carrying on even an occasional relationship with her.

And since some women find her desirable, and she's never been too choosy...

Friga has no visible means of support, aside from crime.

Never has.

She's done robbery, trafficking—any job that turns up and pays well enough.

Her physique is too distinctive for her to work as a scammer or a con artist.

She's killed a couple of times.

Out of anger, not for work or for pleasure.

She isn't a professional killer or a psychopath.

She's spent eight hellish long years of her life in Body Spares, sentenced for various offenses.

She doesn't remember much about those years... She only knows that she doesn't want to get sentenced again.

That's her motivation for setting out on the Voyage.

People say she has a daughter, a little girl, by the name of Leilah, but that she doesn't much care about her.

She may be coarse and uneducated and have a limited vocabulary, but she's a perfect survivor, and a natural leader.

She always knows what to do in every situation.

And she does it without a word of complaint.

The Two Men

They are Adam and Jowe.

Adam is tall, young, gangly, and clumsy.

He uses artificial lenses because he wore out his own eyes long ago staring at holoscreens and browsing through technical reference manuals that are so old, they're actually printed on paper.

Adam can build anything with nothing but trash, patience, and inventiveness.

From a hyperengine to a high-powered ruby laser.

Some say he could manage even if there weren't any trash available. . .

He's a super-handyman.

A genius of technobricolage, convinced that his talent is pitifully wasted on building illegal arms and other brilliant doohickeys.

His usual clients are people like Friga.

He's just gotten out of eight months in Body Spares on account of some masers he made, which later on were supplied to some Yakuzas.

And Body Spares wasn't what you might call his cup of tea.

He was conscious almost the whole time he served as a "horse."

He was mounted by a guzoid from Regulus who was very interested in extreme experiences.

Purely sexual and other sorts.

He survived.

But he still has scars. . .

He dreads having to go through something like that again, which he knows will be very hard for him to avoid given the only kind of life he's ever been able to live.

Though his sentence also had its upside.

That was how he met Jowe.

Jowe is still young, but his face already looks like a weathered chunk of rock.

Jowe would be handsome, with his golden bangs and his big blue eyes, if they weren't as icy as the blue of chrome-vanadium steel.

Jowe has dead eyes.

The eyes of a person whose soul must have frozen.

His eyes look like the sort that have seen everything there is to see about pain, betrayal, disappointment. . . and more.

Jowe is intelligent, seems well educated, has delicate, sensitive, skillful hands, like an artist's.

He never talks about his past.

In general, Jowe rarely talks. . .

Jowe just gazes straight ahead, at the stars.

And his gaze is terrifyingly empty, doesn't hold much hope.

Barely even a motivation to keep on living.

Even Friga, who isn't afraid of anyone or anything, sometimes gets a chill around Jowe.

The idea of the Voyage was Jowe's, and when he speaks of it, the words that emerge from his lips sound like beauty itself.

The Idea of the Voyage

The Voyage is the Exodus.

Like in the Bible.

Escaping from the kingdom of Pharaoh in search of the Promised Land.

In the Promised Land there are clusters of grapes so large it takes two men to lift them, and there's work and opportunity for all.

The rivers flow with milk and honey, and every enterprising man can achieve his dreams of wealth.

The Promised Land is any land but Earth.

Humans aren't exactly the Chosen People, but. . .

The Promised Land belongs to the Philistines, and nobody promised it to the people of Earth.

The Philistines are the power behind Pharaoh's throne.

Xenoids who manipulate the Planetary Tourism Agency puppet and who despise the Earthlings.

Philistines who don't want humans to enjoy the same quality of life that they do, because they fear their worlds might be polluted by the inferior race.

The xenoids are mighty in arms and money, so sword and purse are unlikely methods to win victories against them and their Planetary Security puppets.

What's left is shrewdness and cunning.

That is, entering the Promised Land by stealth.

Taking advantage of the fact that not all Philistines think alike, that there are some who patrol the borders of their kingdoms looking for hands to work in their fields.

The fact that there are always a few "compassionate" sorts who take in runaway humans and, in exchange for the runaways' virtual slave labor in their factories, keep them hidden for three years and three days.

After that period, if the human can show that he has remained among the Philistines the whole time, he gets a chance to become a citizen of the Promised Land.

A second-class citizen, of course.

But at least that's something, and it's better to suffer directly under the yoke of the Philistines than to do it under their puppet Pharaoh.

Better the Promised Land than its virtual colony, Earth.

Shrewdness and cunning, then, mean escaping.

The Voyage means Escaping.

Escaping: Distance

Escaping is no easy matter.

There are two huge obstacles: Distance and Surveillance.

Distance is a serious business all by itself.

To get to the Promised Land you must first cross some desert.

The stars that the worlds of the xenoids orbit are light-years away.

They are separated from Earth by an endless desert of empty space, which hyperships cross in a matter of seconds.

But only xenoids have the technology to build safe hyperships.

Though hyperengine construction is well within the reach of many human "super-handymen" such as Adam, the steering and power control systems are another kettle of fish.

A homemade hyperengine built on Earth works only once... and the ship that uses it can return to ordinary space almost anywhere.

Maybe near a solar system full of xenoids, maybe a thousand parsecs from any stellar bodies.

Or in the middle of a gas nebula, or inside a globular cluster.

Fortunately, the structure of the hyperengine itself prevents it from working very close to large masses.

There's no danger of materializing in a space that's already occupied by a sun or planet.

The flip side is that in order to activate a homemade hyperengine without control systems, you first have to get some distance away from the plane of the ecliptic containing the Sun, Earth, and the other planets.

The only way to get far enough away is by conventional propulsion, relying on the law of action and reaction.

Ballistically, the safest trajectory for getting as far away from the plane of the ecliptic as quickly as possible with minimum fuel consumption is by traveling almost perpendicular to Earth's orbit.

The safe zone is no more than twenty arcminutes wide.

In the semisecret, semitechnical jargon of those who aim to make the Voyage, this route is called the Escape Tunnel.

Naturally, Planetary Security is also familiar with it and keeps it under constant surveillance.

Surveillance: Planetary Security

Planetary Security was created, and exists, to maintain control.

Control is, among other things, stopping Voyages by any means.

Any means add up to a multi-level system.

The first level includes everything from surprise raids in search of the hideouts where homemade ships are built, to generous payments to an extensive network of informants who are retained to locate those hideouts, to ultratight controls on all the raw materials and instruments used to manufacture space engine parts.

The second level is the network of Earth-based radars that rake the atmosphere with their invisible fingers day and night, distinguishing between commercial aerobus flights and any Unidentified Flying Object taking off from the planet.

The third level is the system of orbiting radars that similarly distinguish between shuttles bearing passengers or cargo to hyperships waiting at docking points and any Unidentified Flying Object that attains escape velocity.

The main players at these last two levels are the high-tech patrol ships that the xenoids supply to Planetary Security.

With crews of six, these super-aerodynamic, Mach 3 suborbital patrol ships are loaded with weaponry.

If an Unidentified Flying Object turns out to be a homemade ship headed for the Escape Tunnel, the crews on every patrol ship have instructions to open fire and destroy it.

After, of course, trying to communicate by radio first, and after warning the craft that it absolutely must return to Earth.

Generally speaking, the primitive communications gear on a homemade ship is completely incapable of working while the ship climbs into orbit, when it is subjected to an acceleration of several g and enveloped by static.

So the Planetary Security guys often forget the step of trying to communicate, or simply skip it.

And they fire on the homemade ships without further ado.

If the ships manage to slip through the first three levels of the surveillance system, there's still the fourth and final one.

The hardest one.

After a few modifications, suborbital patrol ships designed for operating in or near the atmosphere can also be effective in deep space.

Their crews reduced to three men each, to carry the maximum

fuel loads possible, modified patrol ships orbit in the vicinity of the Escape Tunnel on shifts lasting several weeks, scrutinizing the Tunnel with their sensitive instruments all the while.

Surveillance like this is, obviously, very difficult to elude.

But there's always a possibility.

Friga, Adam, and Jowe are gambling it all on that possibility.

And on their knowledge of earlier attempts, to make their own plan better.

Earlier Attempts: The Folklore of the Voyage

Now that several dozen people have attempted it, and even succeeded in one case out of fifty, aficionados have a wealth of technical information on the Voyage.

Information that, of course, is shared only by word of mouth.

It harly needs to be said that any mention of the Escape Tunnel is superforbidden and ultracensored.

The data come from three main sources.

Positive feedback from the few lucky ones who managed to get to the xenoid worlds and were later able to tell how they had done it.

Also, feedback from the members of their "support staff" who stayed behind on Earth, spreading information in the form of rumors about the most successful techniques and ship models.

And as negative feedback, stories about how the unsuccessful ones managed so badly.

If all the folklore on the Voyage and Voyage Vehicles were compiled in one place, it would take terabytes of memory to store it.

There's been a bit of everything.

Ships camouflaged as commercial aerobuses to circumvent earth-based surveillance.

Using solar sails, a form of passive propulsion almost undetectable to a patrol ship, to get inside the Escape Tunnel unnoticed.

Ships with several "disposable, single-use" hyperengines, to increase the chances of getting somewhere by being able to make more than one hyperspace jump.

Vehicles tricked out with handcrafted armor, and loaded with illegal weaponry such as lasers and masers, to resist and respond to any attack by Planetary Security ships.

Modular ships that break into independent small craft in order to confuse the pursuing patrols, or, if that turns out to be impossible, so the pilots might escape with their lives back to Earth, able to try it again in the future.

Vehicles with onboard anabiosis systems so the crew can remain in suspended animation. . . for all eternity, if their luck runs out and they return to three-dimensional space too far from a xenoid settlement. . .

Yes, there's been a bit of everything.

Based on all these brilliant and desperate solutions, Friga, Adam, and Jowe have designed and built, with nearly endless ingenuity and patience, their own passport to happiness.

Their escape vehicle, which they have christened the *Hope*.

The *Hope*: The Vehicle

The *Hope* is a genuine marvel of improvisation.

It ought to have the old saying, "Necessity is the mother of invention," written in gold across its bow.

The plan for getting it into the Escape Tunnel is likewise a wonder of deception, cunning. . . and optimism.

The *Hope* will lift off camouflaged inside a tremendous weather balloon, in order to trick ground-based radars.

The four square kilometers of reflective synplast required for this mimicry came from the loot taken in a robbery that Frida pulled off years ago at a grodo-owned import warehouse.

What luck she never found a buyer for all that material. . .

On reaching the ionosphere, the *Hope* will drop the balloon disguise and head into orbit along a regular commercial route.

Its exterior looks surprisingly like the hull of a Cetian-built shuttle of the Tornado class, one of the most common spacecraft in every terrestrial astroport.

Working with practically waste material, Adam and Jowe have painstakingly created a very passable imitation of the perfect outer finish typical of xenoid technology.

The looks of the *Hope* is half technological miracle, half sculpture: a work of bricolage and a work of art.

Thanks to her contacts and with the help of just a few credits, Friga was able to acquire the communications gear from an actual Tornado-class shuttle that was being decommissioned.

Adam fixed it up, good as new.

Now it can link to several astroports.

Thinking ahead, Adam has put in dozens of hours listening in on the conversations of traffic controllers and shuttle pilots.

When the time comes, he's certain he'll be able to imitate their simple technical jargon. . .

With that, and with the communications codes (which did indeed cost Friga quite a lot, in spite of all her ties), they expect to elude the second level of surveillance.

Any patrol ships that see or hear them would have to be magicians to so much as suspect that the *Hope* isn't just an everyday shuttle headed for orbit to dock with a hypership.

But if they do, still, all is not lost.

Under its apparently defenseless imitation Tornado-class skin, the *Hope* conceals a system of pulsating force fields. It's not the nearly invulnerable armor plating of a xenoid-built patrol ship, but it should be able to take a good deal of punishment.

Andit has a few high-powered lasers for responding to the particle-beam weapons of Planetary Security ships.

That's how they hope to reach the Escape Tunnel without too much structural damage or loss of fuel.

Once there, hyperspace. . . And then, everything else.

Hyperspace—And Then Everything Else

Friga, Adam, and Jowe would have preferred to have more hyperengines, but the weaponry and the energy generators for the force shields left only enough room for two.

One to get them far away from the solar system. . . The other in case they get too far from everything.

But, on the other hand, they have a suspended animation system, which Adam has brilliantly modified.

The "super-handyman" guarantees that it will keep all three of them in perfect anabiosis for at least five hundred years.

At least in theory, if neither hyperengine brings them luck, five centuries should be more than enough time for the *Hope* to drift to some port.

Some port with xenoids.

Xenoids of good will, if at all possible.

Xenoids of Good Will

Friga has no scientific-technical training, or any other education.

Nevertheless, she's confident that her physical strength, her stamina, her lack of scruples, and her leadership qualities will make her valuable to any xenoid boss involved in not entirely legal activities.

She knows she could be the best capo in the universe.

If not, she's still willing to make the voyage and stick it out anyway

Adam places high hopes on his incredible skill as a technotinkerer. Though he doesn't say so to anyone, he's sort of skeptical about his utility in xenoid consumer society, where nothing gets fixed but everything is used until it breaks and then is simply thrown away.

But he aims to learn how to build things; since he already knows how to repair them...

In any case, the real trump card for both of them is Jowe.

And his mysterious friend, Moy.

Jowe and Moy

Jowe doesn't talk about Moy very much. Like, not at all.

He's only said that Moy is an artist, an old friend of his, who's had luck with the xenoids.

But everything indicates that they were close friends.

Maybe more than friends, Friga and Adam sometimes think, with the wickedness of the street.

Because it's pretty rare for someone, no matter how well-off economically, to wire money orders worth nearly a million credits to a mere friend.

The remittances that Moy sends have financed the construction of the *Hope*, the purchase of provisions, the suspended animation system, the fuel, and the weaponry.

And none of it came cheap.

Even so, there's a few credits left over...

Friga has declared that what's left is an "emergency fund" for unexpected contingencies.

Credits are credits, from Betelgeuse to Aldebaran, and if no nice xenoids turn up, disposed to keeping them concealed for three years and three days...

It's good to have some reserves.

The key thing is that, along with money, Moy constantly sends messages along the lines of "Come right away" and "I need you here" and "I'm so lonely" and "Just get here, whatever it costs."

Jowe doesn't tell them whether Moy knows that, like anyone ever sentenced to Body Spares, he'll never be given permission to leave Earth legally.

But Friga and Adam are sure that Moy realizes his money is helping Jowe get back to him the only way he can.

By leaving Earth's atmosphere and the solar system illegally.

Friga and Adam are also sure that this Moy will intercede on Jowe's behalf once he's far from Earth.

And on their behalf, too, while he's at it.

Which is why they've taken on the greater part of the hard work.

Because, Jowe might be the one who came up with the idea of the Voyage, but he hasn't done much to make it a concrete reality.

You might say, all he's done has been to add a couple of stylish touches to the *Hope*.

And lately, nothing at all.

Because, while Friga and Adam are sweating away, rechecking things that have already been checked a thousand times and gathering provisions and tools for every eventuality, Jowe just wanders about idly, staring at the sky.

And his dead eyes only light up with a sparkle when they mention how close it is to the day of departure.

The Day of Departure

Lift-off has been cleverly scheduled for Sunday night.

There's always plenty of weekend traffic, and the exhausted air traffic controllers can hardly wait for the relative calm of Monday.

The morning before D-Day, H-Hour, each of the three crewmembers of the *Hope* wants to be alone.

Adam stays onboard the *Hope*.

His child, his creature. . . the best piece of work he's ever done.

He proudly runs his hand over its patched plastisteel armor and its heterodox control panel.

He daydreams of a future when he will design and manufacture prototypes of high-velocity ships for some xenoid corporation. . .

Every now and then he looks outside the hangar that hides the *Hope* from prying eyes and catches a glimpse of Jowe, walking along the horizon.

The hangar is just a large shed on a small island in Hudson Bay.

In the middle of a bunch of buildings, which thirty years ago formed a town, which grew up around a chemical plant.

Later the xenoids shut the plant down because of the pollution, and the town died.

There's not a soul for miles around.

Not a human soul, that is.

There are swarms of gulls and rats building nests and romping in the empty buildings and tall chimneys of the dead plant, which will probably soon be demolished.

The sea roars and breaks against the beach, which is as unspoiled as if man had never existed on the face of the Earth.

Jowe is wandering down the line of surf, skipping stones across the water and shouting words that Adam can't make out, between the wind and the distance.

Could be anger. Or frustration. Or hope.

Or all of it together.

As evening falls, Jowe comes back, silent, unsmiling.

Almost voiceless.

Adam shrugs: little as he normally talks, there's not much difference. . .

When it's two hours before lift-off and Friga hasn't shown up yet, the men start to worry.

One hour to lift-off, Adam, chain-smoking one cigarette after another, mutters that if they have to leave without her. . .

Jowe looks at him without a word; they both know they'll wait.

Half an hour before time's up, Friga returns.

She is limping, her clothing in tatters.

Bruised bump over one eye, her lip split, a black eye, and red, swollen knuckles.

In the soot covering her face there are traces of tears.

But she smiles almost beatifically.

They don't ask whether she's coming back from a fight or from making love.

They know that for Friga, there's not much difference.

But they both suspect that her daughter must have something to do with that happy smile.

And no doubt with the tears as well.

It must be hard to leave your family behind, no matter how little you care about them...

Of course, neither of them says any of this.

Sometimes Friga can be very... sensitive.

Nervous, they take the *Hope* from the hangar and start filling the enormous pear of the balloon disguise.

Fifteen minutes later, when everything is ready, Adam and Friga board.

Jowe, not caring whether they see him, kneels down, kisses the sandy Earth of the island, and collects a little in a small bag, which he stuffs into his pocket.

Then he starts the time fuse that will release the balloon from its moorings, and he too boards.

Now they can lift off.

Lift-off

After a tense half-minute, the fuse works perfectly.

The anchor ties break and the balloon rises at a dizzying speed.

Inside, the three fugitives shout for joy, leaping and hugging.

Friga gives thanks to God.

To any god, nobody cares which.

They're on their way.

The altimeter reads 1, 2, 5, 10, 15, 20, 30, 35 kilometers, and Adam, listening so closely to his headphones that sometimes he gets confused by the sound of his heart beating, hears no alarms going off in the ether.

Everything's going fine.

Though on two occasions they freeze when the *bleep, bleep* of the radar receiver indicates that they are being tracked by a terrestrial radar.

At an altitude of forty-five kilometers, Friga fires the *Hope*'s plasma reactors.

The exhaust, burning at hundreds of degrees, sets the skin of the balloon ablaze and rips through it.

Well-placed explosive charges detonate and finish opening the balloon like the peel of a squashed banana.

Weather balloons normally use hydrogen for lift, since it is cheap and effective.

The ballon disguising the *Hope* used helium.

It is slightly less effective—and much more expensive.

But if they had used hydrogen, the explosion when the engines switched on could have destroyed the *Hope* before they reached orbit.

Adam had thought of that.

As expected, when the balloon rips open, they go into a spiraling fall.

They lose altitude and free themselves from the rest of the balloon's skin.

Finally, the *Hope*'s sturdy delta wings find support in the thin upper atmosphere, and the spiral turns into a dive.

At an increasing speed, but completely under control.

Acceleration forces grow: two *g*, three *g*.

Friga counts to ten, lowers the ailerons, and gives full power to the reactors.

More cheers when the *Hope* describes an elegant curve upward.

Just exclamations; g-forces prevent the woman and the two men from getting out of their overstuffed hydraulic armchairs.

Feeling his jowls down around his waist, Adam thinks how much easier it would have been if they had artificial gravity and an antigrav propulsion unit, like a real Tornado class...

Only the xenoids make them, and their importation to Earth is too tightly controlled...

So it was always mere speculation.

Over the headphones of all three comes a question from a controller at some astroport:

"Unidentified Tornado-class shuttle, Gander Astroport here. Attention: you have entered the Regulus corridor... Your trajectory is odd... Are you having trouble? Please identify yourself."

Adam gulps: the moment of truth is here.

The Moment of Truth

Gander lies within the realm of possibility, though Toronto had seemed more likely, given the latitude.

Trying to keep his voice from being overly distorted by the five *g* of inertial lift into orbit, Adam gives the answer they had previously agreed upon:

"Gander, Tornado LZ-35 from Wellington here. Have jet stream and problems with ailerons. Collision with weather balloon, destruction likely. Requesting guide beam to the point of embarkation for Regulus and free corridor."

For an instant there is no response.

Just the crackle of static filling the cabin.

The fugitives look at each other, going pale.

Is everything lost?

So soon?

Friga fiddles with the triggers of the ship's weaponry and nervously watches the radar screen, as if expecting to see a suborbital patrol ship appear at any moment.

At least she'll make them pay a high price for her life.

Jowe turns pale but doesn't move a muscle.

Adam sweats; could he have made some mistake?

He's sure he hasn't: it's very unlikely that the controller would check up on them with Wellington, New Zealand, on the other side of the planet, and who would be crazy enough to enter an orbital corridor if everything wasn't one hundred percent in order?. . .

"Tornado LZ-35, Gander here. Guide beam activated. The corridor is free. We detect the falling remnants of the balloon. You'll have to be more careful! Have your ship checked over at the point of embarkation, and give my regards to Regulus."

The road is clear.

Incredulous but relieved, Friga releases the triggers with a sigh and focuses once more on the controls of the *Hope*.

For now, the danger is past.

Or so it seems. . .

Just as they reach escape velocity, all the homemade welds on the *Hope* begin to vibrate.

It seems like the vehicle will be torn to pieces at any moment.

Friga turns to look at the shipbuilder questioningly.

"It'll hold up, I swear it will!" Adam shouts, as terrified as the pilot but trying to fill her with confidence.

Jowe is unfazed.

Finally the display shows 11.2 kilometers per second, and Friga turns off the plasma reactors to let them rest and cool off.

Their supply of hydrogen is eighty-five percent spent.

But they're already in hyperbolic escape orbit.

Every second takes them farther and farther from Earth.

A minute passes.

On the radar screen, the great echo marking the point of embarkation for Regulus, where hyperships wait for their passengers to arrive on shuttles to take them to that distant star, is being left behind.

But another echo, much smaller and faster, is growing closer.

It isn't coming from the atmosphere of Earth.

It's coming from another orbit.

A patrol ship.

Friga swears and turns on the hydrogen collector field to reactivate the reactors.

Jowe calmly calculates the relative trajectories and velocities of both space vehicles.

Adam complains about his bad luck: did they have to get detected so quickly?

Friga reminds him that only the weak believe in luck.

The invisible magnetic maw of the collector field which stretches out before the *Hope* traps the hydrogen atoms floating in space at a rate of one or two per cubic meter.

The remaining fifteen percent of hydrogen in the tanks would be enough to reignite and heat the reactors, but not much more.

The collector field becomes more effective as their speed grows: twenty seconds later, it has already stabilized the rate of supply to the engines.

The ship is capturing and consuming hydrogen at the same rate.

Jowe breaks his silence to state hoarsely that the patrol ship is gaining on them.

Adam, hysterical, tells him the Planetary Security guys have antigravity-based inertial engines, which don't need an external source of fuel and don't have to be warmed up. . . but even so, they won't get caught, because they're way ahead.

Jowe disagrees.

According to his calculations, the patrol ship is following a flaw-less interception orbit: it will reach firing range before the *Hope* has entered far enough inside the Escape Tunnel to activate the hyper-engine and get it to work.

And that will be more or less within an hour.

Adam blows up and says that as far as he's concerned, Jowe can go to hell right now: all he has to do is open the airlock, enter it, and jump into space, if he's so scared.

Friga quiets them with her booming voice, reminding them that it's just a patrol ship and that the *Hope* is armed and armored...

She fiddles with the triggers again.

The patrol ship must have positively ID'd them as a fugitive ship by now: it is keeping complete radio silence while continuing to ap-proach.

Just in case, Adam throws up a curtain of interference to keep their pursuer from asking other Planetary Security ships for help.

Manipulating the controls with the dexterity of a pianist, Friga corrects the *Hope's* course with plasma jets at full blast.

At ever-increasing velocity, the ship leaves the plane of the ecliptic; in a couple of hours it will be far enough away for hyperspace travel.

If the patrol ship doesn't destroy it first.

It hasn't even asked them to surrender.

Not that they'd surrender without a struggle.

A dogfight is inevitable.

The Dogfight

The hour passes. Friga, impatient, burns with a desire to open fire.

Despite the *Hope's* significant initial advantage, the faster-moving Planetary Security ship has significantly closed the gap between them.

Jowe reminds Friga that the masers onboard the *Hope* have a range of one or two kilometers farther than the particle projectile cannons that patrol ships carry.

But on the other hand, they'll need nearly half a minute to recharge after each shot, compared with just ten seconds for the enemy's weapon.

Adam nods and looks expressionlessly at their pilot-leader.

Friga smiles: at least she'll have the advantages of surprise and taking the first shot, and she intends to make the most of them.

Besides, she has a few tricks and secrets up her sleeve. . .

Xenoids may have built the patrol ships, but that doesn't mean their design is perfect. . .

She doesn't aim at the Planetary Security ship's ultra-armored cabin or at its super-protected inertial engine, but at the gun-ports from which its terrible weapons emerge.

When the distance-to-target indicator reaches the set point, she squeezes the triggers on her masers with determination.

Then immediately flicks off the engines.

They stop accelerating, and in the sudden weightlessness they all float, restrained only by their seat straps, and they are unable to observe the effect of their shots on the other ship.

"Turn the engines on! Why did you do that?" Adam shrieks hysterically.

On the radar screen, the enemy looks completely unharmed.

"Turning off the reactors is logical; it saves power for our shields, and changing our rate of acceleration should make it harder for them to calculate our position," Jowe replies. "Fasten your seatbelt, Adam. . ."

Eight seconds after carrying out its attack, the *Hope* becomes the target of the charged-particle beam fired by the patrol ship.

On radar, the shot looks like a stream of bright dots linking the two ships for nearly a whole second.

In spite of the force field network that serves as their shield, the impact is right on target—and disastrous for the *Hope*.

The homemade ship's plastishield plates rip from stem to stern, structural reinforcements shatter, the hydrogen tanks (fortunately almost empty now) explode and send huge flames into the void.

The worst of all is that the force field inexplicably ceases to function.

Adam, terrified, bangs away desperately at the system control keyboard, trying to reactivate it.

Without success. . .

"One more like that and the voyage is over," says Jowe, strangely calm.

Friga says nothing, just watches as her weapons recharge: if she has to die, she'll go down fighting.

Apparently, her stratagem didn't work. . .

The adversary will take its second and final shot before the *Hope* can respond.

And with no force shield, it will destroy them for sure.

Time's almost up: seven seconds, eight, nine, now. . .

The woman and the men close their eyes. . .

Three seconds later, they're still alive.

Apparently, the enemy couldn't fire. . .

On the radar screen, the patrol ship is taking evasive action.

It seems to be surrounded by myriads of blinking bright dots.

Friga gives a savage war cry and opens fire again.

"I knew it!" she roars, laughing. "If I could just damage the insulation on their particle projection cannon, their first shot would be their last! Take that, Planetary Security!"

The two men realize that their pursuer did fire.

The bright dots are its "cannon balls": charged particles.

They couldn't be projected as intended because Friga's shot had shortcircuited their weapon.

And, attracted by the static electricity of the patrol ship's own hull, they are gathering around it, while its force shield prevents them from adhering.

The second shot by the *Hope's* masers has no visible effect.

All the same, the enemy retreats, prudently.

There are no other patrol ships on radar.

With no more pursuers to evade, no need for haste, Friga does not turn the reactors back on.

They follow their inertial trajectory to the Escape Tunnel.

The three would-be hyperspace travelers, with infinity and eternity before them, release themselves from their seats and play like little kids in the weightlessness.

They'll repair the damage caused by the patrol ship's attack later.

For now, they have to release some tension.

To forget, at least for a few moments, that compared with what comes next, everything they've done so far is just that: child's play.

Their personal skill and the precautions they've taken may have made all the difference so far, but everything will depend on sheer luck when they enter the Russian roulette of hyperspace.

And, even more so, when they exit it. . .

Hyperspace

They're back in their overstuffed armchairs, panting.

On the radar, far away, two dots, getting closer.

Friga and Adam are exhausted from their extravehicular activity, in spacesuits as homemade as the rest of the ship.

Muscles that they were never aware of before ache horribly now after two hours spent repairing the damage from the dogfight.

They're paying the price for their inexperience, and they know it.

But how could they have practiced moving in space without antigrav simulators or costly tanks?

In any case, they're hoping they won't have to do it again.

Very soon, the *Hope*, more patched-up than ever, will be activating one of its two "disposable" hyperengines.

The three of them, now free—almost—smile despite their worries: the two distant dots on the radar are almost certainly two more patrol ships on their way here.

But they'll be very far from the solar system before any of the Planetary Security ships can get close enough.

"For freedom," Frida says solemnly, turning on the hyperengine.

Though they've heard so much about the sensation of going into hyperspace transit, the three are overwhelmed by it.

"It's like they're turning me inside out," thinks Friga, not very good with images. "As if I had my insides outside and my outsides inside."

"As if all the molecules in my body were iron filings arranged around a magnet. . . and suddenly they switched the polarity of the magnetic field," Adam speculates.

Jowe's mind is blank.

For him, it's just an agonizing new experience.

But nothing as bad as his memories.

The spatio-temporal contraction lasts a thousand years or just one long second.

Then the homemade hyperengine conks out and they return to three-dimensional space.

They have no idea where.

In any case, not very far.

To keep from putting them at risk (and also limited by the cramped space onboard the *Hope*), Adam didn't make either of the twin hyperengines very powerful.

Wherever they are, it can't be more than fifty light-years from Earth.

Very nervous, they check the readings on the computer connected to the instruments.

After noting the brightest stars and comparing them with the parallax and distance readings saved in its memory, the computer positively identifies the ship's position.

Shouts of joy.

Which die away quickly, as the holographic map looms up before their eyes.

Near the constellation of the Whale. . . but eight light-years from the nearest star, which, to be precise, is Tau Ceti.

"So close to paradise, without hitting it!" Adam whines, banging furiously on a bulkhead.

"There's still anabiosis," says their leader, trying to stay level-headed. "It's just eight light-years. At the highest acceleration rate we can squeeze from the engines, if no asteroids get in the way we'll get to Tau Ceti within. . ."—she makes a very rough calculation—"a century and a half. Sorry about Moy, Jowe, but there's no other way out. We ought to save the other hyperengine as a last resort. Besides, it's dangerous; we might end up even farther away. . ."

Adam starts to let out a scream of dismay, and Friga silences him by covering his mouth with her enormous hand.

Jowe takes one quick glance at the holographic map.

"A century and a half. . ." he sighs. "Poor Moy. . . Maybe things will have improved some by the time we arrive. There's nothing else to discuss; let's head to the freezers. It'll be anabiosis, then."

Anabiosis

A first-rate hypership carries suspended animation freezers only as a last resort.

Same way the ships sailing the oceans in olden times used to carry lifeboats or life-rafts.

Their freezers are high-tech: comfortable, safe, individual.

So that, if something unfortunately goes wrong and a traveler dies, the others won't suffer the same fate.

The *Hope* has three freezers that are actually one divided into three compartments.

Instead of three independent biological monitoring systems, it only has three interconnected subroutines.

There wasn't enough money or space or time for more.

On the other hand, since the ship would only be used for one voyage, Adam was able to adapt each compartment to the physical parameters of its potential occupant.

One is long and wide, for Friga.

Another, long and narrow, for himself.

The third, the smallest, is for Jowe.

Their leader is the first to take her clothes off, climb into her nook, and put on her biosensors.

But she waits until the others follow her lead before injecting herself with the mixture of antifreeze and metabolism-inhibitor drugs.

Adam programs the automatic controls of the *Hope* to bring them out of their frozen sleep as soon as the shining lights of Tau Ceti are close enough.

And to steer them prudently away from any dangerous asteroids.

As soon as all three are in their "coffins," cautious Friga watches to see that both men have stuck in their syringes before she does.

When Adam feels the drowsiness and the cold running through his veins, he activates the second phase.

The cryogel comes bubbling into their coffins.

The drowsiness of cold is overtaking them. . .

The conjunction of the low-temperature colloid, the antifreeze, and the metabolic inhibitors will reduce them to unconsciousness and keep their vital functions virtually suspended while the *Hope* slowly consumes light-minutes, light-days, and finally whole light-years.

Theoretically. . .

Friga is the first to realize that something's gone wrong.

In spite of the drug in her veins, the cold stabs at her with icy needles that will not let her lapse into unconsciousness.

A few seconds later, the discomfort is turning into pain.

Pain, pain...

Her entire body is cold, but it burns.

And her still-active lungs need air.

Air that they can't get, with her whole body submerged in cryogel.

Air, air...

Friga gasps desperately, and a huge gulp of the frozen substance enters her mouth, her stomach, and her lungs.

It's as bitter as death...

The drug is jumbling her thoughts: death?

She's drowning!

And she has to live!

Panic overcomes her: she twists, struggles, swallows more gulps of the repulsive, frozen mixture that envelops her in place of the life-saving air she needs.

Her lungs ache and terror commands her to flee.

Flee, out, into the air, whatever the cost.

Calm down, there's a way out...

Her fingers feel around for the latch to open the lid.

The latch won't open.

Adam outdid himself on the security system: cryogel is very expensive, and the coffins are designed so that they can't be opened until the pumps have extracted the last drop of frozen colloid from them.

Not even from the inside...

And there's no command for activating the pumps before the deadline set on the computer expires.

Friga, overwhelmed by claustrophobia, beats furiously against the coffin's transparent steel-glass housing.

As if through a veil of terror, she feels the banging of the two dying men who are also struggling to escape.

The steel-glass in the lid is a very resistant material.

A coffin.

Buried alive, dead, dead. . .

No!

The huge muscles of the woman with a man's strength strain until their fibers are at the breaking point.

And they produce a miracle.

The steel-glass in the lid is a very resistant material. . . much more resistant than the synplast joints around the rim of the freezer.

The entire lid comes off, cryogel goes flying, and Friga, half-suffocated, rolls onto the floor, her whole body aching and half-frozen.

But alive!

She coughs, expelling the bitter colloid from her lungs.

She *breathes*. . . and runs to help the others.

Swaying from the shock of her near asphyxiation, the drug-induced drowsiness clouding her mental processes, she only manages to pick up a hydraulic wrench. . . and break the two men's freezer lids.

Adam is already still, his mouth and eyes open.

The surprise on his face is like the look of a fish out of water.

Jowe is struggling, with the cold obstinacy of instinct, but with less and less strength.

When he gets out, he and Friga, half-fainting, try clumsily and desperately to revive their "super-handyman."

They know that their lives depend on his skill. . .

Cardiac massage, electric defibrillator, the same neurostimulant that they both injected into themselves with trembling fingers to erase the stupefaction brought on by the metabolic inhibitors.

Nothing works.

Adam has drowned, and he stays dead.

Worn out by their futile struggle, naked, sticky with cryogel, covered with bruises, the surviving man and woman fall asleep, weeping and splashing over the lanky cadaver.

They have no strength for more.

Much less to face the crisis.

The Crisis

Six hours later, encased in his improvised shroud, what had been Adam goes tumbling off through the hatch.

Friga and Jowe watch it go, silently.

There's nothing to be said. . .

Their provisions will last two weeks.

They scrape off the cryogel, already half solidified, clean the grubby deck, check the instruments.

For three days they try to repair the suspended animation system.

The broken lids on the freezer are the easy part. . .

But meticulous Jowe discovers, and shows to Friga, the real problem.

The patrol ship's attack damaged the Freon tubing, and some of the refrigerant leaked.

The cryogel never cooled down to the temperature (near absolute zero) necessary for bringing about anabiosis.

They could fix the tubing, but they have no stores of Freon.

Or of cryogel.

Maybe Adam could have rigged something up. . .

Adam is dead.

Friga blasts her bad luck, curses God and the Virgin and all the saints, asks Satan and Moloch and Zeus, anybody, for help, breaks things.

Jowe, quiet, watches her with dead eyes.

When the woman lets her fury abate from sheer weariness, Jowe touches her on the shoulder and points to the controls of the one remaining hyperengine.

Friga looks at him furiously, as if she'd like to squash him, but gives an almost imperceptible nod.

They both know that they're down to their last resort now.

The Last Resort

Friga's fingers tremble above the activation switch for the hyper-engine.

Under her breath she chants a meaningless prayer in which she asks all the gods to watch over her, and glances at Jowe from the corner of her eye.

Jowe's lips aren't moving.

His eyes, as dead as ever.

She switches on the hyperengine.

This second time, the strange sensations of spatio-temporal contraction no longer surprise the two survivors of the *Hope*.

Now they can almost wallow in the vertigo and disorientation of the hyperspace transit.

After an indeterminate time, the second and last engine also quits, and three-dimensional space once more receives the *Hope*.

Friga and Jowe repress any possible rejoicing (after all, they're still alive!) as they wait for the onboard computer to identify their new position.

As the data begin to form a holographic image, Friga breathes easier.

It looks like they're in luck.

A star with several planets that look very promising. . . And the *Hope* is almost inside the system.

It will only take a few hours to reach any of these planets with the plasma reactors.

Friga doesn't know much about astronomy.

Jowe, a little more.

That is why he grows pale as the data continue appearing and forming the map.

That G-type main-sequence star and the constellations surrounding it are familiar to him. . .

Too familiar.

Friga, who's feeling safe now, can't understand why her companion's face keeps growing longer and longer.

Until the two dots appear on the radar, and the authoritarian voice rings in her headphones:

"Unidentified ship, Planetary Security patrol ship VV.98 here. Prepare for boarding. Offer no resistance or you will be destroyed."

Then the strong woman understands, and she howls, punching the control panel.

"Nooo. . .! Not the rebound effect! It's not fair!"

It's Not Fair

Friga has calmed down. . . seemingly.

She drums her fingers against the control panel, and now and then strokes the minimachine gun and the vibroblade she keeps hidden in her clothing.

Jowe stares into the infinite, saying nothing.

Why bother?

In her paroxysm of fury, Friga already said it all.

"We can't possibly have such bad luck! As vast as the cosmos is, coming right back here! Adam only mentioned the rebound effect as a curiosity! Something that happens one time out of ten thousand!"

Jowe stares at the cosmos, and nobody could know what he's thinking.

Probably laughing about the ironic fate that brought them so close to freedom, only to deal them this masterstroke now.

Or thinking about how frustrated his friend Moy will be, waiting for him in Ningando.

Or about the long years awaiting him and Friga in Body Spares when they're sentenced for attempted unlawful departure from the planet.

But he doesn't say anything.

Just like Friga, when the first patrol ship boards the *Hope*, he passively, meekly lets himself be led away by Planetary Security agents.

They don't even handcuff them.

Why bother?

In space, there's nowhere to run.

Like her, he stares out the porthole at the battered and abandoned homemade ship, watching it shrink as the patrol ship pulls away under the power of its inertial engine.

When the explosive charges that the agents placed on their ship before abandoning it blow the *Hope* to pieces, Jowe keeps on watching the bits, unspeaking.

From his right eye, a single tear falls.

Friga doesn't waste her energy on tears.

She takes advantage of the moment of the explosion to whip out her weapons, then quickly and deftly elbows aside both agents restraining her.

Now she's free.

Free

Frida is the sort of woman who never surrenders.

She knew that the damaged *Hope* couldn't escape, and it couldn't fight two patrol ships at once while keeping her alive.

That's the only reason she let them take her away.

Patrol ship versus patrol ship is a more even match.

And she's already aboard one of them...

She only has to get rid of three crewmembers.

Her against three: child's play.

She's fought against worst odds.

Onboard a patrol ship, there's even artificial gravity, like being on Earth.

That makes things easier.

Friga has never been beaten in hand-to-hand combat.

She machine-guns the farthest one in the belly.

Sticks the vibroblade into another one's chest before he can finish drawing his gun.

Struck by the third, she grips his neck in a stranglehold with her powerful arm, and squeezes, and squeezes, at the same time smashing his face with her knee.

Three seconds later, the Planetary Security guy is still struggling, though he should be strangled already and his neck should be broken.

Friga wonders why his blood isn't spilling out and staining the floor like it should.

This agent has a strong neck. . .

And where's Jowe?

Why isn't he helping out?

That's when she feels the blow to the back of her head.

Surprised and hurting, she turns around just in time to catch the next pistol-whip right in the face.

She falls, letting go of her captive, unable to understand how someone with a vibroblade plunged hilt-deep in his chest can strike with such force.

She's about to get up, but the agent with his belly blasted open by machine-gun fire steps on her fingers and then kicks her.

Friga comprehends two things before fainting.

The first comes from the gleam of metal under the pseudoguts of the supposed Planetary Security agent.

That he isn't a human being, but a huborg.

Just like the other two.

At least she wasn't defeated by humans. . .

The second thing, as she wanders into the fog of unconsciousness, comes to her when she looks out through a porthole and identifies what she sees floating off into the vastness of space.

If she weren't so tired. . . if the darkness weren't so welcoming. . . she'd laugh uproariously.

Because now she knows where Jowe is.

Because, in spite of it all, in a way he's made it.

He'll never be sent back to Body Spares.

Now his destination is the infinite.

No spacesuit, frozen, a corpse.

But free.

At last, once and for all, completely *free*.

October 3, 1998

Somewhere, Tomorrow. . .

Once, Earth was brimming with futurologists.

Once, when Contact was just a nightmare to be found in the books of a few pessimistic science fiction writers. . .

Back then, futurologists seemed to have a monopoly on optimism. It wasn't a fact that any point in the past was always better. The future would always be brighter, more human, richer, more ecological, more. . .

Or, otherwise, it would simply not be.

The most pessimistic of these latter-day augurs only went so far as to imagine the possibility that *Homo sapiens*, with their nuclear weapons (or their biological weapons, or their waste—there were several apocalypses to choose from), would destroy their civilization. And maybe the planet as a whole, while they were at it, but how many actors care what happens on stage after they exit the scene?

In any case, the decision about the future depended entirely on man. The choices seemed very limited: either rational development at a dizzying pace, or suicide.

But the xenoids showed up, and apparently they didn't know about futurology and didn't care. At least, not human futurology.

Following the xenoids' Ultimatum, the augurs lost their monopoly on the future. So did the rest of the human race.

All that *Homo sapiens* had left was the present, like a bone thrown to a dog to gnaw on after its master has gorged on all the meat.

No more "predictions of the world fifty years from now." Or ten years. . . or even tomorrow.

Every morning, every human wakes up in fear and hope, discovering, to his dismay but also relief, that he is still there. It was no nightmare. The xenoids exist, and they're the masters. And nobody knows what they'll decide tomorrow.

Social workers, Body Spares, erasing the memories of humans who travel off Earth, the Auyar huborgs taking the place of fallible humans in Planetary Security, mass-produced mestizos, Earth's history and ecology sold wholesale...

Nobody could have imagined it before.

Nobody knows what will come next.

Even the descendants of those pessimistic science fiction writers have stopped imagining and writing, overwhelmed by the dizzying madness of reality.

But just as a man condemned to death knows that no pardon will come, everybody knows that this situation is just a strange interregnum, that it can't last long.

And everybody is scared; if it's hard now, what will it be like later?

Better the frying pan you know than the fire you don't...

Some visionaries try desperately to find a way out.

Earth discovering some new form of superultralight propulsion and abandoning the solar system and the galaxy, getting far away from the xenoid vultures who gnaw our livers every night, only for us to have them grow back the next day.

Earth discovering the ultimate weapon and threatening the galaxy with annihilation if they don't let us emerge from underdevelopment once and for all.

Earth discovering the ultimate drug to stop death and aging, and giving it to the galaxy in exchange for being allowed to have our own, self-determined future.

But the scientist-serfs toiling away in their laboratory-slave barracks know all too well that science won't be the solution. No matter what gets invented, there aren't enough resources to deploy it on a large enough scale to compete with the xenoids.

Others speak of human dignity and propose mass suicide for Earth. Better not to be than to be slaves.

But psychologists know all too well that life and the instinct for self-preservation are too strong. Much stronger than pride and despair... The entire Earth will not become a new Numantia or a new Sagunto. Better slaves of the xenoid Romans than dead...

Others, even more divorced from reality, dream of the galactic act of altruism that will at some future date give this terrestrial colony its freedom to develop. As England so graciously did for India at the end of World War II.

They forget that Queen Elizabeth II only sent her last viceroy, Lord Louis Mountbatten, to give the subcontinent its independence when she could no longer control it. When neither the Englishmen nor their sepoys could continue to lord over millions of people.

So long as the xenoid Englishmen and their Planetary Tourism Agency sepoys control Earth, there will be no independence. Nobody gives up the goose that lays the golden eggs until he's forced to.

Some put their faith in time, which can wear away stone, so that decadence may capture the exhausted old xenoid races and make their empire fall, much as Rome collapsed.

Historians disagree: no empire falls on its own, if it has no shrieking barbarians hammering on the doors of its city walls. Spartacus' rebellion was heroic, but it failed...

Others believe in even more illogical and unlikely things. In the Second Coming of Christ (or of Muhammad, or of Buddha, or of Joseph Smith...) as a Lion, not a Lamb, to drive out the demonic non-human races from the world of His children.

Or that God, or Something Cosmic and Indefinable called (for lack of a better name) "homeostatic justice," will inevitably punish the xenoids' wickedness and highhandedness with stellar cataclysms and devastating plagues, compared with which the magenta illness of Colossa will seem like a minor rash.

But even the most orthodox believers are starting to believe that God, if He does exist, might not be on the humans' side...

Other trust that a mighty and overpowering race will appear from beyond the galaxy, enslaving all the Milky Way and putting the masters and servants of today at the same level...

Many sects hold and secret ideas and theories and indulge in endless debates about the possible futures of Earth and the galaxy. Nobody lifts a finger to bring about the futures they say they believe in.

Of course, it's not all talk and no action...

The famously irredentist Xenophobe Union for Earthling Liberation does act. Though their motto, "It matters not if a hundred humans die, so long as one single xenoid dies or leaves," seemingly ignores the fact that there are many more xenoids than there are humans, their bombs and attacks at least annoy the planet's extraterrestrial masters.

The bad part is that the Union, like many pre-Contact terrorist organizations, has nothing resembling a liberation strategy. Just tactics, and not very brilliant ones at that. Nearly a hundred humans do die for every xenoid... Planetary Security is much more efficient.

They have no plan for taking the power now held by the Planetary Tourism Agency, nor would they know how to keep it... Following the ideas of Bakunin and Nechayev, they just keep trying over and over again to jab their bee stings into the monstrous oppressor's tough hide. And, like bees, they often die trying. And the monster scratches at the stings, smiles, and keeps on going.

The Xenophobe Union for Earthling Liberation has even been accused many times of playing into the xenoids' hands, serving only as an outlet for human aggression and frustration. Draining to death the forces that should be organizing to struggle for life...

The unidentified leaders of the Union haven't even gone to the trouble of refuting these charges.

Many think they wouldn't be able to...

Life goes on, the years go by, the present seems like it will last forever and always be the same in spite of all the changes that give the impression that Earth is moving into the future.

Ordinary humans, the famous "moral majority," are tired of impossible futures even before they get here.

The question remains: What fate awaits a race that has lost faith in the future, idolizes the past, and puts up with the present?

It seems the futurologists were wrong, and in reality, for Earth, everything before Contact was better.

Homo sapiens, forever trapped in a present that doesn't belong to them and they don't determine, can only aspire to one thing: that the hypothetical and frightful future will never arrive. That the present will last forever.

Fearing that, as things stand, any change can only be for the worse. . .

The Platinum Card

He appeared in my life on a Tuesday in August, in the middle of the afternoon. One of those summer days when heat is like a sticky spider's web that you can't get off you.

The stifling air above the asphalt played at looking like water or a mirror in the distance. All Barrio 13 looked lethargic. I had left my Abuela sunk in her alcoholic dreams after her third bottle of Seven Rats vodka, and had gone down to hang out with my gang.

They had just finished blowing up a fire hydrant with a smidge of plastic explosives that Dingo picked up off the street after the latest Triad robbery. All us kids were having a great time goofing around in the gush of water that filled half the street. More kids than ever. Even a few sullen adults decided to join in: it was so hot, and there aren't any air conditioners or swimming pools in Barrio 13. They were almost smiling as they came out of the water, looking ten years younger.

We were having even more fun because we knew it wouldn't last. Less than half an hour later the buglickers from Planetary Security showed up with the repair crew. To run us off and look for whoever was responsible for the "sabotage" while the others were fixing the leak.

He showed up wrapped in a gray overcoat, trying not to draw attention. Sort of hard to do when you're ten feet tall and your reddish Colossaur armor is peeking out through the folds of your clothes. Really hard to do on Earth. Impossible here in New Cali, Barrio 13, where we can smell a xenoid ten light-years off, even if he's mounting a human "horse" from Body Spares. Which wasn't the case.

When Dingo saw that it was a Colossaur and that he was alone, he gave a signal and the triplets ran out to ask the visitor for "some credits, Your Excellency, please."

If he had been from any other race and not a native of Colossa, maybe we would have all ganged up on him. To beat him up and rob him, of course; what else could a xenoid wandering around alone in Barrio 13 expect?

But fifteen kids are no match for one of those armored monsters, not even in the sort of dirty fight we all love. Better use cunning, not strength.

Bubo, Babo, and Bibe were the best beggars in the gang: they knew how to make genuine-looking wounds with printer ink and sandpaper. Their specialty: Colossaurs. They're always moved by what they think are magenta disease sores, and their guilt complex makes them more generous. Since the virus is endemic among them, and they were the ones who brought it to this planet. . .

How come I wasn't suspicious of him from the start? He didn't try to shoo the triplets away for fear of disease, like all the others of his race do. But he didn't give them a single credit, either. Very strange. . . And since everything strange is suspicious, it was very likely we would have tried stoning him right there. Just to frighten him so he'd run off. We couldn't have even tickled those armored plates—even rifle shots just bounce off of them.

Then, in that hoarse voice they all have, he said, "Kids, I'm looking for Leilah, Friga's daughter. They said she lives around here. . ."

That's when we stopped playing and gathered around him, feeling surprised and keeping quiet but trying not to look too interested. The first thing you learn on the street is that giving away your emotions is always a bad move.

Some of the guys in the gang had joined so recently they only knew me by my street name, Liya. The ones who did know me stared out of the corners of their eyes. Like they were inspecting me, checking to see how much I might be worth, for that xenoid to show so much interest in me, how much woman there was in the nine-year-old girl I was. And it wasn't much at all. I pretended I didn't notice them sizing me up.

Even if I hadn't seen Dingo make a sign, I'm not such an idiot I would have identified myself just like that to the first xenoid who came around looking for me. In Barrio 13, when they come from the outside looking for you, it's hardly ever for anything good.

Of course, I had no way to know that this day and this Colossaur were going to change my life forever.

"Leilah. . . Sounds familiar," Dingo said grudgingly, looking down at the ground.

"Do you guys know her?" the Colossaur insisted.

"Maybe yeah, maybe no." Our gang leader sort of casually stuck his hand out palm-up, one of the few gestures that doesn't need any translation anywhere in the galaxy. Money always talks, same on Earth as on Colossa.

And moving so fast we could barely see it, the xenoid grabbed him around the waist with his huge three-fingered hand and hoisted him in the air. His tiny sunken eyes shined when he looked at him from close up, and though some of the guys picked up rocks, something told me Dingo wasn't in any real danger.

"I like that. . . Business sense from a young age," he told Dingo, nearly sticking his tongue into the short, bristly chestnut hair that gave him his street name. "You people will inherit the Earth. . . or what's left of it when we finish." He brought Dingo closer to his snout. Dingo wrinkled his nose: must have smelled bad.

"What's your name, future businessman?" asked the Colossaur.

"Jeremí. . . Dingo." Dingo was scared to death. But as the head of the gang he had to look just the opposite, or every snot-nosed brat would challenge him to a fight for the leadership. If he survived this one.

"Ah. Jeremías, and they call you Dingo?" The wide mouth filled with sharp teeth bent in a caricature of a smile. "Look, Jeremías, you look like an intelligent kid, and I'd love to have a nice long talk with you... but I don't have much time." He pointed at us with his other hand. "Which of them is Leilah? I'm not going to eat her, and I'm not from Planetary Security. I have some business that might concern her..."

"I could..." Dingo dared suggest, seeing a chance for the gang to maybe make a profit and trying to get back some of his authority, which had been placed in doubt.

"I'm sure you could, perfectly well... But she's the one I want," the Colossaur shook his head. "For, let's say... sentimental reasons."

"Leilah's still a virgin. I have an eleven-year-old sister who'd be cheaper for you," piped up Silk, who'd never exactly been subtle or had a sense of timing. He'd basically just admitted that I was there, the moron.

"Shut up, stupid!" I hissed, furious, and jumped him, trying to pull his cap down over his nose.

The part about my virginity was true... But it wasn't the sort of thing a girl was supposed to let a guy talk about in front of the whole gang. And it's not like it did Silk any good to go around saying it: the two of us were steady, and everybody knew it... So if I was still a virgin, it was mainly his fault. Ten years old and still not able to get up an erection that was worth the trouble. Aside from his baby face and his corn-silk hair, Silk was a perfect idiot. I don't know what I saw in him...

He resisted, of course, and we wrestled. He was stronger, but I was angrier, and I would've gotten him in the end. But before I could pull his cap all the way down to his neck, the Colossaur grabbed me with his other hand and picked me up to look me over.

I stuck out my tongue and put on my best Down syndrome face, cursing the moment I decided to start playing in the hydrant water. I'm normally so dirty that nobody notices my face... We call it "Barrio 13 makeup." It's very handy for keeping people from giving you a second glance, and keeping those Cetian pigs who're always hunting for little girls from carrying you off to one of their slave brothels.

My Abuela always told me that my coffee eyes and chocolate skin would be my downfall one of these days. And if this wasn't the day. . .

"Hello, Leilah," the monster said to me. He was trying desperately to sound polite.

"She's not Leilah!" the whole gang screamed together, even Dingo. "She's. . ."—and that's when they really gave me away, because some of them said "Liya," my street name, others "Mary Jane," which is like saying John Doe or Juan Pérez. That is, nobody.

I was done for.

"Ah, well. If she isn't Leilah, she'll do just as well." The Colossaur set Dingo down and gave him something. "Here you go, chief. . . For your trouble. You have half an hour to use it up. . . Then I'll report it missing and they'll close the account."

Dingo's eyes shone with greed when he realized it was a gold card. The bank only gives them to people who have more than a hundred thousand credits in their accounts. . . and not to all of them, either. I'd never seen one outside of a holodrama.

"But. . . she. . ." He pointed at me, insisting almost as a formality, but his impatient feet gave away his desire to run off with his fortune and forget about me. The dirty bastard. . .

I looked at him, sulking. Judas! I would have insulted him, but I wasn't sure I could say three words in a row without starting to cry. All that talk about group solidarity, all that "One for all and all for one," all that "us against the world," but he was selling me for a few credits, the rat! I was going to crack his skull with a rock, and the gang would be mine. . . if I got out of this.

For a second everything seemed to stand still.

"The buglickers!" Babo screamed, and fifteen kids ran off at top speed before the armored Planetary Security aerobus could land in the middle of the asphalt. For the first time in my life I was glad to see them. If that's how the gang was going to betray me, at least the Law wouldn't let me be kidnapped in my own neighborhood. Now this xenoid would know what's what. . . I only had to ask them for help, and. . .

I thought better of it and kept quiet.

My captor greeted my supposed saviors with a slight wave of his free hand and walked off holding me tight against his chest, like it was nothing. Sure. A xenoid, even if he's wearing a recently severed human head as a hat, will always be just fine, everything in order, for his lackeys the buglickers. When it comes down to it, they're the masters, the ones who pay their salaries. And we people in the Numbered Barrios are basically just human trash.

The Colossaur went striding off. Farther and farther from my street and Barrio 13. He seemed to know where he was going. . . and I didn't like that one bit, if you know what I mean. It isn't what you'd expect from a xenoid. They're supposed to get lost every couple of seconds in our urban labyrinths, and give us poor natives a chance to make a living. . .

Later on I would find out that he knew much more about the good and the bad of my planet than I did.

His carapace was so rough, it was scraping my knees. . . I couldn't hold back any longer, and the tears started to flow.

I was furious with myself, but I decided that if I was going to cry, I'd really sob my eyes out, so three seconds later I was bawling like a baby goat that just got weaned. If it didn't stop him from taking me off my turf, at least it should bother him a little. . . and that would give me a better chance to escape.

It worked. He suddenly set me down on my feet, though he kept his heavy hand draped, kind of casually, across my shoulder.

He told me, "Look, Leilah, I don't go around stealing little girls, and I'm not one of those gourmets that like the taste of human flesh. But since it looks like you won't come with me without making a fuss, I'll tell it to you straight. I came to Earth on. . . on vacation, and I need a clever, intelligent girl to help me. I know you won't be losing anything, because you've got nothing to lose. Even your alcoholic grandmother will come out of this with more vodka than she could drink in ten years. I'll pay you well, and you'll also get to travel all over your planet for free. And I promise, I'll never touch you. I know that sounds strange and that you don't believe me. . . That's good. I imagine that a naïve girl wouldn't have made it to your age. But you'll have to believe me. Because even if you don't, I'm very obstinate when I've made up my mind. . . and I'm not going to let you leave. Even if you cry louder," he commented when I took my bawling up a notch (what else could I do?). "But look, so you'll see that things won't be all that bad with me." He dug in his coat pocket and took out something that gleamed with a metallic sheen. "Give me your hand, Leilah. Please. . ."

I hesitated an instant. From the corner of my eye, I was only staring at the huge paw holding me by the shoulder.

If he'd been a Planetary Security agent, I would have bit off a couple of fingers (I have good teeth) and while he screamed and bled I would have lost sight of him forever.

But you'd only try biting a Colossaur on the hand if you wanted to save money on the dentist. It wouldn't do any good, anyway. You could lose all your teeth and he'd never notice.

Besides, this guy seemed so totally determined to find me wherever I was hiding. . .

Reluctantly, I finally stuck out my hand.

In Barrio 13, you learn fast to accept things the way they are. . . otherwise you never get a chance to learn anything else.

He took my fingers, pressed them against the shiny object, and then gave it to me.

I was stupefied.

It was a platinum credit card.

The kind banks give to people who have a million credits or more in their accounts. I had hardly even heard about them. I didn't know any human who had one.

It had to be a trick, or a mistake. . .

"It was a blank card, Leilah, but now that I've recorded your finger-prints on it, you're the only one who'll have access to that account," he explained, then snorted. "Now you can run away if you want to, and make me go through all the trouble of finding you again. Or you can come with me, nice and friendly, and enjoy my gift."

I stared and stared at the card. It looked genuine. Of course, since I'd never seen one before, I didn't have any basis for comparison.

I looked at the xenoid. The truth was, he'd been very friendly, given his position, my own, and the circumstances. . .

"I guess you must be thinking this might be a ploy," he grunted. "But you must see that if I wanted to rape you, eat you, or send you to a slave brothel, I wouldn't go to so much trouble with you. I wouldn't risk losing so much money. . ."

"I want to make sure this card is genuine," I said, trying to make my voice sound steady.

"Certainly, princess." He showed me his four rows of teeth. "Will you come with me? You know better than I do that there aren't any credit machines here in Barrio 13. . . There wouldn't be many custom-ers for them, I guess." He let go of my shoulder and held out his hand as if he expected me to take it.

I pretended not to notice, of course. I wasn't born yesterday, to let somebody walk me by the hand through the streets, and anyway I didn't want to seem too friendly. A girl has her dignity.

I rubbed my shoulder. They really are strong, those Colossaurs.

"Do you hand out credit cards to every kid you meet? Why were you looking for me? What's your name?" I fired off the three ques-tions one after the other, like a minimachine gun.

He presented me with his caricature of a smile.

"Sometimes. The one your little friend—Dingo, wasn't it?—took doesn't have much on it. A couple thousand. . . Anyway, it'll be a for-tune to him and the rest of your friends, don't you think?" He emphasized the word "friends" ironically, and my reaction was what you might expect.

"Those rats. . ." I muttered, remembering how they'd abandoned me.

"Your second question, I'd rather keep quiet about—for now," the xenoid went on. "But you'll find out later on, I promise. Someday. . . Let's say it was for reasons of. . . nostalgia. Not for you, of course; I've never seen you before in my life."

"For my mother?" I speculated, intrigued.

I only had one holovideo of her, and holonet recordings about her trials and sentences. And my Abuela didn't talk about her much to me, not even on the rare occasions she was sober. But knowing the kind of life she led, it wouldn't have surprised me at all if this xenoid had known her. Even intimately. . . If anybody could find my mother's huge muscles attractive, it would probably be a Colossaur male. And Friga didn't have an ugly face, to tell the truth. Abuela always said I was her living portrait.

"Could be," he said, mysteriously. "As for my name. . . I'm afraid you humans find it unpronounceable. But I had a. . . a great friend who called me Ettubrute. . ."

"I don't like it—too long," I said right away. "Can I call you Ettu? How long do I have to stay with you? Can I tell my Abuela?"

He grunted a few times, like a dog barking; apparently that's his race's idea of laughter.

"Do you always ask questions three at a time?" he said. "Sure. . . Ettu is fine. About how long, I guess a month should be enough. And you can call whoever you want. . . Liya. Come on." And he set off walking at his fast but heavy pace.

I let him get a few yards ahead before I followed. I didn't want him to think I was dying to go with him, either. A girl has her pride, and after being practically kidnapped she has to keep a certain. . . distance.

But he'd called me by my street name, the one I picked myself.

Adults never do that.

At least, not my Abuela. She always calls me Leilita and makes me feel like a baby, even though I'm nine years old.

Ettu seemed different. Like someone who'd take me seriously and forget about my stupid age. The idea of spending a month with him was starting to sound interesting, at least.

* * *

I went with him to his hotel. After the gold card and the platinum card, it didn't shock me to find him staying in the New Cali Galaxy itself. The doorman frowned when he saw me walk in, as you might have expected—and that was after I'd taken that fire-hydrant bath and was looking almost presentable. I bet he thought I was a little xenoid from some unknown race, not a nine-year-old girl.

At first I tried to act like I was used to all that superluxury. But I couldn't keep my jaw from dropping for more than three seconds. I was almost drooling in amazement, and I kept tripping over my own feet trying to look at everything while I walked.

There were six levels to the lobby, and the middle three floated in the air without any visible supports. Stable antigrav technology. So expensive, no other building in the city has it that I know of.

Cryogel waterfalls cooling the place down nicely.

Vending machines for drinks, drugs, every piece of junk that could have occurred to me. . . and lots I've never imagined.

Thousands of xenoid tourists entering, leaving, jabbering in a thousand dialects. Social workers and their disguised male counterparts swarmed all over, more or less brazenly approaching every visitor who came near.

The Planetary Security pigs in their dress uniforms looked almost friendly, almost trustworthy. . . but they kept their eyes peeled, and they didn't miss a trick.

I saw them incapacitate a young man with an elegant flick of the electroclub when he tried protesting the stingy sum a dolled-up Centaurian lady had paid him for his services. While he flopped down onto the carpeted floor, the buglickers greeted her slavishly, and she stepped unperturbed over his limp body. Flesh to be used and discarded, she must have been thinking. Earth was a good place...

Private aerobus drivers were whispering their prices, always lower than what the Planetary Tourism Agency charges. People selling fake folklore junk were displaying their merchandise mysteriously in the folds of their overcoats. None of them should have been there, in theory. But they all paid a percentage to the buglickers for their relative impunity.

You could find the whole tourist trap freak show of every street in the city there in that lobby, only more refined and more concentrated. Of the whole Earth, even.

Ettu passed right through that vile bedlam like an icebreaker through an polar sea. Xenoid or human, whoever didn't get out of the way of that determined hulk was shoved aside without a second glance. The basic etiquette of force.

He took me to the spa and handed me over to two experts who obviously owed their goddess-like bodies and doll-like faces to nanosurgery. All smiles, they toiled to scrub nine years of grime off me. The water, the gel, and the ultrasound were delicious, and I would even have enjoyed the hydromassage if it weren't for the fact that as soon as the Colossaur stepped out for a second, the sluts started asking me how I'd met him and who I was... with a hint of envy that I didn't like one bit. And I really hated the provocative way they suddenly started to caress me. Asking if I wanted rings on my nipples, an exotic hairdo for my pubis...

I don't know if they were pedophiles, lesbians, or just trying to get me to recognize their erotic skills so I'd convince Ettu to use them. . . But I decided a long time before that when I was ready to lose my virginity, I'd rather do it with a man. Dingo always said gay sex is like dessert—refined and superfluous, exquisite. But straight sex is like meat and potatoes: what really counts, what feeds you.

He'd know. He always said he'd go in for freelance social work as soon as he turned fourteen. . . and he had all the required equipment. And no scruples.

Luckily, Ettu showed up in time to save me. He brought me a plastisilk sweater and a pair of self-sealing boots my exact size, and when I whispered to him what the bath attendants had insinuated, he got me out of that spa as fast as he could. He hardly left them a tip.

In the changing room, he gave me the clothes he'd bought for me and told me to get dressed. He didn't even watch me dressing, which really confused me. I had gotten the idea, I don't know why, that maybe he was the type who only enjoyed watching other people. . .

With my squeaking-new clothes and the platinum card safely tucked deep in my pocket, I went with Ettu to the hotel shops. He let me enter first, while he waited for a few seconds, enjoying the show.

When I entered, the looks I got from the saleswomen (more goddess-bodies and doll-faces—apparently plastic surgeons mass-produce them for the Galaxy hotels) weren't exactly friendly. What's this little girl doing here? Toys are another department! There's only expensive, super-exclusive things here! One even tried shooing me off with a languid wave of her perfectly manicured hand, the way you'd shoo a bothersome insect. But a girl doesn't survive Barrio 13 by worrying much about how people look at her. Condescending gazes and scornful gestures don't break bones. I have eyes, too—and insolent ones, my Abuela says. I made do with sticking my tongue out at them all and then ignoring them. I had plenty to look at. . .

Then Ettu walked in, patted my hair kind of casually, and they stood up straight and immediately put on their professional smiling masks. If I was with him, nothing was off limits for me.

Running around the store, selecting this and that, was like the birthday I'd never had. I bought everything I'd always dreamed of: urban camouflage outfits, mirrored dresses, spinning skirts, high-speed leather pants, a color-shifting dress, shoes with hydraulic soles... Even a long plastisilver dress, which of course they didn't carry in my size, but the cybertailor trimmed and mended it in a few seconds with his nanomanipulators. If the Colossaur planned to take me with him everywhere, a more grownup dress might come in handy. Maybe he wouldn't always want to be seen with a nine-year-old girl dressed like a jungle explorer or a jetskate racer...

When it became obvious that I wasn't just looking, far from it, the saleswomen's looks went from scornful to envious and intrigued. Suddenly attentive, they gathered around to "help" me. I continued to ignore them. Ettu winked at me and we both laughed. Some social workers shopping nearby came over, attracted by that barking sound of his, so obviously xenoid, smelling a potential client with credits to burn. But I held tight to his hand and looked at them defiantly, as if to make clear that this one was mine. And we laughed again.

The ice was broken.

Though I still hadn't realized that it wasn't just a dream. Maybe that's why I was so calm.

The platinum card did have credits on it. Lots, apparently. I could tell when it was time to pay. The employees' attitudes, already obliging and astonished, became absolutely servile when I showed them my treasure. What does young Madame desire? Would she like to see our perfumes? Might we accompany her to the toy department?

What disgusting people!

The worst is that you could tell their friendliness wasn't the least bit sincere, that they were burning with envy, wondering: What does this skinny little kid have that we don't? What does he see in her?

Ettu told me we were going to the restaurant, and I didn't dare refuse anything he wanted, though I would have preferred to eat something light, by myself, anywhere... There had already been too many emotions for the first day.

On our way to that gourmand's paradise we passed by the toyshop. My eyes almost popped out of my head, seeing all those marvels, but I put on my bravest face and walked right on by. If Ettu wanted a girl who acted grownup, he'd have her. And I could always slip out early in the morning and look at all those things... and even buy something, with a bit of luck, if my card hadn't used up its magic yet.

I couldn't get used to the idea that the platinum card and the account behind it were really mine. Mainly, I think, because I knew I hadn't done anything to deserve it—and I didn't want to think about what I might have to do. As nice as Ettu might seem, by the age of nine a girl has already long figured out that nothing's free in this life. And possibly in no other life, either—if there are other lives.

Dinner was more a theater performance than anything. Platinum and jade cutlery. A table big as an astroport landing strip. Six waiters in their ridiculous penguin suits just to serve the two of us. And talking the whole time in a language that had nothing in common with Planetary, which I only learned a couple of weeks later was French. The language of haute cuisine.

And the menu... If I had eaten a different dish every day, it would have taken me a year to try half the dishes that appeared in a holoimage over the table. And they all looked so generous and appetizing it made my mouth water, but I couldn't decide which to order.

In the end I trusted Ettu, who ordered a Chicken Bellomonte for me, the same thing he got for himself. Except he asked for nine servings. And he ate so fast, he was almost done when I was still absent-mindedly gnawing the last bits off the bones of my chicken, wiping my fingers on the immaculate natural silk tablecloth under the horrified gaze of the waiters.

And the wines... For me, who had never tried anything but my Abuela's Seven Rats vodka and the explosive concoctions that the gang brewed up in the still that Dingo built, they didn't taste like alcohol, but something different, very different. And delicious. I drank so much that Ettu had to restrain me... after I had mixed red wine and Champagne, port and Madeira, Tokay and Bordeaux, one glass from each bottle, constantly fearing it was all just a dream from which I'd awake at any moment.

I was feeling deliciously tipsy when Ettu brought me up to his suite. His room was so big, they could have played several Voxl games there at once. And the bed—round, enormous, central, dominating the scene.

I remember thinking in my stupor that if my virginity was the price for living a few more nights like this one... it was a good price. And I stumblingly pulled off my clothes, not caring whether he saw me, and lay down face up on the bed, opening my legs as wide as I could, and likewise squeezing my eyes and fists as tight as I could.

If it was going to happen, let's get it over with quick, and better now when I'll barely notice...

But when I woke up the next day, I was in the same position... alone. No blood on the sheets, no pain in my insides. Ettu hadn't slept in that enormous bed.

There was a smaller door on one side of the vast bedroom, shut and locked. I couldn't open it.

And when I got a horrible suspicion and ran to check my pocket ... The platinum card was right there where I'd left it the night before.

From that moment I trusted Ettu completely. I didn't understand why he was doing it, but at least I knew why he wasn't doing it. Don't look a gift horse in the mouth. When you're living in paradise, you don't ask too many questions. Especially if you're from Barrio 13, which is to say, from hell.

For five days Ettu let me wander around freely, as if he were getting me used to the wonders of the Galaxy.

It was strange and delightful to be able to behave for once like a little girl, without always having to think about the consequences or the price that had to be paid for everything.

I swam in each of the six pools, from the huge one that was open to everyone to the small, superprivate hot pool, where I cavorted naked around three bored Cetian and human couples and a contemplative polyp from Aldebaran that remained underwater.

I ate as much candy and ice cream as a nine-year-old girl can digest without any stomach disasters. I bought enough toys for a whole elementary boarding school. Magazines and books I'd always wanted to read, from holographic comic books to the classics that grownups talk about, which I didn't have the time or the desire to do more than leaf through.

I wore myself out in the hotel's magnificent gym, more playing with the equipment than really exercising my childish muscles.

I spent hours in front of the suite's enormous holoscreen, flipping from channel to channel among the thousands that I had free holonet access to as a hotel guest. I saw holodramas that were on their thousandth episode, documentaries about the flora and fauna of Earth and other worlds, dance and theater spectaculars that bored me, concerts of those traditional music groups that all the xenoids love, cartoons, and all sorts of pornography for every taste.

During my frenzy of trying everything and acquiring everything, Ettu was only a fleeting reddish presence I barely glimpsed when he was entering or leaving my suite and locking himself behind his secret door. I gave him friendly smiles, but I didn't know what to say to him, and I couldn't think of any good topics of conversation. An indiscrete question might put an end to this fantastic dream forever, and I wasn't about to risk it. He seemed very busy, but he was always observing me. And that toothy grin of his seemed permanently painted on his thickset face. As if to say, "Keep it up, Liya—what you're doing is great, but there's still more..."

And there was more.

By the fifth day, I was like that grodo in the fable who, after crossing a vast desert, thought his thirst was endless, so he dived headfirst into a lake, planning to drink it all. And after drinking for three days and three nights, he discovered that the lake level hadn't gone down so much as a centimeter. And yet, not only had his thirst disappeared. . . so had his desire to drink any more water, ever.

The material world, the world of luxuries and objects I'd never had, didn't do me any good if I was alone. My new possessions were worthless if I couldn't show them off, brag about them, share them with others, watch them be astonished about it all. And most of all, the fact that it had been so easy to get it all, the fact that I hadn't had to pay anything for the treasures cramming my room, took away most of their value.

On the sixth day I ran away. I used my platinum card to get a cybertaxi, a wide aerobus that I packed full of toys, clothes, candy, books. . . and even so, I had to leave some behind. And I went back to Barrio 13. Where else?

I had already talked with my Abuela, but she was prudent and as allergic to the mob of kids as any other woman, so in the middle of her drunken stupor she'd had enough common sense not to tell anyone where I was. Whereas I was so naïve, I asked them to let me off right there on the street, instead of at my house, when I saw the gang—my gang—playing.

Everything would be just like before, except better. . .

I was ready to forgive them. I had to.

They had sold me to a Colossaur. They were worse than rats, but they were my rats. The only real family I had—much more family than my alcoholic Abuela. Ettu, in spite of his tolerant generosity, was nothing but a strange xenoid who was up to something weird with all the interest he showed in me. . .

For Dingo and the rest of the gang, my return was a total surprise. Alive, happy, and loaded with marvels. When the cybertaxi let me off in front of them, they stopped playing soccer and just stared at me. As if they didn't believe it, as if I were just a ghost.

As if I had to be dead.

"Hey, guys," I said, happy. "Did you miss me?"

Then, without a word, without Dingo giving them any sort of signal, they all ran at me. I thought they were going to hug me, to congratulate me for my cleverness and my good luck. But, too late, I saw the anger twisting their faces.

They fell on me. Kicking me, biting me, spitting on me, shouting at me. Ripping everything I had so happily brought to share with them out of my hands. I felt their hatred, their envy, and their simple need to destroy me so they could keep on being themselves. And those feelings were like a monstrous shell that turned them into something very different from the gang, my gang.

I wasn't one of them anymore, and this was their way of showing me. In a way they had killed me by selling me to that xenoid. They had thrown me out of their world, which up until five days earlier had also been mine. I should have at least had the decency to stay dead. Not to remind them of what they hadn't had any choice but to do.

We children are capable of endless cruelty. Because we don't have anything to tell us, deep down inside, "That's enough, stop." And in Barrio 13, grownups tend not to get involved in kids' business. If they kill one? Okay... one less mouth to feed. One less who'll end up with the Triads or the Yakuza when he grows up.

At first, greed made Dingo and the others restrain their rancor. They controlled themselves to keep from breaking any of the "riches" that I had so naïvely brought them. Perhaps if I had shown complete submission it would have appeased them—I now know that this is how it works in the group rituals of lower primates such as baboons. But when Babo tried to rip the clothes off of me, when I kept my platinum card in my pocket, and I resisted, they forgot everything else and turned into bloodthirsty rats.

Surrounded by the smells of broken perfume bottles, trampled chocolates, caviar dumped on the ground, and wine spilling from smashed bottles, thirty hands and thirty feet went at my body. I fought like mad, like the girl accustomed to Barrio 13 gang fights that I was. But when I tasted my own blood running from my broken lips and split nose, and I realized that they would never stop, I was terrified like never before in my life. I screamed, begging for the help I feared would never come.

I screamed and shouted for my Abuela, for my mother, for the neighbors, for Planetary Security, for anyone who would help me, for mercy.

I screamed for Ettu, when I couldn't take the pain any more.

It was killing me.

Then he showed up.

He was swift, brutal, and effective. Two swipes of the tail, one blow of the hand, two kicks, and one snap, and the gang fled in terror. My Colossaur angel, without a word, led me by the hand like a father leads his daughter, and practically dragged me out of there.

I was bleeding, had a dislocated shoulder, and felt dazed by the pain and the shock, but I'll never forget the spectacle of two of the triplets twisted into unnatural, broken positions on the asphalt, and the body of Dingo, headless.

Dingo, the leader of my gang.

The same gang that had attacked me...

It couldn't be. If it had all been a dream, this had to be a nightmare.

When I got back to the suite, I slept almost fifteen hours straight. Maybe they gave me some drug, but I needed it. I have a vague memory of Ettu and the three hotel doctors caring for me, the sharp jab of pain when they snapped my arm back in place. Afterwards, through a fog, being moved and lifted somewhere.

When I woke up, I was in another almost identical suite, but half a world away. According to the brochure, it was also the Galaxy—but in Tokyo. I dug into my pocket, looking for the blessed card... and it wasn't there.

I remembered that Babo and the others hadn't managed to snatch it from me. So it had been him. The Lord gave it to me, the Lord took it away... Cursed be the Lord. Cursed be the xenoid Lord, who saves my life and takes from me the possibility of enjoying it.

That was the end of my buying frenzy. And the ice floes that had almost completely melted loomed up once more between us.

Ettu continued to pay unflinchingly for every meal, every item I needed—or that he realized or thought I needed—though I never asked him for anything again. I felt that when he took away the platinum card, he took away his trust, so why should I give him mine? He was a xenoid, I was a human. No trust was possible...

The silent, roving period had begun.

After Tokyo there was no more rest. We traveled as if we were pursuing something, or fleeing something. Ettu talked and talked, revealing the world to me, the Earth I had never known. I just followed him everywhere, quiet, but like an affectionate puppy that follows in its master's footsteps. Though it was less affection than fear. Fear of losing him, too, after he had taken my gang away from me.

Fear because I knew how useless I was, since Ettu could manage on his own perfectly well. He didn't need anyone's help to rid himself of the moochers who crowded around in every city, or the people offering him a "pretty girl, real cheap, will do everything," or a "good room with antigrav and holonet connection, good price," or "traditional food, satisfaction guaranteed, cooked naturally, organic ingredients." He didn't even pay attention to the ones who came up to him pretending to be old friends or to have a predilection for his race, much less to those who talked about terrestrial hospitality and then wanted at all costs to invite him to their house. None of the vultures who always circle round the xenos, all the same in every city on Earth, could faze him.

We never slept two nights in the same hotel. After the Tokyo Galaxy he preferred simpler, more anonymous hostels. Maybe he wanted to go unnoticed. . . or he might have had some other reason. He never consulted with me about his decision. It couldn't have been to save money, because he kept spending it hand over fist.

In any case, even the grubbiest hotel (and we never spent the night in one that was actually grubby) would have been much better than my tiny apartment in Barrio 13. Ninety-seven square feet, including bath and kitchen, filled with the smell of my Abuela's alcohol, vomit, and old age, day and night. . .

Tokyo, Kuala Lumpur, New Bombay, Beijing, Florence, Berlin, Stockholm, New Paris, Barcelona, New York, Havana, New Sao Paulo, Buenos Aires. . . In less than a month, we tied a bow around the world.

The key question was still the same: what did Ettu need me for? It wasn't to be a guide for him: at the age of nine, I'd never left New Cali, hardly even the microworld of Barrio 13. He knew how to get around better than me in every city we passed through.

In each city we repeated the same routine. Arrive, find a hotel, eat, drop off the luggage. . . and wander. We walked around looking at everything, for hours at a time, snubbing the taxis and aerobuses. Until my legs started to ache, when he, always perceptive, would carry me on his armored shoulder, though I never complained. Or thanked him.

He was never interested in the nightclubs where his people hung out, or the shows for tourists, or any part of the well-planned spider's web for emptying xenoid bank accounts that the Planetary Tourism Agency had woven around the planet.

His thing was the past. And of the past, art.

He seemed thirsty to look, to touch, to measure step by step every portion of Earth's artistic past. He knew so much about human architecture and its convoluted relationship with history! He talked to me about every fountain, every palace, every plaza and monument, with a sense of wonder, of respect, and at the same time of bitterness, which at the time I grasped or understood only in the vaguest way.

He seemed to know it all. Whichever city it was, he knew where to go and what to find.

The austere sand gardens of the Zen monasteries and the graceful palaces of the Japanese. The lovely pagodas and ornate wooden palaces in China. The stupas and the temples bursting with reliefs in India. The orgy of curves in the Arab mosques and minarets, the orgasm of color in Florentine marbles and cupolas. The solidity of German cathedrals, the profuse richness of the Spanish Baroque, the fake Eiffel Tower and its steel stylishness, the symphony of cement and glass in Scandinavian and Catalan modernism. The fusion of European spirit and indigenous patience in Brazil, the pretentious Europeanization of the palaces and avenues in Buenos Aires, the fiesta of colors in Caribbean eclecticism. And to sum up the world, the Steel Babel, where all styles cross paths and are refined by their dizzying combinations.

New York. That's where we would stay. . .

There was still much more. . .

Ettu talked about the bold human feat of conquering height and volume, overcoming the resistance of form, using only inadequate primitive materials. But he passed by the ultramodern living edifices of grodo architecture, not built but grown, without a glance. He disdained the perfect glass-steel and synplast angles of astroports in favor of the musty glory of medieval European castles. For him, human architecture had had its childhood, youth, mature adulthood. . . and its senile decay was the obscene and perfunctory perfection that had been brought to Earth by all the races of the galaxy.

In museums, he looked at paintings and sculptures, and sometimes even talked to them, with the sort of affection and familiarity you see between old friends. The Chinese bronzes, the delicate Japanese calligrams, the erotic reliefs of the Hindu temple at Konark, the Greek Orthodox icons and the unique brilliance of Flemish primitives—for him, it was all a cause of wonder. The unbridled colors in paintings by the blacks of Africa and America, the abstractions of European modernism... he preferred it all to the cold geometry of the Cetians' networks of lights, the Centaurians' fractal kaleidoscopes, the living surfaces of grodo bioarchitecture. The beauty of imperfection, of life, was what human pictorial art was all about for him.

I've lost many of his words, but some of them remain etched in my memory, like drops of water that splash from the stream and sprinkle the rock and so remain for a while. Insufficient in themselves, isolated, but giving an idea of the torrent.

I listened shyly, amazed that an all-powerful xenoid would pay so much attention to our dead and obsolete art. I didn't understand his obsession with unearthing our past glories. It made no sense in him, one of the masters of the present and future. His rapture over colors was stupid, since as everybody knew, his species could only see shades of gray, not the miracle of colors.

I understood a little better when I met some other Colossaurs, beasts concerned only with force and power, for whom art was a waste of time and a stupid weakness.

Then I began to comprehend Ettu.

His tragedy was to have been born in the wrong star system, under the wrong sun, in the wrong time.

Not long ago, much later, I read about a king, Ludwig of Bavaria, and I realized that one of the descriptions applied to him would have fit Ettu perfectly: mad for beauty.

He was a stranger among his own kind, a freak, a leper, a pariah. And the arts of the rest of the galaxy were too elevated, abstract, and perfect for his crude yet refined and terribly heightened sensitivities. The history of human art was exactly what he would have wanted his own history to be. Elemental, imperfect, sometimes naïve, feeling and stumbling its way to what others already knew from the start. But vital, never giving up. . .

And of course, there was his human friend, the mysterious Moy. . .

In Barrio 13, nobody asks questions about anybody's past. I didn't either, but curiosity demanded that I learn more, and I simply listened more closely.

Sometimes he talked to Moy as if he were there. At first it terrified me—a crazy Colossaur isn't exactly the safest person in the universe to be around. But later, picking up bits here and bits there, putting together this monologue and that, the puzzle began to take shape, and I calmed down.

Moy had been a human artist, he was dead, and Ettu knew it perfectly well. He had been Moy's agent, the one who made him famous. He was also, after a fashion, his friend. No matter where they went, they were each as lonely as a drop of water in the desert. . . They ended up getting intimate. Logical, right?

That would have been enough for me, once. In Barrio 13, a girl learns that when you dig until you get to the bottom of anything, you'll find sex. . . and that's it. It can be dangerous to your sanity to wonder what lies beyond. It's almost always something slobbery, gross, malignant, yet pathetic. Like a wad of phlegm that comes to life and tries to speak.

All the same, I felt I knew enough about Ettu for nothing to gross me out. I kept listening between the lines.

That's how I found out it was Moy who named him Ettubrute, early in their relationship. Later, what started off as a caustic joke must have turned into a kind of affectionate nickname.

In any case, it was clear that their relationship was never obvious or easy. They pretended at mutual hatred, but they needed one another. Moy was always complaining that his agent exploited him, but he never questioned any of his numbers. Ettu pretended to put up with the human only because of the money he made from him, but it was his vitality and his very presence that gave him the strength to bear his fate as a hopeless creampuff from a race, a world, and an ethic of brutal titans like Colossa.

I never found out what kind of art Moy made. I suppose he was a painter or an architect, given Ettu's tastes. Colossaurs may have very keen ears, but they have no sense of rhythm or melody, so they lack even the most basic skills needed for producing or appreciating music. And among humans, the olfactory arts were never our forte.

Moy, the painter or architect, did something with his body, something impressive, savagely beautiful and risky. Something that wore him out so much that he almost died every day, or something like that. Ettu admired his talent and his complete devotion. And his bravery. But he was always ready to protect him from anything—especially from himself. Moy became addicted to telecrack, and Ettu got him over his dependence.

I guess neither of them really realized how much they needed each other. . . until it was too late.

But I only discovered the why and the how of that "too late" afterward. At the end.

When we'd been all over Earth, when Ettu seemed to realize that a thousand lives wouldn't be enough for him to see the whole history of human art, only then did we settle in New York. The house he rented on Staten Island was remote, huge, and safe, and I immediately christened it the Castle. And he devoted himself to artists.

It seemed logical to me. After the dead art of past eras, the living creators.

Logical. I couldn't imagine how terribly logical it was.

We started frequenting exhibits and performances by the most famous artists of the moment. Well, not exactly the most famous. The most famous ones who still lived on Earth.

I learned the meaning of the word "patron" when I saw him in action. Though he was a very odd patron.

He gave his credits away lavishly, without drawing up contracts, without committing himself to support anyone's career. But they were just small contributions—"to relieve the artist's situation," as he put it himself while smiling his toothy grin.

I couldn't see the sense in what he was doing. Was he planning to devote himself seriously to the art business? The big xenoid dealers had cornered the market on exports from Earth, as everyone knew. Ettu could buy all the art produced on the planet; if he didn't get the okay from the galactic sharks in the field, no collector would buy any of it from him.

And if he was really aiming to help human artists, why toss around these relatively insignificant amounts, which might relieve their lives for a month or two but not longer? Why not pick three or four truly talented artists and give them some real support?

Not long ago I saw the fishers in the Bay of Fundy. Before spreading their nets, they dumped the guts and scraps from their previous catch into the water. This clever operation, which attracted all the fish eager to devour the blood and entrails of their unfortunate peers, is called "baiting."

Ettu did know exactly what he wanted. And how to get it. But I did not understand what that was until later. Much less why he wanted it. Though in practice, those amounted to the same thing.

While the Colossaur was playing patron, our trust blossomed again. As if to make up for lost time, we became closer than ever.

After pretending to be distant and pretentious at every art show, Ettu would let off steam with me. He enjoyed being just as childish as me, dropping the serious talk and the businessman mask. We played a lot. I soon realized that under that armored carapace of his, he was more of a playful puppy than a terrible machine of destruction like the one I'd seen when he saved me from my former gang.

He loved to carry me on his back, playing horsey with me. Day by day, I found it easier to see him not as a dangerous, almighty xenoid but as my ideal accomplice in all sorts of games and pranks. Slowly, without imposing himself, he pulled off the miracle of getting me to stop missing the companionship of Dingo and the others, which I could never get back now.

When we went to art shows and the high-society afterparties, he dressed me like a miniature woman, like a living doll, and I went along with the masquerade, feigning a grownup's serious and affected dignity and taking great care of my clothes. When I got bored of all the chatter about abstruse theories like transmodernism and holofigurative representation, all it took was a glance at Ettu's tiny eyes for me to understand that it was all a kind of secret grand masquerade, in which only we were real and only we knew there was nothing behind the others' masks. A brief annoyance we had to put up with before going on with genuine life. The life of games and jokes in the Castle.

When I turned ten, he threw a surprise party for me that caused a commotion all over New York. All the artists and their minions came. Many of them gave me works of theirs as presents... I still have some: today they're worth hundreds of thousands of credits, given that the artists who made them won't produce any more...

Only one thing was missing: children. It wouldn't have cost Ettu anything to invite three or four dozen kids from any gang in Queens or Harlem, but he didn't want to. In any case, I had already learned my lesson. Childhood is too precious to share with someone just because you both share the same age.

All my apprehensions about his intentions died once and for all that day. The following week, as a magnificent post-birthday celebration, he skipped exhibits and inaugurations and devoted all his time to me. We went to a thousand amusement parks around the city, bought or rented all sorts of pets and riding animals, which wandered grunting and stamping around the enormous lawns of the Castle, driving to distraction the efficient and expensive huborg servants that Ettu had gotten from the Auyars, paying six month's rent in advance.

Because it soon became obvious that things might go on much longer than the "couple of months" he had mentioned to me at first. Ettu seemed to be in no hurry.

On the contrary, he grew more interested each day in my desires and plans for the future, as if he were expecting us to spend several years together.

I wasn't sure what I wanted to be. Ballerina, painter, shuttle flight attendant, executive? Professions that were only a dream for a girl from Barrio 13 now seemed within my reach. And boringly real.

"Liya, one way or another, you have your whole life ahead of you," he always told me, stroking my head and cutting short my indecisive ruminations. "For now, enjoy life, find out about things, learn. You'll have to choose later, when you're grown."

And did I ever find out and learn! Ettu found the best alternative education programs for me. Education through play, which only the children of the big shareholders in the Planetary Tourism Agency had access to, the sort of education I'd never even dreamed of in Barrio 13.

He even arranged to have some facts about the history of Earth translated for me from the educational materials of other races. That could have cost him some stiff fines, maybe even a memory erasure, if he'd been caught. The facts about how xenoids viewed my race were stark and cruel in their schematic coldness. But they only confirmed what Xenophobe Union for Earthling Liberation leaflets constantly repeat, what every human learns almost subconsciously from childhood: they weren't our friends, they were our masters.

But to see it written by the xenoids themselves, without all their altruistic rhetoric, was very hard. You always dreamed that it was all just slander, mistakes in Earth's administration, problems with the transfer of power. . .

At first I didn't understand why Ettu revealed it all to me. Revealed the truth, no less terrible for always having been intuitively known.

"Do you feel guilty for me?" I asked him in a fury after stomping on one of the more explicit and difficult holovideos about the political economy of the galactic races toward Earth. "Because just being born on Colossa gave you all the privileges I'll never aspire to as a human?"

And he smiled.

But I wanted to wound him, and I kept at it. "Do you think adopting me as your daughter will make me forgive the whole galaxy in your name? Do you think I'll ever love you?"

Then he got serious and told me in a carefully neutral tone of voice, "Liya, I don't like talking about this. There's something I've never told you: I can't have children. I'm not... fit. On Colossa, only the biggest and strongest have the right to leave descendants. They let me live—but they sterilized me."

Of course, I already knew in practical terms what "sterilized" meant: what the Planetary Security guys did when they flew over my barrio with their radiation transmitters "so the shit won't overflow," as they put it. Lots of adults protested, yelled, got angry. But the social workers and most of the young people just shrugged and laughed, joking that at least they wouldn't have to worry about the venereal disease that lasts nine months, followed by a lifelong convalescence.

After my tantrums and my hatefulness, I always went back to him. He was the only one I had... And in a way, I felt... pity? affection?... for him. Those aren't as different as you might think.

I knew he was alone, much more alone than me. I was on my own planet at least, where I wasn't anybody, but I was one of many nobodies. He was a stranger, and always would be. A stranger on his own world, where they didn't consider him Colossaur enough to let him reproduce, a stranger here on Earth, where he was too Colossaur to be anything else.

We didn't talk much about it. In the middle of our talks about games, about the human history that I was starting to find more fascinating than the best stories, because on top of everything else it was real, sometimes a word about it slipped in. It always sounded strangely alien, and it would practically paralyze us to hear it. Like we were trying to understand the odd word, wondering where it had come from and what it meant, as if we didn't both know perfectly well.

Children. . . Friends. . . Race. . . Belonging. . . Loneliness. . . Love. . .

No, it wasn't the words but the ideas they contained that spread the icy silences when I would endeavor to come up with something else to talk about, as if trying to avoid the iceberg whose reflection I saw gleaming in Ettu's little eyes.

One day he brought the first artist home. They talked for a while, Ettu listlessly and the other almost in a frenzy. Then Ettu invited him upstairs, and they spent a long time in his apartments. Not in the inner sanctum that he never let me enter, but in his bedroom, with the enormous bed that I knew he never slept in.

Later the artist, a pompous little genius of the holoprojections, came down strutting around smugly, but with a strange expression on his face, a mixture of disgust and terror. And Ettu said goodbye with a sad—yet final—smile.

I ran upstairs, with a horrible suspicion. . . The bed was unmade, as if someone very large and very heavy had been romping in the sheets. Strange liquids were staining the silk. And the smell of sex, which I knew so well, mixed with Ettu's acrid and cloying scent.

He surprised me there, and I said nothing. I don't exactly know why, but I felt. . . betrayed. I thought it was because he had introduced the grownup world into the childhood paradise of the house. But, deep down, I knew it was something else.

Jealousy.

Why them and not me?

I wasn't such a little girl as I'd been months earlier. . .

I tore the costly silk sheets in a fury, my eyes moist, like a wronged woman. And I peed on the mattress, vengeful as a hurt child. The following day, Ettu instructed the huborgs never to let me enter his suite until they had finished erasing all traces of his encounters with artists.

I never again found traces of what I thought of as his repulsive xenoid lechery.

Oh, if I had only suspected the truth. . .

Artists continued to visit. After a while they became a routine. Always different, always urgent, hopeful, skeptical but clinging to that possibility. When I saw them arrive I'd withdraw, as if to express my disapproval of all that. Ettu always had long conversations with them. Sometimes they went upstairs, sometimes not. When he sent artists off without inviting them into his bedroom, their faces had the look of being devastated but, at the same time, sort of relieved. When artists came downstairs after a while, they seemed happy. . . but always with that shadow of disgust.

As if they'd sold their souls to the devil, it occurred to me to think one time.

I naturally pretended to be playing, though I was really spying all the while. I tried to find out what it was that made some of them eligible for his pleasure and so prizeworthy while others didn't deserve that "honor." My feminine instinct told me that the whole pantomime of a long conversation, then going upstairs or not, was very important to Ettu. And that the key lay in the questions he asked and the answers he got.

One day, dying of curiosity, I dared to bring up the subject directly. What was all that? What was he up to? Why make them go upstairs if he was going to give them money? Couldn't he do that just as well downstairs? Was this what he came to Earth looking for? Why the whole masquerade of acting mad for beauty, hiding the fact that he was only interested in easy, cheap sex, like all the others? Wouldn't it have been easier, cheaper, and more sincere just to ask them?

"Sometimes, especially when dealing with difficult issues, the easiest road isn't the best," he answered, very serious, looking me straight in the eye.

That confused me.

It was strange, contradictory. As if I'd suddenly discovered another Ettu. I'd been innocently living with him for months, and he'd never tried anything. I hadn't seen that he had any lovers, either. And now, all this interest in sex.

It all came down to sex, always: the perennial means of exchange between humans and xenoids. What every tourist came to find on Earth. But—my playmate, too? Practically my adoptive father, so taciturn at times and other times so communicative?

We never brought up the subject again.

As the scene was constantly repeated—artists showing up buried in debt, heading upstairs after the interview with Ettu and later coming down contented, or else being sent packing—I ended up accepting the inevitable. Yes, sex. He might be a very special sort, but it was still all about sex. Ettu only liked adult human artists. And his respect for me no longer seemed like respect but scorn. The only reason he didn't touch me was that he wasn't attracted.

So why did he love me, then? The eternal question.

That night I ran away. I didn't have the platinum card, but I had a couple of regular ones. With enough money on them to. . .

To do what? I knew all too well that I had no place to go home to. Even though my Abuela still lived in Barrio 13, accepting my frequent remittances so she could keep on happily destroying her liver, I no longer belonged there. And what's even worse, after those months of traveling around the planet and living this new life in the Castle, I was starting to doubt whether I belonged anywhere.

If there was any place in the world for me, it was with Ettu. If I cared about anyone and if there was anyone who cared about me, it was him. But that was precisely what I felt least disposed to accept.

I rented a room in a third-rate hotel... In theory a minor shouldn't be able to do that, but credits work wonders in practice.

The first night, I could hardly sleep. I was restless, tossing and turning all night long. I was furious. Jealous. Of Ettu, much as it angered me to admit it. Why other men and women, and not me? Wasn't I woman enough for him? Lots of guys would pay a fortune to enjoy a ten-year-old virgin eager to stop being one. That stupid Colossaur and his obsession with beauty—not that the artists were so handsome. Being able to create beauty didn't make them special or better. They were rotten inside, and he knew it as well as I did. I was more beautiful than all of them together...

The next night I put on my most womanly dress and went to Lolita, a nightclub known as a hangout for teenagers of both sexes—and for xenoids more or less interested in pedophilia.

I drank one kind of wine after another, like that first night in the New Cali Galaxy restaurant. Maybe it was because I was so coldly determined to get drunk that I never fully lost consciousness of what I was doing.

I danced for hours, with humans and grodos, Cetians and Centaurians. I put my whole soul, with all the anger and confusion I was feeling, into every movement; I was the star that night. Everybody was watching me, and I got plenty of propositions. Fewer than I was expecting, I admit. Apparently my obvious need for sex, here and now, frightened away most potential clients.

I smiled politely at each offer, and that was all. I was waiting for him. Just him. Stupid me, completely forgetting that Colossaurs can barely grasp the meaning of music. He never would have gone to a place like that. Or maybe that was why I was so hoping he would come looking for me there... Even if just to have him bring me home like a naughty runaway girl. Because it would have meant that he cared a little about me. That he took me a little bit seriously. That he loved me a little... since I hated to admit that I was the one who loved him.

He didn't come. I wanted to forget. If it wasn't him, somebody like him would do. That had to be my night, and no stupid armored Colossaur was going to mess it up for me by not showing up. I kept on drinking; I smoked pot, sniffed coke. I even let a Centaurian who showed more interest than the others give me a dose of telecrack, which fortunately must have been fake.

And at the break of dawn, when I was about to faint from sheer exhaustion, I left with him. For a third-rate hotel, the sort that stinks of half-rotten food and dry semen. Every city has hundreds of these hotels, where xenoids of few means rent one-night rooms to enjoy sex with humans.

I hardly felt him make me a woman. It wasn't as wonderful or as painful as I'd heard. I didn't enjoy it much, and it didn't make me ache. It just... happened. Afterwards I fell asleep, smiling about my triumph, but wanting to cry.

In the morning the Centaurian was gone. Taking my cards and clothes with him, of course. I didn't feel like reporting him—after all, he'd almost done me a favor. And it wouldn't have done any good, anyway: apart from the fact that he was a real xenoid and I was just a human, if he'd ever told me his name I'd forgotten.

My head ached as if some monster inside my brain were trying to enter the world through the bones in my skull. And I was dying of thirst, but there wasn't even a glass of water in the room. My legs ached too, but not much. What did bother me was my stomach, where the humanoid's blue semen had dried and formed a crust that was starting to itch. I took a shower, and with a few stitches turned the pillowcases into an improvised garment, not very elegant but good enough to pass for a poorly made dress. Luckily he had left my shoes. Maybe he thought he wouldn't find them easy to sell...

When I went downstairs, Ettu was waiting for me. Sitting calmly in the lobby. As if nothing had happened. He only asked, "Done? How was it? Happy now?"

I looked at him with anger, with hatred. There were so many things I wanted to tell him. Why had he let me do it? Why hadn't he ripped that Centaurian louse to shreds before he even touched me? Why hadn't it been him?

What was I? Why did he bring me with him, like one more object, since he didn't need a guide to the planet, since he knew it better than most of us, its inhabitants?

But I said nothing. And right then, the idea came to me.

If he doesn't like virgins, maybe now. . .

That night I waited up for him. After the daily artist-beggar left, happy and disgusted, and before Ettu could shut himself up in his mysterious room, I ran upstairs and confronted him.

The huge round unmade bed lay between us like the arena between two gladiators. I had made myself up like I had always seen the social workers in my barrio do: waterproof cosmetics forming a virtual mask to cover my face, long fake eyelashes, shiny hair.

I was naked, the subtle allergen stiffening my nipples, the aroma of the perfume that I had spread over my carefully straightened pubic hair filling the whole suite.

I was tired of waiting. If he didn't do it, I would take the first step.

"Ettu. . . I'm not a girl anymore," I remember telling him.

And I stepped forward. My high-heeled shoes wobbling on the springy mattress.

I was ready to do anything.

"You've been very kind to me, Ettu. I want to pay you." I kept talking. "I don't want to owe you anything. . ."

Looking him in the eye the whole time, defiantly. . . but quite ready to start weeping if he scorned me.

Ettu said nothing. He walked right past, toward his secret room, opening the door.

I ran after him. I almost tripped because of the stupid stilettos that I didn't know how to walk in.

I wanted to go in; he stopped me. I only got a slight glimpse of medical equipment, antigrav stretchers, and bottles of serum, before his enormous body blocked my view.

"Ettu, I love you. . ." I insisted, pressing my body against his reddish carapace, banging my fists against his armored abdomen, grinding my pubis against him. With the desperation of a cat in heat and the blind obstinacy of the young girl I still was. And crying unrestrainedly.

He stretched out his enormous tridactyl hand and picked me up, like on the first day. It seemed to take more effort. Either I weighed more, or he was weaker.

He looked at me for a long time, and his eyes shined.

Then, in one motion, he tossed me on the bed the way you might toss something that you disdain, that's no good. The shoes with the stiletto heels clattered as they hit the floor, freed from my feet.

I thought he was furious and I shuddered, thinking of my grief. Then I suddenly remembered Dingo's head and the twisted bodies of the triplets, and I grew afraid. I curled into a ball to protect myself. I realized I was naked as a worm, ridiculous, my precious mask of acting the grownup woman broken.

In one step he was there, and I closed my eyes, expecting the blow.

But his voice sounded strangely sad as he said, "No, Liya. . . Not you. Forgive me, if you can. . . I think things with you haven't turned out the way I planned. I've let myself go too far. Goodbye."

Then he shut the door, and I stayed there crying, and fell asleep crying. But crying from happiness. He had forgiven me! Everything would go back to the way it was before, or better, and maybe, with time, he would. . .

The next day, when I woke up, I found the mysterious room open. And empty. There wasn't a trace of the well-stocked medical lab I had glimpsed.

Ettu wasn't there. Not in the room, not anywhere in the house.

I made inquiries. Planetary Security is very efficient in New York.

They had seen him take a cybertaxi to Manhattan, the place where shuttles launch, late that morning. Walking slowly, as if he were tired. With no luggage.

His name was in the registry at the embarkation point for Colossa. He had left Earth to return to his world.

Perhaps running away from me...

I knew I'd never see him again.

Then everything became a nightmare. Except for the educational programs and other details, the Castle and the animals and almost everything was in his name. I could hardly keep anything—it all went to the government. A ten-year-old girl has no legal personhood.

Less than two weeks later, with no more luggage than a few thousand credits and a box of educational holovideos, I was sent by a Planetary Security aerobus back to Barrio 13 in New Cali. Back to the tiny one-bedroom apartment, my Abuela, and her constant drinking.

Of course, I wasn't the same any more.

We soon had to move. I had nurtured the hope that the gang and the rest of the barrio would forgive and forget. But when they scrawled the word "Buglicker" in excrement across our front door, after fleeting shadows on a street corner threw rocks at me twice, and a group on jetskates ran over my Abuela in one of her drunken stupors and broke her hip, I knew I was marked. Forever.

We left Barrio 13 for Barrio 5, higher rents and quieter neighbors. So quiet they didn't even have gangs. I spent all day with the holovideos, learning, trying to fill the gaps in my education... trying not to think about everything I'd left behind. Especially not about Ettu. Now it really did seem like a dream. A lovely dream, the sort you feel sorry to wake from when it ends. My Abuela was drinking up hundreds of credits every night and lurching home at dawn to beg for more. I never denied her; it was easier than listening to her complaints and threats. Maybe I also had the cynical hope that she would drink enough that cirrhosis would soon free me from her... and I wasn't wrong.

"There's no hope, unless you can afford a liver transplant. And you don't look like you could," said the old doctor in Social Assistance when I took her to the hospital after finding her unconscious and burning with fever, and her aged skin as yellow as parchment.

The doctor barely glanced under her eyelids before saying, cynically and harshly but without euphemisms, "Galloping cirrhosis, I'd say. How many bottles a day did she drink? Most likely she won't regain consciousness. You're the granddaughter, right? Well, you choose for her: a week of suffering and expensive drugs, or euthanasia now."

I chose euthanasia. At the age of forty-two, my Abuela had drunk and lived enough. Now it was my turn. Without her, it would be easier.

Though I didn't know what would become of me. I always knew that a girl born in Barrio 13 doesn't have many options. . . but it's harder after seeing everything you're going to lose.

I continued to miss Ettu. I felt it was my fault everything had gone wrong and come to an end. By trying to turn him into a lover, something tangible, I had lost the closest thing to a father or a friend I'd ever had. I didn't really understand why I'd done what I did, why he was what he was. . . but I didn't care. I was ready to do anything if it would bring him back. . . To follow him on foot to the end of the world, to make his bed every time he finished enjoying his repulsive artists, even to stop asking him any more questions, ever.

In the hospital, while I was filling out the forms to have my Abuela cremated, I found out about the epidemic. And I started putting two and two together.

The magenta illness, the terrible venereal disease of Colossaurs, was wreaking havoc in the artist community. Some fifty of them had died, their flesh covered almost entirely with the purple sores that were the stigma of the disease. The Health Department of Planetary Security couldn't understand the cause of the contagious outbreak that the disease seemed to be following and was adopting measures to fight the plague while searching desperately for the illness's new vector. Because it seemed unlikely that it could have been transmitted by the usual means...

Even before I heard their names and saw their faces, I already knew who they were. In the final stages of the disease, their faces didn't show much of that satisfaction I'd seen on them when they came downstairs from Ettu's bedroom. But they did show the same disgust, and a horrible despair.

Naturally, they never told how they had acquired the disease. They just painted, worked, created like crazy, knowing the end was near. At least they got that much out of the price they'd paid Ettu for their lives and health. And then they died.

One day the package arrived. By Hyperspace Shipping, direct from Colossa. I knew who it was from long before I opened it, of course. But the contents truly surprised me.

A letter, on plain paper, written by hand. A thick, wobbly hand. It wasn't very long.

Hi, Liya. How are you? They tell me you're doing okay. Sorry about your Abuela. But without her, your life will probably be more... bearable. A lone wolf always gets ahead... And pardon me if I sound inhuman. Don't forget what I am.

I've seen the news from Earth. I think you'll have already figured out that I'm the vector they're looking for. And that it won't do much good for you inform them. Magenta illness is incurable... And anyway, by the time this letter is in your hands, nobody will be able to take any measures against me.

I carried the disease for years... without knowing it. Apparently, sterilization makes us Colossaurs more prone to developing it. It was as an asymptomatic carrier that I gave it to Moy. And not even all the money the two of us made could keep his flesh from being covered in magenta pustules and then dissolving. I killed him, Liya.

Nobody but me, who loved him so much, killed him, one of the few people I really cared about in this life.

In his last days he wanted to have one of the few humans he valued by his side. A guy named Jowe... An artist. He told me to spare no expenses to get him there. Maybe you've heard of him. He was the other one who died in the Escape Tunnel, along with Friga, your mother, trying to leave the solar system unlawfully. Because the terrestrial government wouldn't allow him to come to Ningando, where Moy waited for him to the end...

But I didn't find out any of this until I got to Earth. When Moy died, and the first symptoms of the illness were already weakening me, I felt lonely and decided to look for this Jowe. Maybe he would look like Moy, and having our absent friend in common would serve as a bridge. All I wanted was a little affection during my final days, you understand?

But Jowe was dead, and the last person connected to him was your mother. I don't know what kind of relationship they had, and I don't care. When I found out that Friga had left a daughter behind, I set off to find you. You are, in a way, the only thing I have left.

At that time, I still hadn't come up with my plan for revenge. The idea came to me while we were traveling the world, one night when I was thinking how sad it was that such a rich planet should also be so poor. Revenge. I had to take revenge for Moy. Revenge on whom? For what? How was it those artists' fault that Earth was poor? you must be wondering. And I could answer you: no fault at all. Just that I was alone and furious, despised by my own people and not accepted by yours, about to die. Stupid reasons, don't you think?

But they were guilty. Guilty of selling their art because they were hungry, of betraying the history of their world, of not seeing beauty. So my revenge, from a certain point of view, was simple justice.

In case you care to know, I didn't act indiscriminately, either. Of all the needy artists who came to beg me for help, I only responded to the ones who had known Moy or Jowe. And not all of them, either. Only the ones who could barely remember them. . . Most of them miserable that they had achieved a degree of success they didn't deserve. Ambitious sorts who really didn't even need my modest financial help very much. . . but who were already so used to selling themselves that they approached me almost as a reflex action, having heard of easy money. Worse rats than the lowest social workers. The fact that they still lived and sometimes prospered, while Moy and Jowe had already fallen by the wayside, also condemned them.

The magenta illness is extraordinarily contagious. It was because of that, not because I didn't find you attractive, that I never paid attention to your advances. I may have noticed your intentions before you were aware of them yourself. And I admit, there were times when I seriously considered the idea. . . But you weren't guilty of anything. You were the only way for me to feel that everything I was doing wasn't just irrational destruction and fierce revenge.

I hope you do well. I hope that when you pick your vocation you will listen to your heart's desires, and not be looking for money or applause. And, even if you do choose to be an engineer or a flight attendant, I hope that art will be important to you some day. As it was for Moy, for Jowe, whom I never knew. . . and for me.

I hope you don't hate me. That you can understand me, just a little bit at least. That you understand that, in my own way, I loved you like the children they wouldn't let me have.

Remember me, Liya. But live your own life. Here, as a goodbye present, is a little something to help you. After all, Moy made me rich. . . and I had to pick an heir. That, by the way, might be the answer to why I needed you so much. . .

Take good care of yourself,

Ettu

PS. You always treated me as male. The truth is that, although my race has seven sexes, I'm more like your mother and you than Jowe or Moy. But I liked it when you called me "him." It made me feel like more of a... protector.

Wrapped inside was a small, oblong object. My platinum card. That was six months ago.

Now I'm living in a small penthouse in New Sydney, studying hard for the aptitude test I have to take to get into the Baryshnikov School of Modern Dance. I have rhythm and flexibility, according to the private tutor I hired, but I need a lot more style. And I'll need at least as much luck if I want to compete for one of the school's coveted slots with the teenagers who've been going to dance school practically since they learned to walk. But I trust my luck. If I don't make it this year, I'll still have next year. And the next one, and the next. With his card, Ettu gave me all the time in the world.

This isn't a nosy neighborhood, and no one here can connect me with the girl Planetary Security is secretly looking for as the accomplice of the Colossaur "epidemic vector." I'm growing up, I've changed my hairstyle... and in a couple of years, I won't look anything like that skinny, four-foot-eleven Liya.

The platinum card pays all my bills. Though I avoid showing it whenever possible; people might ask questions I wouldn't want to answer. Not long ago, I started using an ordinary plastic card with just ten thousand credits on it. It attracts less attention around here.

I've picked a new name for myself: Ettuya... The reason is obvious.

I'm always thinking about him, about Moy, about Jowe, about my mother... And it's funny, but when I do so, I feel less alone.

Also, I live across the street from a fourteen-year-old boy who's not bad at all. He's studying to get into the Da Vinci Fine Arts School, and we've crossed paths a couple of times. He looks like the son of very rich parents...

One of these days I'm going to ask him out. Probably, no matter how rich his family is, he'll be amazed to see I have a platinum card.

He'd be even more amazed if he heard the whole story. But I don't plan to tell it to him, of course. Most likely they'd never believe a word of it, and I hate to be called a liar.

I'll tell them I'm the daughter of a couple who died in an accident, and that their insurance paid for it. . . Or something like that. Anything that doesn't sound as unbelievable as the truth.

The truth. . . Well, I hardly believe it myself, even now. . . From a girl in a Barrio 13 gang to the owner of a platinum card, by the work and grace of a xenoid! And without even going to bed with him.

And they say that reality can't beat fantasy. . .

October 8, 1998

Acknowledgments

This book is indebted to many people. Some, because their lives served as its inspirations and raw material. Others, because their works or comments did the same. Though making their names public will not cancel out the debt owed them, I think it may help. . . a little.

For their lives:

To Yanet from San Miguel del Padrón and her two sisters. To Mayelín, Elda's former sister-in-law. And to the other "social workers" of L Street between 23rd and 25th.

To the Arte Calle group. To Cuenca and the other artists of the '80s who left to live from their performance art under other skies.

To the Cuban volleyball teams, male and female. To Duke Hernández, Roberto Urrutia, and other members of "the champions."

To my friends Adolfo and Ariel, ex-policemen, for explaining the rules of the game to me.

To the Biology majors of the Class 1991 (including me) who ended up in Aquaculture, Fishing Bureaus, and Spawning Stations. To those who stayed in the field of science. To those who left for some conference and never came back. To those who are driving old taxis or selling pizzas. To all the Cuban scientists who ever had to pass aptitude and attitude assessment tests.

To my friend Vlado, who rowed into the Escape Tunnel but returned to tell me the tale. To all the makeshift sailors of the summer of '94. Especially to those who never made it.

To Danilo Manera, foreigner, Italian, for trying to understand us. For becoming another victim of the disease called Cubanitis. And most of all, for giving me the platinum card of his friendship.

To Cuba and to all its people, because we still do believe in the future in spite of it all, because we have faith in ourselves.

For their works and comments:

To Domingo Santos, because his collection of short stories, *Futuro imperfecto*, gave me the idea for this book, years ago.

To Frederik Pohl, because his story "The Day the Icicle Works Closed" made me think of what a nightmare Body Spares would be.

To Plinio Apuleyo Mendoza, Carlos Alberto Montaner, and Alvaro Vargas Llosa, because it was thanks to their polemic in *Guide to the Perfect Latin American Idiot* that I decided to read *Open Veins of Latin America* to find out if they were right and it was so awful.

To Eduardo Galeano, for *Open Veins of Latin America*. Which turned out to be just the opposite.

To Roberto Urías, for his story "Infórmese, por favor," to which "Aptitude Assessment" is an explicit tribute.

To Ronaldo Menéndez, because his story "Otro Lado" gave me the original idea for "Escape Tunnel," and his story "Una ciudad, un pájaro, una guagua" was the inspiration for "Platinum Card." And also for being, aside from all difference in theories and aesthetics, a terrific storyteller and a friend.

To Eduardo Heras León, "El Chino," because his reading of "Performing Death" convinced me that science fiction could attract non-fans if it was well written and had something to say. Because his spirit was what turned this book from a project to a reality.

To Carlos, for his punctual and unsparing criticism. To Fabricio, for his measured, almost pedantic attitude as a connoisseur and friend. To Vlado for his wild enthusiasm and the liberties he took with my original. To Michel (Umbro), to Guillermo, to Ariel, to Roberto Estrada, to all the fans of science fiction who read my work and believed in me.

To Sandra, who read "Social Worker" and told me she'd had it up to here with *jineteras* and didn't want to keep reading. I hope she'll change her mind. . . some day.

To Yailín, who thought "Performing Death" was a horrible story and refused to illustrate it. For having the courage to express her opinion even though many of her friends disagreed with her.

To Milana, in the distance, for many things that cannot fit in a list of acknowledgments. Just because.

About the Author and Translator

Born José Miguel Sánchez Gómez, YOSS assumed his pen name in 1988, when he won the Premio David in the science fiction category for *Timshel*. Since then, he has gone on to become one of Cuba's most iconic literary figures—as the author of more than twenty acclaimed books, as a champion of science fiction through his workshops in Cuba and around the world, and as the lead singer of the heavy metal band Tenaz. Alongside novels, Yoss produces essays, reviews, and anthologies, and actively promotes the Cuban science fiction literary workshops, Espiral and Espacio Abierto.

* * *

When he isn't translating, DAVID FRYE teaches Latin American culture and society at the University of Michigan. Translations include *First New Chronicle and Good Government* by Felipe Guaman Poma de Ayala (Peru, 1615); *The Mangy Parrot* by José Joaquín Fernandez de Lizardi (Mexico, 1816), for which he received a National Endowment for the Arts Fellowship; *Writing across Cultures: Narrative Transculturation in Latin America* by Ángel Rama (Uruguay, 1982), and several Cuban and Spanish novels and poems.